HOW TO DISAPPEAR

BY SHARON HUSS ROAT

HARPER TEEN
An Imprint of HarperCollins*Publishers*

**For anyone who has ever felt left out
or overlooked or not good enough**

HarperTeen is an imprint of HarperCollins Publishers.

This is a work of fiction. The characters, incidents, and dialogues are products of the author's imagination and are not to be construed as real. Any resemblance to actual events or persons, living or dead, is entirely coincidental.

ISBN 978-0-06-229175-2

Typography by Kate J. Engbring
17 18 19 20 21 PC/LSCH 10 9 8 7 6 5 4 3 2 1

First Edition

1

STANDING BY MY LOCKER, I can already feel the sweat circles forming on my T-shirt. *Nobody can see that,* I assure myself. Not through the enormous sweater I'm wearing, or beneath my nearly impenetrable wall-o-hair.

Still, I pull the drab-yellow knit away from my armpits. My mother took one look at me this morning and managed *not* to mention what she was probably thinking—that I won't win any popularity contests dressed like a giant blob of Dijon mustard.

Instead, she joked, "Are you in there?" and kind of paused while spreading the Grey Poupon on my sandwich, her eyes flitting between the jar and my sweater.

She's subtle like that.

And I'm perfectly aware this is not my best color. It doesn't make my hazel eyes "pop" or help me stand out in the crowd. In fact, this particular shade of brownish-yellow is a perfect complement to both my hair and the painted-block walls of our school. Which is exactly why I'm wearing it. If the dare I'm about to attempt goes badly, I'll be able to blend into my surroundings and disappear before anyone notices.

My best friend, Jenna, is making me do this. We were Face-Timing last night from our respective bedrooms, mine in its usual place, and hers in the very far away state of Wisconsin, where she now lives. Her mom got a really good job there, so their family moved in mid-August, a couple of weeks before the start of our sophomore year.

"I'm worried about you," she said.

I leaned out of view, so all she could see was my cat, named Kat, curled into a tabby fuzz ball on the bed.

"It's been two months." Jenna put her face extra close to the screen and whispered, "Have you spoken to anyone in two months?"

"I speak to you," I said.

"A real person."

"You're not a real person?"

"You know what I mean." She tipped her phone sideways and propped it on a dresser, giving me a panoramic view of her new bedroom, which I hated on principle. "A real *live* person. Not your parents. And teachers don't count."

I tried to think of the last time I spoke to someone at school, aside from mumbling "sorry" when I got bumped into or whispering "bless you" when the kid next to me sneezed. For pretty much as long as I can remember, Jenna has been the only person I ever really talk to. When it comes to communicating with anyone else, she has always spoken for both of us. Even if someone directs their question to me. I hesitate, and she jumps in to answer. It's just the way we are. Like how I always tied her shoes for her. I was better at it, so she never really learned. Now she just buys shoes that buckle or zip or slip on.

And I don't talk.

"All you have to do is say hi," said Jenna. "That's how we became friends, isn't it? You said hi and the rest is history."

"I was five," I said. "I didn't know any better."

She laughed. "So, pretend you're five again. You're sitting cross-legged in the grass chewing on a Popsicle stick when a girl with tragically unfortunate bangs walks out of the house across the street. She looks like somebody cut her hair with a machete. Say hi to the poor thing."

I sighed. "It's not that easy. You know how I am."

Her face filled the screen again. "I know exactly how you are. That's why you need to do this. Or you'll spend the rest of high school alone and miserable. Hiding in the bathroom, probably."

She *did* know me.

So I promised to say hi to somebody at school today. And the somebody I've selected as recipient of my greeting is Hallie Bryce. Her locker is right next to mine, which regularly puts her within earshot of whatever sound I can force from my vocal cords. I won't have to go out of my way or approach anyone.

I clear my throat to make sure it's still working, and that's when I spot Hallie's gloriously perfect dancer bun gliding down the hall toward me. Immediately, my pulse is pounding in my ears.

She reaches her locker and squats down to enter the combination. It's not really a squat, though, what she's doing. The proper term is *grand plié*, which I learned from her Instagram, which is composed entirely of ballet photos. (Mostly of herself on pointe in various locations where you wouldn't normally find a ballerina. In a tree. On the beach. Against a backdrop of urban decay.) I don't "follow" follow her. As in, I haven't clicked on the follow button or anything. I'm more of a lurk-in-the-shadows kind of girl. Not in any creepy way—in more of an admiring-from-afar, "I wish I could be like this" sort of way.

So, here she is plié-squatting right next to me, and all I have to do is say that one tiny word to fulfill my mission. I'm not even asking myself for a full-on "Hello" or anything insane like "How are you?"

Just "Hi."

Hallie glances up at me then. One of her beautifully curved eyebrows arches high on her forehead. She's waiting. Because I'm staring. I know I am, but I can't seem to stop, or move, or otherwise behave like a normal person. Her brows pull together in a V-shape and her head tilts slightly to the side.

"Did you say something?" She knows I haven't said anything. She's just being nice.

I throw my eyes to the floor. Forget saying hi. It's all I can do *not* to hyperventilate.

She sighs, stands, clicks her locker shut, and pirouettes down the hall. Okay, maybe she just walks, but in that ballerina way of hers—toes pointed, feet turned out. I watch her go, exhaling the tightness from my chest. There's a moment of relief as my fear subsides, but it's quickly replaced by a feeling I like to call "I suck."

One simple thing. That's all I had to do.

I drag my gaze to the interior of my locker, to the photo of me and Jenna taped on the back wall. We are standing arm in arm. I'm wearing her pink camisole dress that was too tight but she insisted fit me perfectly, and we're smiling with all our teeth.

I touch the picture, because it helps. I don't know why. Only seven hours to go, and I'll be on the bus home, texting her. I'll confess my failure, but she'll still be my friend. She told me so when she moved away, that we won't let the distance come between us. We'll finish high school. Graduate. Go to college together. Be roommates. Just like we've always planned.

I close my locker and head toward my first class, concentrating on not tripping or getting slammed by a backpack or poked in the eye with a drumstick. The latter is a realistic threat, because Adrian Ahn is walking in front of me, twirling actual drumsticks.

Adrian is the official rock star of Edgar H. Richardson High School. He's in a band called East 48. They're good, like mosh-pit-diving-fans-screaming-their-heads-off good. Not that I've seen them in person, but they post videos on YouTube. He's part

Korean and dyes his long hair a darkish red color. Today he's got it twisted into a messy knot with a pencil poked through it. Nobody else could pull that off, but Adrian looks amazing.

My eyes are glued to his man-bun (not *buns*, though they are certainly worth gluing one's eyes to). I'm wondering what would happen if I yanked that pencil out of his hair when he suddenly spins around, throwing a stick in the air as he does a 360 on one heel. I come to an abrupt halt so as not to crash into him, but the kid walking next to me doesn't. He knocks right into Adrian and pushes him away from the drumstick that is currently soaring through the air . . .

Right for my face. My hand shoots up to grab it.

"Whoa!" Adrian says, regaining his balance. "Good catch."

I blink at the drumstick clutched in my outstretched hand. *OMG, I caught Adrian Ahn's drumstick.* And he's speaking to me. This is my chance to talk to somebody. Somebody who spoke to me first!

"Hi!" I blurt. It's the only thing I can think to say, I guess because I spent the morning rehearsing it and working up the nerve to say it to Hallie, but I know immediately it's the wrong thing.

So, of course, I say it again.

"Hi!"

Adrian laughs. "Hi to you, too."

We're stopped in the middle of the hall. Kids jostle me as they step around us.

"Can I, uh . . . get that back?" Adrian tips his chin toward the drumstick in my hand—which I am still holding up in the air like the Statue of Liberty. I quickly push the stick to his chest.

"I, uh . . . yes. Here's your drumstick. I caught it. Self-defense, of course, totally. You could put an eye out with that thing. But here you go. All yours now. Happy to be of service." Oh my God. *Happy to be of service?* Did I actually say that out loud? The word-spew is an occasional side effect of never speaking to anyone. It's like my brain stores up every ridiculous thought I've ever had and then projectile vomits it all over the place.

To make matters worse, I cap it off with a cheerful, "Go forth and prosper!"

Adrian laughs again. "You too, Spock."

I decline to clarify that I wasn't quoting the Vulcan, who actually said, "Live long and prosper," because my brain has thankfully gone into complete lockdown and we are swept away in the throng of students.

This is why you can't have nice things, Vicky. Like friends. Or conversations.

Instead of continuing to my world history class, I duck into the nearest girls' bathroom, trying to tamp down a sudden wave of nausea. I don't succeed and heave into the toilet, holding my hair back with one hand and steadying myself on the toilet roll dispenser with the other.

One of the girls I dashed past on my way in says "Ew" and

7

scurries out. I flush and stare into the toilet bowl, which is now clear and filling with water.

A knock on the stall door startles me. I turn to see a pair of red Converse high-tops on the other side, the yin-yang symbol Sharpied onto their rubber toes. I love that symbol. Jenna and I first discovered it the summer before seventh grade and adopted it as our own secret code. We doodled it everywhere, signed notes with it. We downloaded a custom emoji so we could text it to each other. We even got temporary tattoos of it once and swore we'd get real ones when we were old enough.

The wearer of the yin-yang Converse says, "You okay in there?"

"Fine!" I call out. Too loud. Why am I shouting?

"You sure?" the girl says.

"Yes," I whisper. Too quiet now. I sound like a freak. I wasn't always this bad, or maybe I was and didn't realize it until Jenna left. It's like walking on a balance beam while someone's holding your hand and you're perfectly fine until they suddenly let go and you can't move.

The girl in the red Converse hesitates before pivoting and heading out. I wipe my mouth with toilet paper and flush again. It's too late to get to class on time, so I take a disinfecting wipe from my backpack (I always have a supply on hand) and clean the toilet seat where I'll be spending the next period. The bell hasn't rung yet, but it will any second, and the thought of rushing into class after the bell makes me want to hurl again.

Being late for class is very high on my list of stupid everyday stuff that now terrifies me, aka the Terror List. It's a mental list I've been keeping since the beginning of the year. I add to it whenever something makes me nervous or embarrassed or want to disappear. The list is long enough now that it's become a sort of game for me to remember everything on it, like trying to name all fifty states. It includes:

Starting conversations

Walking into class late

Making eye contact

Assigned seating

Having to choose my own seat

Saying something stupid

Getting called on in class

Finishing a test first

Finishing a test last

Group projects

Individual presentations

The cafeteria

Eating in front of people

Gym class

Sneezing in public

I can now add "Catching drumsticks" to the list. Also, "Not catching drumsticks." Either way, that was going to be humiliating.

After going through the list, I take out my history book. I've discovered that it is big enough to span the width of the toilet seat and provide a slightly less disgusting surface to sit on. I use all of first period to study for my precalc test, which is next period, and also thankfully means I won't have to talk to anybody. I can put my head down and just do the work.

That's pretty much how I spend the rest of the day. Head down. Going to class. Doing the work. I pay attention enough but not too much, so I can escape notice by teachers who only have time to deal with the slackers and the scholars. My sweet spot is that inconspicuous in-between.

The final bell rings at 3:50, which is an hour and a half later than last year since our school switched to a new schedule that's supposed to match the natural sleep cycles of teenagers (according to studies and the fact that everybody was sleeping through first period). By 3:57 I'm on the bus and slinking into my usual seat (the one over the hump of the tire where nobody else ever wants to sit). I pull out my phone to text Jenna.

You there?
You'll never believe what happened today.

She doesn't answer right away. Her day ends about ten minutes after mine even though we live two time zones apart, because her school still starts at the crack of dawn. I check her Instagram while I wait for her to get to her bus and see my text, but there's nothing new since the kissy-face selfie she posted last night.

I embarrassed myself spectacularly today.

You probably heard people laughing all the way in Wisconsin.

Still no reply. I scroll through her Instagram feed, which is like a glossary of facial expressions. Yesterday was a wink. The day before was wide-eyed surprise. She started her account when she moved to Wisconsin, as a way of staying in touch with me. Now she's got more than a hundred followers, and likes from complete strangers.

I narrow my eyes at the interlopers and go back to texting.

Ugh. I really shouldn't be allowed to leave the house.

It would be better for everyone.

Maybe I could claim I have one of those diseases that require you to be raised inside an airtight bubble.

Like the girl in that book. Avoid all contact with the outside world. Online contact only. No cute guys showing up outside my window, either. (Which would never happen to me anyway let's be honest.)

I'm prepared to continue babbling about my future in containment when I finally see her thought bubble pop up.

. . .

She's alive!
OMG, what happened?
It's humiliating.
Tell me.
Promise you won't laugh?
I won't laugh.

I can almost imagine her saying it, leaning her shoulder against mine on the bus seat, huddling in close to listen. Texting is not the same; it never will be. But at least she's there. I exhale the stress knotting my shoulders and recount the story of my failed attempt to say hi to Hallie Bryce, in excruciating detail.

Hallie thinks I'm a complete idiot now.
No she doesn't.
Yeah, I'm pretty sure she does.
She's not like that. She's super nice.
Even nice people know an idiot when they see one. Plus that's not even the worst part.

I take a deep breath and text out the catastrophe of Adrian and the drumsticks. The word vomit. The Statue of Liberty. The going forth and prospering. When I'm finished, Jenna's ". . ." bubble pops up, but it's taking forever for her message to come through. Probably because she's laughing so hard she can't type. Or maybe she's trying to find a nice way to tell me I am, indeed, an idiot. Finally:

> Okay, that was actually awesome and hilarious.
> **Are you high?**
> No, I'm serious. Adrian probably thinks you're funny, as in FUN.
> **I don't think so.**
> You caught his drumsticks! That's so cool.
> **I told him to GO FORTH AND PROSPER.**
> I know! Brilliant.
> **Are you kidding me?**
> I'm serious. You're so funny!

She assures me it was funny in a good way, as in clever and witty. Not funny in an everyone-is-laughing-at-you way. I am not convinced. Sometimes I don't think she realizes how hard it is for me to do all the talking for myself, to step into her shoes. *The shoes I no longer tie for her.* But she coaxes me down from the ledge of "I suck" until I am standing on the slightly more solid ground of "maybe it's not as bad as I think."

Even better, she takes my mind off my own troubles by

13

drawing me in to her world, which is way more interesting than mine.

> These kids in the back of the bus keep looking at me.
>
> **Boy kids or girl kids?**
>
> One guy. Two girls.
>
> **Looking at you how? Good or bad?**
>
> Not sure.

We monitor the situation for a few more minutes. The guy is cute, she says, and possibly flirting. The girls are cute, too. Also possibly flirting. I advise her to slide lower in her seat so they can't see her, but mostly so I can have her to myself.

I keep her texting as long as I can, until I am off the bus and in my house and sitting at the kitchen counter, drinking the fruit smoothie my mother made for me. Finally, Jenna texts that she has to go. I reply with a sad-face emoji. She sends a kissy-heart-winky face. I unicorn-birthday-cake-thumbs-up her back. It's silly, but we've been doing it since we got our first phones when we were twelve. She ends as we always do, with the yin-yang symbol. And in that moment, all is right with my world. It's as if she's there next to my balance beam again, holding my hand to make sure I don't fall.

I **WAKE UP THE NEXT** morning to a cheesy, two-thumbs-up grin on Jenna's Instagram, which I take as a personal pep talk. She tagged it #sayhi #beawesome #yougotthis. I click the little heart icon (first like!) and head to the kitchen for breakfast. Mom has left a plate of fresh croissants. It's Wednesday, her early morning workout day. My father doesn't leave for his office for another hour, so he shuffles out to join me.

He pours us both a cup of coffee and sits next to me and we eat and drink in silence. He never forces me to chat, and doesn't even notice what I'm wearing. Today's brown hooded sweatshirt with the pocket in front does not inspire a mention of the marsupial exhibit at the zoo, like it did with Mom the last time I wore it. If he thinks I resemble a kangaroo, he doesn't let on.

I like Wednesdays.

My father's calm stays with me on the bus and all the way to my locker. I'm feeling pretty good, having managed to avoid both Hallie and Adrian in the hall, but the bottom drops out of my stomach when I walk into world history. There's a substitute teacher, which means an attendance roll call. Add it to the Terror List. Even if it only requires me to bark out a single word, I can never decide whether it should be "here!" or "present!"

I'm pondering that decision when I notice the guy seated next to me sort of leaning toward my desk. I'm pretty sure he's the one who knocked into Adrian yesterday, causing the whole drumstick incident. His name is Lipton Gregory. I've heard him explaining that it's a family name on his mother's side, not related to the tea company. But kids still call him "Tea Bag" sometimes.

Lipton clears his throat, and I turn my face a teensy bit more in his direction without establishing eye contact.

"*Frankenstein*," he says.

"Excuse me?" I shoot him a quick glance, then eyes to the floor.

"What you said to Adrian in the hall yesterday. 'Go forth and prosper.'" He taps his pencil. "It's from *Frankenstein*, not *Star Trek*."

I blush, absolutely mortified that someone was listening to my babbling enough to quote it back to me. And remembered to do so a whole day later.

"Right," I say. "*Frankenstein*. Mary Shelley." Can't speak. In complete. Sentences. Apparently.

"It's from the introduction, right?" He swipes the screen of his cell phone and reads from it: "'I bid my hideous progeny go forth and prosper.' She was talking about her book."

"Right," I say again.

"Not Spock." Lipton beams at me, nodding. "Mary Shelley."

And that's when I realize the sub is shouting my name, which I must've missed the first time he called for me at a more reasonable volume. "Decker! Vicky Decker!"

I can't remember if I was going to say "here" or "present" so I shout the first word that pops into my head, which is "Frankenstein!"

The class erupts in laughter as I turn every shade of beet and quickly correct myself: "Here! Present!"

The laughter continues when Jeremy Everling's name is called, and he shouts "Dracula!" Then Brandon Fischer says "Werewolf!" and Ellie Good squeals "Mummy!" and so on, though Lipton Gregory very politely says, "Present."

It's not on my list—being laughed at—because that one goes without saying. The being-laughed-at is what makes all the rest of it so terrifying. I let my hair fall around my face and sink into a puddle behind my notebook.

The sub hushes everyone, but cannot silence the roar in my ears. It's grown louder and more frequent since Jenna left two months ago, like an army of zombie vacuum cleaners that will not die. I open my book and pretend to read the assignment Mr. Braxley left for us, but I can't focus. A small, folded square of paper appears in front of me. I don't look up to see where it came from. It's a joke, no doubt. A picture of Frankenstein. Neck bolts and all. I should brush it to the floor, or slide it to the back of my book.

I'm not exactly sure how long I've been staring at it when I hear Lipton clear his throat. I glance over and he darts his eyes at the square of paper and back at me.

Oh.

I unfold it. There are two words scrawled inside.

I'm sorry.

I hold the note in my hand for the rest of the class and try to clear my mind of any strange words I might inadvertently blurt out if asked another question. All I can think is, if Jenna had been here, she would've answered for me. She would've heard the sub calling my name and said, "She's here!" And Frankenstein would never have happened.

I should've said "that's okay" or at least smiled at Lipton when he passed me the note of apology, but I don't think of it until later when I'm sitting on my book-on-the-toilet-seat in the bathroom eating a sandwich. Which is gross, I know, but the cafeteria and I are presently estranged and there's nowhere else to go. I spent second period in here, and then decided I might as well stay through until lunch. The girl in the red Converse high-tops comes in and I scoot my backpack in front of my feet so she won't recognize my shoes and think I live here. Even if I kind of do.

After three hours, my butt hurts and I'm starting to feel claustrophobic. The idea of staying in this stall any longer is getting worse than the prospect of leaving, so I gather my things at the next bell and make my way to fifth-period English. We're reading *1984* together so it's quiet and nobody looks at me, not even Hallie Bryce, who sits two seats up and one seat over. She holds her book at eye level rather than hunching over it like everyone else. A couple of girls behind her to the right are imitating her, sitting all prim with their books in the air and giggling, until Mrs. Day scowls at them.

Hallie doesn't seem to notice or care. She just keeps reading with her impeccable posture. I guess when you're that perfect, it doesn't matter what anyone else thinks.

About five minutes before class is over the door opens and one of the students who helps in the office delivers a yellow slip to our teacher and scurries out.

"Vicky Decker?" Mrs. Day's eyes drift around the room. She looks right past me, which is exactly what I hope for in most situations. Except now it just means everyone else has to turn and point me out to her. They're like a synchronized swimming team featuring me at the middle of their formation.

"Vicky?" Mrs. Day waves the yellow slip at me. "For you."

Add it to the list: getting a yellow slip. So embarrassing. I slide out of my desk and walk to the front, my face burning. Back at my seat, I read the slip, which is from Mrs. Greene, the school psychologist. It's an appointment for tomorrow at nine fifteen. Right in the middle of first period.

Yippee.

***

I make it through last period and practically fall onto the bus, where I text Jenna the whole agonizing story of my day.

She doesn't text back for a really long time. Longer than usual. I start to worry something's happened to her. A bus accident. Or worse, the kids in the back she's been telling me about have messed with her. Stolen her phone, maybe. Which means . . . ugh. My humiliating texts about Lipton and *Frankenstein* and my guidance appointment are now being read by . . . someone not Jenna.

JENNA? You there?

I'm so relieved when the "..." appears, I could cry. I stare at the screen, waiting. The bus ride home is almost over and I'm holding my phone in both hands as if squeezing it tighter will make the message come through faster. Finally it is there in a blip and it says . . .

LOL

LOL? What does she mean, LOL? I scroll backward, worried I missed something funny. Maybe while I was dumping all the depressing details of my day, she shared something humorous that happened to her? Or maybe . . . did I make a joke I've forgotten?

20

But no. There's nothing.

Someone shoves my shoulder.

I look up, and *crap*, we're at my house. I grab my backpack and scurry up the aisle and down the steps and out the door to the curb. The bus rumbles away. I stand there catching my breath for a minute, then start across the driveway to our front porch, my backpack banging against my leg. Our house is a brick ranch with a gray roof. My mother keeps our shrubbery neatly trimmed at all times, the flower beds mulched and weeded and blooming with seasonally appropriate colors—orange and yellow chrysanthemums at present, perfect fall colors. She fusses over things like that because the house itself is so plain, she always says. Low and unassuming and overshadowed by its fancier two-story neighbors, like Jenna's old house, which sits across the street diagonally from ours.

I try not to look at it too much. It seems so empty, even though new people are living there now.

My phone starts buzzing in my hand. It's Jenna. I let it ring a few times so it doesn't seem like I'm waiting for her call, even though I am.

"Hey."

"Vicky. Oh my God." There's still a laugh in her voice.

"It wasn't funny," I say. "At all."

She snickers. "Actually, it kind of was. *Frankenstein*? I'm dying."

"You're laughing at me."

"I'm laughing WITH you," she insists.

"Wouldn't that require me to be laughing? Because I clearly am not." I pace the driveway. "I made a complete fool of myself, and everyone was laughing at me, and you're the only one I can talk to about it, and now you're laughing at me, too."

"I'm sorry," Jenna says. "I didn't realize you were so upset."

How could she not realize? She usually knows what I'm feeling before I do.

I drop my backpack on the front porch and sit on the step. "I was worried something happened to you on the bus."

"Well . . ." There's a singsong to her voice. "Remember that guy I told you about?"

"The one who was looking at you in a bad way, with the two girls?"

"I said I wasn't sure if it was bad or good," she says. "Turns out it was good. They invited me to sit with them. Well, he did. Tristan."

"In the back of the bus?"

"I know, it's so cliché. Cool kids in the back of the bus. But they are. Totally cool."

I force a smile. "Tell me everything," I say. "So I can live vicuriously through you."

She laughs. "You mean vicariously?"

"Right. Vicariously." I always mess up that word because it seems like *curious* should be the root of it, since it comes from being curious about how someone else lives. I should know, since I spend most of my time that way.

"It's not that exciting. We rode the bus and they asked me where I was from and stuff like that. I told them all about you."

"You did?" My pulse quickens just knowing they were talking about me. "What did you say?"

"Just how we've been friends since kindergarten. How much I miss you. That I can't tie my shoes without you." She laughs. "Tristan didn't believe me so he untied his sneakers and made me show him."

"How you can't tie shoes?"

"Yeah," she says. "I just rolled the laces into a ball and shoved them into his sock."

I laugh, strangely relieved.

"I'm pretty sure they won't be inviting me to sit with them again," she says. "But I have a picture. Bus selfies are a thing out here, apparently."

"Ooh, show me."

"Okay. I'll send it as soon as we hang up."

We chat a little longer, then say good-bye, and the photo comes through as I'm walking into the kitchen. There's Jenna smiling like it's the most exciting moment of her life, surrounded by the faces of Supercuteguy, Supercutegirl, and Supercuteothergirl.

I should be happy for her. I know I should. She's meeting people, making friends. I'd have to be a horrible person not to want that for her. But all I can see is how quickly and easily she is moving on without me.

My mother is in the kitchen at the computer when I walk in. She's on Facebook, where she spends her free time scrolling through the heaping mounds of evidence that I am not nearly as accomplished or impressive as the children of every single other person she knows.

She sees me holding my phone and says, "How's Jenna?"

"Terrible," I say, not sure why I decided to blurt this out.

"Why?" Mom turns from her monitor to face me. "What happened?"

All of a sudden, my eyes start to water. If I tell her the truth, that Jenna is making new friends and I've probably lost the one thing I look forward to every day, which is thirty measly minutes of texting time with my only friend, she'll pity me more than she already does.

I clear my throat. "She's, uh, having a hard time at her new school," I lie. "The kids on her bus are really mean."

Mom's lips turn down in an exaggerated frown. "Aw, poor Jenna."

"Yeah, she's wishing they never moved." I sit at the counter and peel a banana.

Mom studies me like she's never seen someone eat a banana before. "I know it's hard," she finally says. "Maybe a little neighborhood party would help. Invite some classmates' families over."

"Sounds embarrassing."

"Oh, it would be fun."

My eyes slowly widen as I realize she isn't talking about Jenna anymore. "Mom. No."

"What?"

"Please tell me you did not invite kids from school to a party." It hardly bears mentioning that parties are on the Terror List.

"It's just an idea. We could invite the Everlings. And Roberta DiMarco from work. Her daughter Marissa is a junior at Richardson, isn't she?"

Mom turns back to the computer and brings up a full-screen image of Marissa DiMarco and ten other beautiful girls in sexy, short dresses and extremely high heels, standing in a row. The next image shows them paired with their dates for homecoming, boy girl boy girl boy girl boy girl. Then just Marissa and her date, a grinning Adrian Ahn, sans drumsticks. I've already envied the photo on Marissa's Instagram.

"She seems like such a nice—"

"Mom."

"You don't like Marissa DiMarco?" My mother's face is pained, as if failing to be an adoring fan of Marissa DiMarco is making it all the more unbearable that I will never *be* Marissa DiMarco.

"I like her just fine," I say. "But I don't need you to set up play-dates for me. I can make my own friends."

She hesitates. Takes a deep breath. "Of course. I know you can."

"So, just . . . don't. Okay?"

Her eyes get kind of squinty, and she nods slowly.

"I can make my own friends," I repeat.

She keeps nodding, but I can tell she doesn't believe me.

"As a matter of fact," I say, "I had a lengthy conversation with Adrian Ahn just yesterday. And . . . some kids in my world history class today."

An eyebrow shoots up. "Really?"

"Yes, *really*."

She moves from the computer to the kitchen sink, and starts washing dishes. "Then why not have some of them over? We can put up the badminton net. You kids could get to know each other . . ."

"Just kill me now."

"Oh, please, Vicky. It won't kill you." She drops the pan she's scrubbing into the soapy water and turns to face me again. "I just want you to get out there and live a little. Is that so bad?"

There is nothing quite so demoralizing as having your middle-aged mother pause from her Facebooking and dishwashing to suggest that you need to get out more. I glare at her until she looks away, then drag my backpack to my room, lock the door, and flop on my bed.

I pull out my phone and stare at the bus selfie again, zooming in on Jenna's face so I can focus on how happy she looks. I try to pretend her smile is for me. But inevitably I swipe to the left and right, to the faces that are the reason for her happiness. New friends, their heads squeezed together, filling the frame. I wouldn't fit even if I was there. And the supercutes are not to blame for that. I have absolutely no reason to dislike them, but I do. They're so perfect. So everything that I am not.

I slump to my desk and plug my phone into the USB port on my computer so I can open the image in Photoshop. Soon it's filling my whole computer screen.

I zoom in on the face of Supercutegirl, her flawless skin. And I can't help myself. I use the pencil tool to give her a ladystache, and then Supercuteothergirl gets a unibrow. Supercuteguy is the recipient of a bad case of acne. I'm just about to go full-on mean girl by making Jenna cross-eyed when my phone buzzes with a text message from her:

Miss you so much. Wish you were here.

I sit back in my chair and close my eyes. I feel a pang of guilt, and shame, and a heavy dose of "I suck." I sigh and text back:

Me too.

I quickly delete the ladystache and the unibrow and the zits. They looked realistic, but I vow to henceforth use my Photo-shop skills for good and not evil. Which gives me an idea—a way to convince my mother I am not completely hopeless and avoid the embarrassment of a please-be-friends-with-my-daughter party.

I click open the Photo Booth on my computer and position

myself in front of it just as Jenna is positioned in the bus selfie. Then I smile like I'm having the time of my life and snap the photo. It takes a few tries to get it right—looking straight into the lens, smiling but not too much, and with my blank wall in the background instead of my cluttered bookshelves.

Then I carefully drop my own image on top of Jenna's so she disappears and I take her place. I use the brush tool to blend it in. And it looks . . . like an obvious fake. Too flat. The lighting's all wrong. In the original photo there's sunshine from the bus window hitting the side of Jenna's face. She's squinting a little bit, and there are shadows.

I try again. I open my curtains and position objects from my room so they cast dark shapes across my chest and shoulders just like in the photo. Kat keeps trying to crawl on my lap. I throw her on the bed a few times and she finally gets the hint and massages my pillow to death before lying down to sleep.

By dinnertime, I've got a photo of myself with Jenna's new friends that—if viewed on my small phone screen—should fool my mother. If she doesn't look too close. Or zoom in too much.

"Here," I say, placing the phone on the kitchen counter as I start setting the table.

She lifts it to her face, and her eyes widen. "Who's this?"

"Some new kids on my bus," I say, taking my phone back before she can inspect it further.

Mom tries to get another look. I flash it at her again.

"Was that today?" She glances down at my sweatshirt. Same as in the photo.

"Yeah. One of them just emailed it to me."

"Well," she says. "They look very nice."

My dad walks in from work then, and asks who looks very nice.

"Nobody," I say.

He doesn't press me for answers like my mother usually does, just shrugs and smiles. We sit down to eat, and it's the best time I've had all day. Mom doesn't think I'm a complete loser for once, and Dad's just happy that Mom's happy.

Even though I know the picture's a fake, seeing myself surrounded by new friends like that? It feels good.

3

THE ALARM ON MY PHONE buzzes and I grope around on my nightstand to swipe it off. I check Instagram when I wake up, even before I turn on my light, to see what manner of selfie Jenna posted the night before.

She used to send me a close-up selfie as soon as she woke up—squinting out of one eye, or yawning, or making some hilarious face. Now she posts them on Instagram before she goes to bed so I can see them in the morning. I don't have an account in my own name so I log on as katthecurriouscat, aka Kat.

But today, it's not one of her usual goofy faces. It's a sexy face.

Dewy lips. Smoky eyes. Loose tendrils of hair perfectly framing her face. This selfie is clearly not for me.

I type "What the . . . ?" in the comment window, then delete it and click the heart instead. I am not the first like. The first like is from tristanistanagram, who I assume is "Tristan from the Bus." I click over to his page but it's private, and there's no way I'm going to request to follow. So, I go back to Jenna's post and try to convince myself it's not meant to be a sexy photo. That she was trying some new makeup and hairstyle she wanted me to see, or was running out of facial expressions so felt the need to try "pouty" or something. I even scroll back over her previous posts to confirm the absence of pouty faces and thus explain the need for one.

That's when I notice something else that's missing, which is all of the goofiest selfies she ever posted. I sit bolt upright in bed, heart thumping, swiping my finger frantically up and down. Where's her zombie face? The pig-nose, eyes-rolled-back face? The just-ate-a-blue-lollipop, tongue-wagging face? The ones that made me LOL, I mean *really* laugh out loud, are gone.

Because she didn't want Tristan or her new friends to see them?

I write "WTH" in the comment window again and again and again so it's a big, long stream of WTHs.

And delete it.

I thought I was losing her yesterday, but when she texted that she missed me I convinced myself it was all my imagination, that we were as solid as ever. Now I'm not so sure.

I get dressed and brush my hair and wash my face and eat three bites of the omelet my mother makes and say "good morning" and "fine" and "bye" and board the bus and go to school.

I try again to convince myself I'm not losing my best friend, mostly because I don't know if I can handle it. The photos she deleted were pretty embarrassing, after all. I'd be mortified if anyone saw *me* making those faces. I never would've posted them in the first place, so I'm kind of a hypocrite to be mad at her for taking them down.

I decide it's okay. It's fine. Move along. Nothing to see here.

I hurry to get to world history before Dracula or the werewolf arrive. I don't even stop at my locker. When I slide into my seat, Lipton is there already having a hushed conversation with Adam Shenkman, who sits in front of him. It thankfully does not involve Frankenstein.

"We need to isolate our stuff," says Lipton. "Go into the wild."

Adam huddles low and does shifty eyes. "Set a warp?"

"Yeah. And whatever you do, don't let that jerk into our faction again. I can't believe he griefed our base."

"Sorry, dude. I thought he was cool, I didn't . . ." Adam stops talking suddenly and nods toward me.

"Don't worry. She's cool," says Lipton. Then he winks at me.

I swear I glanced over at them for maybe a second and now they think I was eavesdropping. Worse, I've been approved to share in their secrets via wink.

"I, uh . . . wasn't . . ." I shake my head. Why am I talking? I'm causing unnecessary sweating here. But words keep coming out. "I have no idea what you were even talking about."

"*Minecraft*," says Lipton. "You play?"

I shake my head again.

Lipton looks genuinely disappointed. "It's not just for little kids, you know."

"I didn't think that," I mumble.

"Good." He smiles. "It's really complex, and the multiplayer servers—"

"Dude." Adam bulges his eyes at Lipton, then stage whispers, "She's not interested."

Lipton glances at me, blushing. "Oh. Sorry. Never mind."

I resume my face-forward-eyes-down stance as our regular teacher, Mr. Braxley, calls the class to order. Jeremy Everling (aka Dracula), of the Everling family my mother is so keen to invite to our house for badminton, raises his hand. "Aren't you going to take attendance?"

He darts a glance at me and snickers.

Braxley ignores him and carries on. Class is going fine—status quo, just the way I like it, until twenty minutes before the end. That's when Mr. Braxley starts clapping to get our attention, since half the class has dozed off.

"Time to choose topics for your group projects!" he declares.

I groan inwardly while the rest of the class groans aloud.

"Up to four students per group. You may choose your own group, but choose wisely," he continues.

I cling to the words "up to" in hopes that I can do the project alone, in my own group of one. Everybody else is scrambling to claim their friends and avoid being the fifth wheel. I'm just trying to hold my lunch down as Mr. Braxley reads off a list of cheerful topics like Attila the Hun and the Black Death.

"Okay, I'm going to say them again." Mr. Braxley peers at us over the top of his reading glasses. "Raise your hand if you want the topic, and you can form a group with the others who want that topic, too."

My heart rate has doubled at this point, and I can feel the sweat circles forming. I'll just wait and see if there's a topic left over. The smartest kids in the class are suddenly very popular, as everyone wants them to do all the work for their group. Nobody's particularly excited about any of the topics. They sort of look to their friends every time one is named, and half-heartedly raise their hands.

Except Lipton. He nearly leaps out of his seat to claim the Battle of Thermopylae as his topic. Adam shrugs and raises his hand, too. Mr. Braxley looks around to see if anyone else wants it.

Lipton smiles at me.

I quickly look down, and Mr. Braxley moves on.

Lipton has a very nice smile, I realize. His teeth are straight and exceptionally white and there's a little gap between the front two. I should've joined his group because now I'm going to be the only one without a group and Mr. Braxley will probably make a big deal about who needs help and it'll be worse than if I just raised my stupid hand for the Battle of Thermopylae.

He calls out three more topics, which get taken amid nudges and hand-raising, and it's finally down to the Siege of Jerusalem. Nobody claims it because there's nobody left but me. Mr. Braxley looks up from his list and says, "Vicky Decker?"

He obviously has no idea who I am, even six weeks into the

school year. But he at least recognizes me as the only person who hasn't raised a hand. He lifts his eyebrows and I give a quick nod, then he writes down my name and starts telling us what we need to do for the project.

I practically go limp with relief that he didn't force anyone to join me or take me onto their team, even though it means I have to do the entire project by myself. I'm getting used to that.

There are still a few minutes of class left, and everyone is chattering with their group members when the intercom starts crackling. A voice is trying to be heard over the noise. "Mr. Braxley? Mr. Braxley?"

In the few seconds it takes him to answer, my stomach lurches into my throat and back down to my feet again, because I suddenly know exactly what this is about. It's almost nine thirty.

My guidance appointment was at nine fifteen.

"Could you please send Vicky Decker to the guidance office?" the voice on the intercom says.

Mr. Braxley answers in the affirmative, and then he and every single other person in the room stare at me. I don't move. I really want to. There is nothing I want more than to be gone from this room, but I am momentarily "deer in headlights" frozen.

Finally, after what seems like hours, Jeremy Everling breaks the silence. "Frankie, you going?"

For a second I think he meant to say "Vicky" but forgot my name, but then everyone's snickering and I realize it's short for Frankenstein.

I *really* can't move now.

Lipton reaches over from his desk and touches my arm and whispers, "Vicky. They called you to the guidance office."

I glance at him, at his kind eyes and his badly cut bangs, which remind me a little bit of Jenna's that first time we met. I hadn't noticed before. And that somehow releases me from my paralysis. I nod at Lipton and begin gathering my things and everyone goes back to talking to one another. I walk to the end of my aisle and around the side and escape out the door.

"You've been missing some classes lately," says Mrs. Greene. She sits at a desk, but swivels to face toward the room, which is furnished with comfy chairs, twinkly lights, and scented candles. She wears her hair in neat, shoulder-length dreadlocks, a patterned scarf wound around her neck. "I just wanted to check in with you and make sure everything's okay."

"Okay."

"Everything's okay?"

"Yes, fine." I try to make my voice calm and unshaky, but my knee keeps bobbing up and down. I force it to stop with the palm of my hand.

"And the missed classes?" She opens a folder in front of her. "Two last week, one Monday, and three yesterday."

"I, um, I wasn't feeling well."

"Did you go to the nurse?" She searches the folder for nonexistent excuse slips from the nurse.

"No, just the bathroom."

"Ah." Mrs. Greene closes the folder and looks at me, a warmth in her eyes. "You know, if something's troubling you—"

"Everything's fine." My knee is jackhammering again. I lift my backpack from the floor and set it on my lap to weigh my leg down. "I'm fine."

She inhales deeply. "How about the next time you feel like skipping a class, you come see me instead. Okay?"

It's *way* better in here than the girls' bathroom. But she'll want to talk about what's wrong with me. Or call a parent-teacher meeting. They do that sometimes. Gather all your teachers and your parents and the counselor and go around the room describing what you're doing wrong and how you can do better. I overheard a kid talking about it once, how it was like an ambush and he just told them whatever they wanted to hear so he could make it stop.

The zombie vacuum cleaners are starting to roar in my head again, and I feel dizzy.

"Hey." Suddenly Mrs. Greene's hand is resting on my arm. I didn't even notice she moved from her desk to sit in the chair next to mine. "Vicky. Breathe," she says. "You don't have to come if you don't want to. It's completely voluntary, and confidential. You don't even have to talk."

I nod and take a few deep breaths. "Okay. I'll do that." *No, I won't.*

She seems satisfied and moves back to her desk to pull some

papers from her file drawer. "I thought you might also like to consider joining a club or activity." She hands a few stapled pages to me. "It's not a requirement, but I'd like to get you into at least one extracurricular. It will be good for your college applications, which we need to start thinking about."

I scan the list. Book Club. Chinese Club. Drama Club. Feminist Club. BPA, EAC, AFS, OTM. So many impossibilities. I had no idea.

"Anything of interest?" she says.

"Not really." I pass the list back to her.

She scans it herself. "Math league?"

I shake my head.

"Handbell choir?"

I shake my head harder.

"Why don't you tell me what does interest you, and maybe I can suggest a match." She sits on her desk corner.

I rest my eyes on Mrs. Greene's hands, which are clasped in front of her. She leans forward, her whole body urging me to speak. "What do you like to do in your free time?" she prompts.

I can't tell her what I did in my free time last night, Photoshopping myself into Jenna's new friendships. And I can't tell her how I spend most other nights, lurking on the social media pages of kids at school who have the kind of life my mother wants for me. It makes me sound like a weirdo stalker.

Which I guess I am.

"I spend a lot of time on my computer," I finally say.

She flips through the stapled pages. "How about Computer Programming Club? Wait, no." She frowns. "They've disbanded. Let's see."

I watch as her eyes scroll down the page, and flip to the next one. And the next. There are a lot of activities at our school, and even she can see that I'm not suited for any of them.

"Gaming?" Her eyes light up.

I shake my head. I don't game. "I taught myself how to use Adobe Illustrator and Photoshop," I offer.

She gives an approving nod, like we're finally onto something, and flips to the last page of her activity booklet. "The yearbook staff is always looking for help," she says. "Editing photos, doing page layouts . . . does that sound of interest?"

"I don't know." The thought of joining an already-formed group is making me want to vomit.

"How about this," says Mrs. Greene. "Try it out. I'll let the editor know you're joining, that you're interested in photography."

"But not taking photos. I can't take photos." I also can't hide the panic that's crept into my voice.

Mrs. Greene makes a calming gesture with her hands. "Okay, no problem. Photo editing and layout, then. Sound good?"

I nod miserably. "Who's the editor?"

"Marissa DiMarco. You'll like her."

I nod. Of course I will. Marissa is perfect. I'll be sharing the same space, breathing the same air. Practically best friends! At least, that's how my mother will look at it. She'll be fantasizing me into those homecoming pictures in no time. If I tell her, that is. Which I won't.

I force a smile for Mrs. Greene. "Can't wait."

* * *

Jenna? Are you there?

Hello?

I guess you're with your new friends. Out with the old, in with the new, right?

Kidding.

Seriously, I'm kidding. Need to talk to you.

Okay, you're not there I guess. Call me later?

Jenna?

Mom's making her signature smoothie in the Cuisinart when I walk into the kitchen, and doesn't notice me sitting there until she turns it off.

"Oh! You scared me."

"Sorry." I watch her pour the frozen-mango-banana-kale-yogurt concoction into a glass. It's thick like soft ice cream, so she hands me a spoon.

"How was school? Anything interesting happen today?"

"Not really." I scoop a spoonful of smoothie into my mouth, then pull my phone out to see if Jenna replied to my texts, but her side of the conversation is still blank.

"How's Jenna?"

"That wasn't Jenna."

Mom's eyebrows shoot off the top of her head. "New friend?"

"Hallie Bryce," I say, surprising myself as much as my mother. Lies beget lies, apparently, and this one fell off my tongue before I even knew it was there. "We're doing a project together. For world history class. The Siege of Jerusalem."

"She's the dancer, right? The ballerina?"

I nod.

Mom beams. "Such a lovely girl. It's so nice you'll have a chance to get to know each other. Maybe you can—"

"Mom." I stop her before she starts fantasizing that Hallie will become my new best friend. "It's just a project. We'll probably do the whole thing online."

"Oh. Well. Anyway. It's nice." She's not grinning quite so exuberantly now, but there's a twinkle in her eye. She's happy to see me interacting with someone. *Anyone.* I guess that's why I made it up in the first place.

I take my smoothie with me through the dining room and living room and all the way down the hall to my bedroom, which is as far as you can get from the kitchen and still be in the house. I close my door, drop my backpack, pet Kat for a minute, and sit at my computer. I've got a dozen or so bookmarked pages I like to visit, some favorite YouTubers like Zoella and Rhyming Rhea, and assorted Instagrams. Some are random interesting people I stumbled across and just like their photos, and others are classmates with whom I have developed a probably unhealthy obsession.

There's Hallie Bryce, of course. Her pictures are so ethereal and peaceful, the way she bends herself to match the shape of tree limbs or tiptoes delicately through the tulips. Today she's doing some kind of backbend pose on a park bench, with one leg pointed skyward. I just can't imagine going out in public, putting on pointe shoes, and contorting myself into these shapes while people walk past. Maybe that's why I'm so infatuated with her Instagram. She's like a superhero to me.

I check in on Raj Radhakrishnan, who posts selfies constantly and always from inside his house rather than anywhere interesting. He's like the anti-Hallie. Yet I can't look away. Every day he stands in the same corner of his living room, posing the exact same way. His shirt changes; his glossy, black hair grows over time and then is suddenly shorter. The room brightens and dims with the weather. It's become a puzzle for me, finding what has changed. Today, an intricately patterned pillow rests on the couch at a different angle. A candle on the table is slightly shorter. I keep looking for a new expression on Raj's face, but it's always the same. Not happy or sad. Just there.

I flip through some other favorites from my school—a girl who knits, another who walks dogs, one with a nail polish and book fetish, a guy who's building a race car. They are solitary but fascinating.

Also fascinating, but in a totally different way, are the popular kids. The OMG-look-how-much-fun-we're-having people. They take selfies with twenty friends crammed into a single picture. They backflip and high-five and tackle-hug and cheesy-grin their way through life. They are confident and fearless and cool.

I end up back on YouTube, at Adrian Ahn's channel. He's posted a new video from last night's East 48 concert. It's not great—taken on someone's phone—but the crowd is going nuts. They're literally bouncing. Jumping up and down like pogo sticks. The music is fast and Adrian is drumming at a frenzied pace, his hair flying. It's invigorating just watching.

The band's logo pulses on the front of Adrian's drum. They got their name from a road near our town. I saw an interview with the lead singer, Rupert, who's from England, talking about how they couldn't come up with a band name. So one day, they were driving along, and decided they'd name the band after the next thing they saw out the window. And they saw the sign for Route 48 East. "We came bloody close to being called 'Lady with a Stroller' or 'Gigantic Cemetery,'" he said.

I crank the volume and watch the video again, bouncing along with the crowd. I can almost feel the floor shaking and the beat pulsing through my bones. Adrian is going completely crazy on the drums and the fans are dancing like mad. I pause the video and take a screen grab. As a photo, it's blurry. But I like the motion of it.

And then I have an idea.

I drag the image into Photoshop, then set up my monitor so the Photo Booth on my computer is pointing toward my blank wall, click the little photo button, and fling myself around so I'm dancing like a lunatic when the photo snaps.

The angle's all wrong, though, and I look slightly deranged with my massive hair flying and my big, baggy sweater billowing. I find a hairband and flip my head upside down, tying my hair into a high ponytail. I dig around in my jewelry box for a pair of dangly earrings my mother bought for me last Christmas. I pull off my sweater to expose the plain black T-shirt underneath.

What I do next would probably earn me some weird stares if anyone was watching. Because I'm flinging myself around, then lunging toward the computer to press the photo button, then flinging myself around again to make sure I'm dancing when the three-second timer goes off. I push the photo button and dance and push the photo button and dance and push the photo button until I have about twenty images to choose from.

Then I catch my breath, select the best photo, and Photoshop myself into the crowd. This one's harder than the bus scene. I have to motion blur my image before layering it over the other, so it looks like I'm really there dancing. The color temperature in my room is different than the purplish hue of the concert, so I have to adjust it to match. Then I use the airbrush tool to blend myself into the scene.

I turn the music back up and stare at the picture and it almost feels real. I'm there. Only I'm not worried that people are laughing at me, or I'm dancing wrong, or I don't belong. I'm at the concert, not caring what anybody thinks.

I'm fiddling with the image, making slight modifications, when my phone starts vibrating across my desk. I scoop it up. It's Jenna.

"You're alive!" I practically sing into the phone, still pumped from my pseudo-adventure. "I thought you were blowing me off."

She doesn't say anything, which is weird, since she called me.

"We must have a bad connection. Can you hear me?"

Nothing. But it's not totally silent. There are muffled voices in the background.

"Jenna!" I shout into the phone. "Are you there?"

No answer.

Did she just butt dial me?

I flop onto my bed, turn the volume on my phone all the way up, and press it to my ear. Someone's bouncing a basketball. There's laughing. One voice is Jenna's. I'd know her laugh anywhere. There's a male voice, too. I catch snippets of conversation.

"Come on," the guy says.

". . . have to go." That's Jenna.

"You just got here."

Bounce. Bounce.

"She's waiting."

I open my mouth to speak, to try and shout loud enough to get her attention, but then I hear his reply.

". . . such a drag . . . Let her wait."

More bouncing. Mumbling. My heart pounds.

". . . needs me," says Jenna. "I'm her only friend."

"So you're just going to text her all day?"

"No." Jenna sounds sulky.

There's a banging noise in the background, like a basketball hitting a board, then more bouncing. It stops, and is replaced by a different sound—like he's slapping a hand against the ball.

"She needs to get a life," he says.

I lift my hand to my mouth, phone still pressed to my ear. The pause before Jenna speaks again is excruciating, but not nearly as painful as what she says next.

"Yeah." She snorts. "I guess it *is* kind of pathetic."

I drop the phone as if it's burning my fingers, my breath coming in short gasps like the hiccups after a hard cry. Tears burn my eyes. I can still hear the mumble of their voices. That damn basketball pounding in my chest. I fumble to turn off the phone, so they won't realize I've been listening.

So I won't hear any more.

It takes a minute to process what just happened. Jenna was talking about *me*. With her new boyfriend. Who thinks I need to get a life. She . . . she told him I'm pathetic? No, she *snorted* that I'm pathetic.

I stare at the phone, my thumb hovering over her number. I'll call her. I'll tell her I heard everything she just said, and how could she say that? She'll say she's sorry. She'll tell me she's done with that guy, that he's a jerk. That she was only agreeing with him because she felt she had to, being new and all.

But I can't press her number, because what if she really *does* think I'm pathetic?

How could she not?

I drop into the chair in front of my computer and stare at the Photoshopped image of myself dancing at the concert. Even though it's all fake, I look . . . good. Like I'm having fun. Not pathetic. If Jenna saw me like this—if she could show her new friends—she wouldn't have to be embarrassed by me.

So I email it to myself. Then I open my phone, and I paste the photo into the text window below my last desperate plea to Jenna. And I write:

Went to the East 48 concert last night! So much fun.

I hit send, then wipe my tears. It only takes a few seconds for that " . . . " bubble to pop up on Jenna's side, then:

OMG! Jealous!

Adrian was amazing.

!!!!!!!

:-)

I can't believe it! Call me!

I don't write any more than that. And I don't call. I'm mad at her for saying what she said, for dismissing me so easily. When my phone rings a few minutes later, I let it go to voice mail. Maybe I'll check it tomorrow, and maybe I won't. Maybe I've fooled her into thinking I'm not so pathetic after all. It will only be a matter of time before she realizes that I still am, that nothing has changed. And worse, that I've lied to her.

But maybe it's best to leave her thinking I'm off doing something fabulous, so she won't feel bad about leaving me behind.

FABULOUS IS NOT HOW I feel the next morning when I press myself against the wall outside the yearbook office, hoping to disappear into the painted concrete blocks. Marissa DiMarco told me to meet her here. She texted this morning before I left for school, which thankfully gave me the opportunity to pack two extra T-shirts as backups for the inevitable sweat-through, which is happening at this very moment.

I see Raj at his locker. Alone. Two other Indian kids walk past and pretty obviously ignore him. His not-happy-not-sad face falters, but only for a second. Then he's back to neutral, shoulders square and walking away. Something is definitely going on there, but I have no idea what. I recognize the green collared shirt he's wearing. It's his favorite, I think, because it appears most often in his selfies.

The fact that I know this pretty much confirms that I am, in fact, a pathetic weirdo stalker.

Lipton walks past, too, and I am studiously averting my eyes when the door to the yearbook office opens and Marissa's head pops out, inches from mine. "There you are. Are you coming in?"

The temperature of my face rises about a thousand degrees. I didn't even think to knock. I just assumed she'd meet me out here, in the hallway . . . because I am an idiot. I follow her in. She sits in a rolling chair and pushes herself across the room.

"Quick tour. This is my desk. That's Beth Ann's and that's Marvo's. Everyone else shares those." She points to the various workstations, some with computers, some without. "I already assigned layout and writing of all the sections, but Mrs. Greene said you could help with photo editing?"

I swallow and nod.

"Great. Our photographers download everything here." She clicks open a folder on her computer screen. "Then somebody, usually me, has to go through and pick out the best stuff. Most of it needs Photoshopping. Not changing what people look like or anything, but brightening the image, cropping, getting rid of anything inappropriate. Maybe you could help with that?"

I nod again.

She rips a blank page from a notebook and scribbles down a series of letters and numbers. "This is the computer password. You can come in whenever you want. Just choose one of the folders from this file, go through the photos, drag the good ones over here."

She demonstrates everything and shows me where to leave

questions on a group chat that other staff members can access. And in the course of about five minutes, I'm officially a member of the Richardson High School Yearbook staff. I can come and go as I please. I don't have to talk to anyone or go to meetings or give high fives or even sit in the same room at the same time as anyone else. I can just slip behind a computer in the corner and do what I do best—watch from the sidelines. I don't even have to do it in a creepy way. It's actually my job. Or my guidance-counselor-sanctioned activity, at least.

The best part? For the first time all year, I'll have a place to eat my lunch that doesn't smell like hair spray and Lysol. The thought of it gets me through my morning classes, and helps me work up the nerve to go back to the yearbook office at lunch period. It is blessedly empty, so I settle in at a computer in the corner, open one of the folders Marissa showed me, and pull out my lunch. Two minutes later, as I'm clicking through images from a field hockey game, the door is flung open and two kids come bursting in. It's Beth Ann Price and Marvo Jones.

They see me and Marvo says, "Hey."

My throat feels tight, so rather than risk trying to speak, I give him a small nod and glance at Beth Ann. She's staring at my . . . feet? I follow her gaze to my shoes, the ones I wear every day, which are tan suede oxfords I found at the thrift store. I hate wearing new shoes, because everyone notices new shoes. Nobody notices a pair that are already a little scuffed.

Except Beth Ann Price, apparently. I tuck my feet under my chair.

"Hey," she says. "Welcome to yearbook."

"Thanks," I whisper. Dammit. Too quiet.

Marvo takes a step toward me to see what I'm working on. "Field hockey?"

I nod.

Beth Ann snorts. "Good luck with that."

My eyes widen. I have no idea what she means.

"Marissa's the captain," Marvo explains. "No pressure."

I swallow and turn back to the photos. Choosing the best ones was the one thing I *wasn't* worried about. I mean, I know a good photo when I see one. I should've realized it wouldn't be that simple. Should I pick all the photos Marissa is in? Will that look like I'm sucking up? Or will it make people think she's an egomaniac, since everyone knows she's the editor? I don't want to piss her off. I have no expectation of becoming friends with her, but I *really* don't want to be enemies. She'll tell Mrs. Greene it isn't working out. I'll be forced to join the handbell choir.

Suddenly, Beth Ann's hand is covering mine, which is shaking as I grip the mouse too tight. I'm rattling the whole table.

"Don't freak out," she says. "I was kidding. Pick the best shots. Just make sure there's one of Marissa, and that she looks halfway decent in it. Treat her like you would any team captain. You'll be fine."

I nod. Try to breathe normally.

She releases my hand and goes to her desk. Marvo sits next to her and they pull out their lunches and start working, talking quietly to each other.

I take a few breaths and flip through the photos. There are hundreds from this single game, and there will be hundreds more from other games. I'm supposed to save only a few from each. I pick the best one I can find of Marissa—just one. She's lunging for the ball with the fiercest expression on her face, lips snarling around her mouth guard. It's a great shot. I crop it a bit, brighten the color and fix the contrast, and dump it into the "best of" folder.

There are two others I like. One of a girl sitting on the bench, leaning her chin on the end of her stick. And another of the team manager dragging a sack of equipment. I save those, too, and dump the rest in the archives folder.

Then I click once more through the few I've selected.

"Good eye," says Marvo, making me jump. He's standing right behind me.

My pulse immediately starts throbbing in my neck. "Thanks," I croak.

"Except you might want to do something about that." He reaches over my shoulder and points at the photo on the screen, at a guy in the stands who is making one of the inappropriate gestures Marissa warned me about.

"Oh." I zoom in and hide the offending finger by cloning a bit of nearby background and covering it with that. It looks like a fist now, like the guy is simply cheering.

"Wow. You're good," says Marvo. "I'm Marvo, by the way. That's Beth Ann." He nods toward where she's standing by the door.

"I'm Vicky." My voice comes out clearly this time, and at a normal volume.

Beth Ann throws the door open and gestures for Marvo to go ahead of her. He gives a little bow and skips out, which makes her laugh. She glances back at me and says, "Later, Vic."

I raise a wobbly hand to wave, but they're already gone.

I've never had a nickname. Vicky isn't even short for Victoria. My given name is Vicky. Nobody's ever called me anything but Vicky.

It feels kind of nice to be someone other than Vicky.

I revel in my new identity all afternoon, imagining a much cooler version of myself saying, "Call me *Vic*" whenever someone asks my name. I'm even looking forward to texting Jenna about it when I get on the bus, until I remember I'm not texting Jenna anymore. Besides, how pathetic is it that I got all excited about someone *abbreviating my name*? Also, I got the shakes over choosing field hockey photos.

Still, I can't resist checking her Instagram, at least. There was nothing new when I looked this morning, but now there is. And for the first time, she's got company for her daily selfie. It's Tristan, his cheek pressed up against hers, and they're both making sexy faces now.

Ugh.

I close the Instagram app and swipe it off the screen so their faces are completely gone, not even hiding in the background sucking my battery life. There are phone messages, though, and a dozen new texts since I sent her the Photoshopped concert pic.

I put the phone to my ear and play the first message.

"Oh. My. God. I can't believe you went to an East 48 concert! By yourself?" She squeals and then laughs. "Seriously, who are you and what have you done with Vicky Decker? Anyway, call me. I need details. Stat."

A pang of guilt twists my stomach. I really fooled her. She's so excited for me. I can almost forget what I overheard on the phone, that she thinks I need to get a life. But that sends another kind of twist through my gut. I press play on her next message.

"Vicky! Where are you? Don't tell me you're hanging out with Adrian Ahn now." Uproarious laughter. Despite the photo, she knows that's not possible. "Who did you go to the concert with? Someone took that photo of you dancing and looking, wow . . . you look so great. Call me, okay? I'll be here all night."

I save the final message until I'm home and sitting in front of my computer. The picture I doctored of myself with Jenna's new bus friends is filling the screen. I can't stand seeing myself with them anymore. They stole my best friend. I don't want anything to do with them. A few clicks reverse all the changes I made, and leaves Jenna in her rightful place.

And me nowhere.

I pull up the East 48 photo. No Jenna. No Jenna's new friends. This one is mine. I'm sorry I even showed it to her, that she thinks I could ever be that girl, dressed like that. Dancing like that. In that ponytail. It's so *not* me, I might as well have purple hair! I take the paintbrush tool and I draw bright purple hair on myself. Then I change the color and add orangey-red streaks. I draw dark glasses on myself. And tattoos. An arm full of bracelets.

None of it looks real. But it turns me into someone else entirely. Someone fun and confident and unafraid. What would it feel like to be that girl? To *make* people look at me instead of always hiding?

I put my computer to sleep and listen to Jenna's final message.

"Hey." The excitement is gone from her voice now. "Are you mad at me or something? I don't know why you're not calling back. I hope everything's okay. So, call me. Vicky?" There's a fidgety silence at the end, and a sigh, and she hangs up.

My heart is pounding now, because of what I'm about to do.

Which is nothing.

I'm not going to call her, or text. Because that will only make it worse. I won't be able to talk to her without crying. Or continuing to lie about the concert. I'll have to tell her the truth, and I really will be pathetic then. I'll be her loser friend back home who sits alone in her bedroom and Photoshops herself into other people's lives.

I'd rather she remember me as that girl dancing at the concert.

5

I'M TOTALLY ZONKED OUT AROUND eleven on Saturday morning when Mom comes into my room all cheerful without even knocking. "Oh, you're still asleep! Sorry. I got you this."

I open one eye as she holds up a Forever 21 bag, then pulls out its contents—a black stretchy top and a neon-yellow skirt. I roll over to face the wall and close my eyes, hoping it's a dream.

Mom says, "You can wear it to the party!" at which point I'm actually hoping this is a nightmare.

I flop back over to face her. "I told you, no party."

"Not us, silly. Marissa DiMarco. It's next weekend." Mom holds the neon skirt up to her waist and looks at it in the mirror. "I ran into her mother at the mall. She thought you might like to go."

"What?" I am now fully awake and living the nightmare. "Why would she think that? I'm not even friends with Marissa."

"I simply mentioned—"

"Nooo. Mom, what did you do?"

"Nothing! She asked how you were doing. All I said was that your best friend Jenna had moved away . . ."

I pull the covers over my head and start whimpering.

". . . And she mentioned the party they were having and maybe you'd like to come."

There is only one thing worse than never being invited to anything, and that's the pity invite. No, wait . . . even worse than the pity invite is the my-mother-made-me-do-it pity invite.

"You're killing me. You are literally trying to kill me."

"You don't have to go if you don't want to," Mom says quietly. "I just thought—"

I play dead under the blanket. No movement. Not even breathing.

My mother sighs. "Well, just think about it."

I wait until she leaves my room and shuts the door before throwing the covers off my face and taking a huge, gasping breath. The new clothes are draped over the chair. While it was nice of her to buy me clothes, my mom clearly doesn't pay attention to what I actually wear. Scratch that—she pays attention, and then buys what she thinks I *should* wear. I pull both pieces out of the bag. Why would she buy me a skirt? I don't even *wear* skirts. And this one? I might as well put a traffic cone around my waist and shout "LOOK AT ME OVER HERE YOOO-HOOO!"

Having the clothes appear in my room is slightly better than an actual shopping trip. My mother has a tendency to shout my name from across the store, waving garments and offering commentary on which part of my figure they will flatter or hide the best. The only upside is, if I agree to an outfit of her choice, I get to go to the thrift store afterward, which is where I buy most of the clothes I actually wear, like my oversized "boyfriend" sweaters—which are just men's sweaters—and my lightly scuffed shoes. Mom *hates* it there. So, she drops me off and I get to shop by myself.

I crawl out of bed and pull on the skirt and top, and shuffle out to the kitchen to show her.

"Oh!" She presses her hands together like *namaste*. "They fit!"

I twirl around and curtsy. "Now can you take me to the thrift store?"

"Are you really going to wear it?"

Of course I'm not—I look like a giant bumblebee—but I at least have to pretend it's a possibility. "Maybe with a sweater?"

She sighs. "Fine. I'll drop you on my way to the grocery store."

I eat breakfast and change into my usual clothes. The neon-yellow-and-black ensemble gets shoved in its bag and tucked into my closet, never to be seen again. Just as we're getting in the car, a text from Jenna lights up my phone.

Need to talk to you.

I fight the urge to text her back. To believe that she actually *needs* me. Because I know that's not true. She's just used to me being there when nobody else is. Which, ironically, is part of the reason she finds me pathetic. *You can't have it both ways, Jenna.* I tuck my phone back into my pocket.

"Everything okay with Jenna?"

"Great." I don't want to attribute too much crap to Jenna, or my mom might call her mom to see if everything's okay. Our moms were never that close because Mrs. Tanner always had a really stressful job and now she's CEO of a company in Wisconsin. I don't think my mom has even spoken to her since they left, and that's how I'd like to keep it.

We pull up to the thrift store, which is an enormous warehouse with a floor-to-ceiling glass storefront where mannequins are displayed, dressed for weddings and business meetings. I always get the urge to sneak into the display and spice them up a bit, with crazy hats and jewelry and glasses and scarves—all the things I would never be brave enough to wear myself.

"I'll pick you up in an hour," says Mom. "Unless you want my help."

"That's okay." I quickly scramble out of the car and head inside. It's better this way, without her cringing at everything I choose. I bypass the women's clothes and head straight for the men's size-large sweaters that offer the most coverage in the least puke-worthy colors. No lilac. No coral.

Boyfriend sweaters are always in style. Right? Hallie Bryce wears them sometimes with just leggings and ballet flats. And her amazing legs, of course.

I find a gray cardigan I can at least pretend I might wear with the neon outfit. It hangs down almost as far as the skirt does. And, oooh, *cashmere*. Score!

My phone buzzes in my pocket. I pull it out and see another text from Jenna.

Never mind.

She "needed" me for, like, ten minutes? I jam the phone back in my pocket and return to the rack, choosing two more sweaters—a navy-blue crewneck and another in olive green. I hug the three sweaters on their hangers to my chest and start for the checkout. Altogether, they'll cost me less than fifteen dollars. I'm tempted to text Jenna because she loves oversized sweaters, too. She'd definitely be jealous of the gray cashmere. But, *never mind*.

My phone buzzes again and I don't want to look at it. I tell myself, *Don't even think about looking at it.* So, of course, I look at it.

Wanted your opinion on this outfit.

There's another "..." bubble beneath it so I wait, staring at the phone. Jenna knows I'm the wrong person to ask about clothes, especially if she wants to look cute. I'm pretty sure that's not really why she texted me. The next comment comes through:

Jossie and Tiff picked it out.

I stare at the cute names of the girls who have replaced me in Jenna's life. Then a photo comes through, featuring Jenna with Supercutegirl and Supercuteothergirl, aka Jossie and Tiff. Seeing her with them feels like sandpaper on a brush burn. They are posing like a trio of sexy anime warriors. But what really gets me is what they're wearing—which is pretty much the same outfit my mom just bought me: Black tops (all slightly different), and neon skirts. Jenna's is bright pink. Supercutegirl's is neon yellow, and Supercuteothergirl's is electric blue. They've also got clunky platform sandals on, with black-and-white patterned socks.

I barely recognize her. Especially when she texts:

Tristan loves it, so I'm all good.

Jenna never used to care what boys thought of her clothes. She'd be more likely to wear something the guys would *not* consider hot on purpose. And the matchy-matchy with friends? She used to roll her eyes when girls came to school like that. She'd say, "Can they not dress themselves?"

It's like she's transformed herself into an entirely different person.

I shove the phone in my back pocket and stumble through the shoe selection, not even wanting shoes. But there's a clunky pair of black platform sandals similar to the ones Jenna and her new friends are wearing, and they call out to me. It's as if they're teasing me, taunting: *You can't wear these! You're not cool enough!* I hook my finger through the straps and carry them toward the register.

The checkout line goes past a special display of items for Halloween. It's mostly kids' stuff—giant footed pajamas that look like lions or bears or dragons. But there are wigs, too. All colors. They start calling to me, too.

I pick up purple and orange ones, kind of nestle them together atop each other. It looks like the Photoshop hair I drew on myself in the East 48 picture.

A sign on the Halloween table reads "Everything $3." I take the wigs. A plastic bin offers sunglasses for $1.50 each. I sift through them and pluck a pair of cat-eye-shaped lenses with thick white rims, and a pair of those X-ray-vision glasses with the red-and-white swirly eyes. I snatch up three more pairs, plus a fistful of bracelets from a huge bowl that says they're twenty-five cents each. My arms are loaded to the point where I can't carry any more.

I'm nervous taking my haul up to the counter, because I'm always nervous at checkout counters. Sometimes the clerks are chatty, and I don't want to explain why I'm buying chunky sandals, two colorful wigs, five pairs of crazy sunglasses, and a dozen bracelets in addition to my usual boring sweaters. I'm not entirely sure myself, except that I'm tired of being me. I want to be someone else and I'm not sure living vicariously—or vicuriously—is going to cut it anymore.

The clerk barely acknowledges my presence, so I needn't have worried. She simply rings up my total, shoves everything in a bag, collects my money, and says, "Next."

I sit on a bench outside to wait for Mom, and carefully arrange my $43.75 worth of purchases so the weirdness is hidden beneath the sweaters.

Kind of like what I do every single day of my life.

When we get home, I run up to my room, shoo Kat out, and lock the door. I gather my hair into a blob and try to cram it all inside the purple wig, but it's sticking out everywhere and looks like I have a massive growth on top of my head. I rummage in my sock drawer for a pair of panty hose I've never worn, and cut off part of one leg to fashion a skullcap. Once I've got my hair all smoothed and tucked inside, I try to put both wigs on at once—orange first, then purple on top. They look ridiculous, like a furry double-decker ice cream cone.

I take them off and study the colorful blobs of hair until I figure out how to make them look the way I'm imagining them in my mind. Then I get to work, carefully cutting strips from the orange wig and gluing them to the scalp of the purple one, like extensions. After a while it starts to look like the hair I drew on my picture in Photoshop, except now with real (fake) hair.

I'm so engrossed in my creation that I barely register my mom calling me for dinner. I attach a last strip of orange hair to the purple wig and carefully stash it in my closet, resting atop a boot so the glue can dry without all the hair getting matted together.

Dad walks in the front door as I come down the hall from my room.

"Hi, sweetheart." He looks tired.

"Hey, Dad." We walk into the kitchen and sit down as Mom puts out the food.

"Good day?" he says, scooping mashed potatoes onto his plate and passing the bowl to me.

"It was okay."

"We went shopping," says Mom, implying that we did this together. "You should model your new outfit for your father."

"Do I have to?" I shoot Dad a pleading look.

"You don't have to," he says, smiling.

Mom gets that pursed-lip expression on her face that signals her annoyance whenever Dad sides with me. "If it were up to you two, nobody would ever do anything around here." She starts clearing the serving dishes even though we've barely started eating.

"Nora. Honey." My father lays a gentle hand on her arm, but she pulls away and carries the food into the kitchen. Dad and I start to eat but Mom doesn't come back. He says, "Maybe you could show me that outfit after all?"

I sigh. "You don't even care about the stupid outfit."

"But your mother does. And it won't hurt you to put it on."

"Fine." I toss my napkin on the table and push my chair back. He always does this. Takes my side, but then caves the second Mom gets upset. "But it also wouldn't hurt her to stop treating me like I'm some kind of Barbie doll she can dress up."

My father closes his eyes briefly, then folds his napkin and lays it on the table next to his plate. He won't say any more, but he'll be disappointed if I don't do what he asked. So I go to my room and I put on the neon skirt and the black top. When I return to the dining room, Mom is all smiles. "Isn't that cute?"

Dad blinks a few times at the neon, clearly doubting its cuteness. "Yes, very nice," he says, nodding.

"Whatever," I mumble. I excuse myself again and return to my room to stand in front of my full-length mirror. I try to imagine myself in that photo with Jenna and the supercutes. I strike a pose. Try a sexy face. *Look like a complete idiot.*

I strap on the clunky sandals to see if that helps. *It doesn't.*

"Honey, do you want to finish your dinner?" my mom calls to me down the hall.

"No, thanks. I'm not hungry anymore."

I hear my mom mumble "Okay, fine" as I go to my closet and check on the wig. The glue is dry, so I try it on, shoving my hair into the stocking skullcap first. It's better, but still not right. The look I'm going for needs to be a little more punk rock, a little less hippie clown. I take a pair of scissors from my desk and start snipping away until I have a jagged explosion of color framing my face. I lift clumps of it with my fingertips and spray it into place with Mom's ultra-stiff hair spray.

Jenna would die laughing . . .

I cut off the thought, go back to what I'm doing. Hiding myself.

Creating someone even Jenna won't recognize. The un-Vicky.

When I finish, I stand in front of the mirror, this time with the wig on. The glare of my pale legs is blinding, and cute ankle socks—even if I had them—won't help. I remember a pair of "snazzy leggings" my mom gave me for my birthday. I dig around in my drawer of misfit clothes until I find them. Black-and-white zigzags. I pull them on and examine my reflection again.

Combined with the crazy wig and the leggings, the skirt now looks too prim. I slip it off and start cutting. The hem goes first; then I slice thick strips all the way up to the waist, like the fringe of a very strange hula skirt. The black top gets a trim, too. But when I put it all back on and stand up straight, I realize I've given myself a bare midriff on one side.

I try tugging the shirt down, but can't hide the triangle of skin that rises about three inches from my belly button to my side. It's the perfect spot for a tattoo (that nobody will ever see), so I Sharpie the circular yin-yang symbol there.

The internet says that Sharpie tattoos stay longer if you dust them with baby powder and spray them with hair spray, so I try that. Then I strap on the platform sandals, dive my hand through the tower of bracelets, and for the final touch, choose from among my eclectic collection of secondhand sunglasses. SpongeBob eyeballs? Peace signs? Or rainbow-colored leopard frames with reflective lenses? I go with the first pair I picked, the dark cat-eye glasses with thick white frames. In honor of Kat.

I. Look. Awesome.

Okay, slightly ridiculous, too. But in a "Go Big or Go Home" sort of way. (Or, in my case, Go Big and Stay Home Because You're Too Chicken to Actually Go Anywhere.)

I prop my phone on the bookshelf and use the timer to take a picture. In my first few attempts I capture images of myself walking away from the camera, because three seconds isn't long enough to get into position. I switch to ten seconds so I can move to the opposite end of the room before it snaps the photo, and take several that way. Just standing there. Head to toe.

Boring.

I'm too still, too scared. *Too Vicky.*

I also realize that the bottom half of my face is completely bare and unchanged. I remedy that with a lipstick I find in a box of mostly-never-used makeup my mother gave me. Now I have a bright red mouth, slightly bigger than my own. I set the camera timer on my phone and try again. And again. And again.

I pose. I spin. I jump. I sway and lean and dip and bend and twirl and wave and smile and laugh. I blow kisses. I press my lips to the palm of my hand and hold the red kiss-mark to the camera.

I take dozens of photos until I am breathless from running back and forth to restart the timer. After downloading all the images to my computer, I click through them, hardly recognizing myself. If it weren't for the presence of my bedroom in the background, nobody would guess it was me. It feels good in the way the East 48 photo did, though I never left my room.

I only left *myself.*

But this time, there's no one to send the photo to, no one to fool into thinking I'm more fun or interesting or special than I am. There's no Jenna on the other end of a text message to say "OMG!"

There's no one out there at all.

So I go to Instagram, where there's always *someone.* Instead of signing in as Kat, I start a new account. I call it "Vicurious." Maybe I want Jenna to find it and know it's me. Or maybe I simply want proof that I exist outside my own bedroom. I drag one of the crazy pictures I just took into Photoshop so I can replace my bedroom with a plain, white background. Then I upload it as my profile picture.

And there I am: 0 Posts; 0 Followers; 0 Following.

I decide to post something, just to see if I get followers, though the very idea of followers makes me nervous. Total strangers watching me? I laugh at myself, since that's exactly what I do to Hallie and Adrian and even Raj. They don't know I'm watching, since I haven't officially followed them, which means anyone could be watching *me* and I wouldn't know it, either.

I'm in disguise, though. I look in the mirror again. Nobody will recognize me. I'm anonymous. Imagined. Not a real person. They can't hurt me if I'm not real. Can they?

I flip through my new pictures again and keep coming back to the very first one I took, where I'm walking away from the camera. Maybe I'm being a coward, using one that doesn't reveal even my fake face, but it captures the emptiness that weighs on me right now. I fiddle with the image in Photoshop, making sure I have a clean, blank background around my whole body. I'm like a cutout doll. Then I search the internet for a place I'd rather be.

A concert or crowd scene would only make me feel lonelier, so I go somewhere my solitude can be appreciated, even envied. I find a photo of an empty beach at sunset, waves gently lapping at the shore, reflecting the tropical sky's orange light. I drop my purple-and-orange-wigged cutout self into the scene—a small figure walking in the distance.

Disappearing.

And I post it. It's amazing how quickly the visual affects me. It's like I'm there. I'm somewhere else. I'm *someone* else. I take off my Vicurious costume, wipe my red lips clean with a tissue, and crawl into bed. Cuddled under my blankets, I take one last look at my alter ego's Instagram, my single lonely post, out there in the void. No likes. No comments. It's a comfortable place to be, but a part of me wishes someone would notice.

I click on the "..." button and slide my thumb to "edit." Then I add a single word:

#alone

6

SOMETHING WAKES ME, BUT I'M too groggy and disoriented to figure out what it is. I glance at the clock—it's two a.m. Just as I'm starting to nod off again, I see a dim flash of light through my closed eyelids, like the headlights of a passing car or a flash of distant lightning. I don't hear an engine or rumble of thunder, so I crack an eye open and look around my room. The light flashes again and . . . it's coming from my phone.

Jenna?

I lunge for it, forgetting. Squinting as my eyes adjust to the brightness of the screen, I quickly realize it's not from Jenna. And it's not a text.

It's a message from Instagram.

Actually, there are several messages from Instagram.

Wait, why is Instagram sending me messages? Then I remember last night and how I opened a new account.

I scramble to sit up in bed, swiping the screen. Vicurious is getting likes. And followers! There are twelve of them, with names like lonelyyygirlll and unlovelyunloved. I remember the hashtag I added right before bed. I click on it, #alone, and oh . . . my . . .

There are 13,150,650 posts with the #alone tag.

I scroll down the photos and see mine—Vicurious on the beach—amid a sea of other images of people in various states of solitude. The pictures are intermingled with what appear to be inspirational quotes. I click on one of them to see what's so quote-worthy about being #alone.

Don't depend too much
on anyone in this world.
Even your shadow leaves you
when you're in darkness.

Oh, God. That's depressing. I click away from it and tap on another and another.

It's sad when you feel alone
in a room full of people.

I am a prisoner in my own mind.

No one needs, wants,
or loves me.

I've found my people, apparently. And they're kind of scaring me. I mean, I can totally relate, but the thoughts they're sharing are ones I try very hard to ignore. Reading them all in one place is like standing on the edge of an abyss, and I can only teeter here for so long before I fall in.

So I back away. I click out to my own page again, to my single post. It has seventeen likes. Seventeen people have enjoyed my photo enough to click on the little red heart. I'm not sure what that means. Do they like that I'm lonely?

I turn my phone completely off so the flash of notifications won't wake me again, and I try to go back to sleep. It's not easy, though, knowing people are watching me, or Vicurious, rather.

But, seventeen people? I probably haven't spoken to that many people in a year. I'm not sure there are even seventeen people who know my name. And though these seventeen people don't know my *real* name, they know a part of me that nobody else does. They like something about me I hardly knew existed.

Comforted by that strange connection, I fall asleep so soundly it takes my mother pounding on my bedroom door to wake me later that morning. And I'm not even annoyed. I'm excited to check in on Vicurious. I wait until after breakfast, though, telling my parents I've got tons of homework. Which I do. But that's not how I plan to spend my day.

For the first time in my life, I feel like I can be part of something. I won't be lurking and watching with nobody knowing

I'm there. Vicurious gets to put herself out in the world, which I never could.

The question, as I'm back in my room and searching the internet, is this: If I could spend a day with anyone, who would it be? Where would I go?

I start dragging photos into an empty folder. Hogwarts. The *Titanic*. The *Tonight Show*. The guard hut at Buckingham Palace. Skydiving over the Grand Canyon. The Great Wall of China. The cosmos. An assortment of red carpets.

In the absolutely-not-crushing-on-him-but-think-he's-super-smart-and-cool department, I decide my first adventure will be with Neil deGrasse Tyson. He's standing at the helm of his space-ship with the cosmos exploding behind him. I select one of the photos of myself I took yesterday, where I'm sort of jumping and making this "Wow!" face, and I Photoshop it into the cosmos picture with Neil. I am copilot of his spaceship.

It takes me a while to get it just right, and looking quasi-real-istic. Not that I expect anyone to believe it's real, but I want it to seem like it could be. If only for me.

When I open Instagram to post the doctored image, I've got a dozen more followers—twenty-four total, and thirteen more likes. I hold my breath, clicking through the notifications to see if I recognize anyone. They're all random names, some who iden-tify specifically with depression or sadness and incorporate it into their handle, like sadgirldreaming and sucks2bsodepressed.

There is no jennaelizabethtanner or marissadimarco or anyone else I know. So I'm able to breathe again. I select the image, and I write a message:

To infinity and beyond!

I'm about to post it when I start worrying about copyright infringement and if it's okay to use someone else's photo like this without getting permission. I mean, people do it all the time, but that doesn't make it right. But I'm thinking the *Cosmos* producers will be cool with it because it's promotion of the show, and a form of fan art. They're probably happy to see people share stuff like this with friends. If anyone complains, though, I'll take it right down.

Still, I let my thumb hover over the "share" tab. This is it. I'm doing it. Sharing an image where you can actually see me. In costume, but still. I close my eyes and press my thumb to the blue bar, holding my breath until it pops up as a real, live post.

Then I wait.

And wait some more.

Nothing happens. No likes or follows or comments. Neil deGrasse Tyson is apparently not that popular with the #alone crowd. I look at the post again. Is there something wrong with it? Not cool or interesting or fun enough? How stupid is it that I care if the internet likes my photo? I'm the one living vicariously here, so it should only matter whether I like it or not, if it makes *me* feel good.

Yet here I am, feeling bad that people aren't liking my photo. They lifted me up last night, those twelve followers and seventeen likes—the fact that they related to me, to my photo. Now they've let me right back down.

As if real-life rejection isn't bad enough, I've got to inflict this alternate universe of scrutiny and neglect upon myself?

My phone beeps then. I perk up, and check the notifications.

sadgirldreaming Love your hair. Can't wait to see where you go next.

And I'm smiling again. With that one kind comment, just one expression of interest, my mood swings back up. Maybe other people need lots of friends, or hordes of fans, but all I really need is one.

I put Vicurious away and pull out my homework for Monday. All the while, I'm thinking about sadgirldreaming's comment. Where will I go next? It's got to be Hogwarts. Because, obviously. That's been my dream since I was nine. I lost count of the number of times I checked the mailbox for my letter of admission. And I've always wanted to ride a hippogriff.

I finish my precalc and make half an effort at studying for my bio exam, then start searching for Buckbeak. I quickly find the iconic movie image of Harry Potter soaring over the Great Lake on the creature's back.

Scanning through the Vicurious photos I took yesterday, I

find one where my hands are thrown in the air like I'm riding a roller coaster. I zoom in to make a cutout of myself and blend it into the movie shot. When I finish, it looks like I'm seated right behind Harry, grinning as Buckbeak's hooves skim the surface of the lake.

I can almost feel the hippogriff's feathers beneath my legs. The wind in my hair. Laughing and hooting along with Harry, on top of the world. I haven't posted it yet when Mom calls me for dinner, so I wait. I want to see the reaction. I rush through my meal and excuse myself with claims of more heaping piles of homework. As soon as I get back to my room, I post the image and stare at the screen for a while, waiting again to see if anyone notices.

Nobody does.

So I post another photo, and another. Vicurious chatting with Jimmy Fallon on the *Tonight Show*. Hanging out on the red carpet at various award ceremonies. I'm terribly underdressed in the shredded neon skirt, so I make them photobombs. Those are relatively easy to Photoshop so I do a bunch. Jennifer Lawrence. Will Smith. Gina Rodriguez. Neil Patrick Harris. Eddie Redmayne. Chris Rock. Gael García Bernal.

It's the height of living vicariously, for me at least. Vicurious can go anywhere, do anything, without ever leaving my room.

"Vicky?" Mom knocks on my door at eleven p.m. "Honey, you've been working hard. Time to get to sleep."

I dim my computer screen and turn off the light so she'll

think I've gone to bed. "Good night," I call out.

"Can I get a hug? I've hardly seen you all day," she says through my door.

"I'm already in bed, Mom." I try to sound as if I'm simply too sleepy to get up to unlock the door, rather than sitting at my desk fully clothed staring at my computer.

"Well, okay then." There's a pause, no retreating footsteps. She's still standing out there, and I hear her sigh.

I start to call out "Love you," but she says "Sleep well" and shuffles off.

I should be tired, but it feels like I've actually spent the past two hours leaping in front of cameras on the red carpet. It's as if I'm meant to exist in a vicarious state. It makes me feel alive.

I flip through the dozen photos I've posted today. Aside from sadgirldreaming, only one or two other followers have liked a photo. Otherwise they've gone unnoticed. And I shouldn't care, except that Vicurious is fabulous and daring and full of life. She deserves to be noticed! I click around to some of the more popular Instagrams and quickly realize what I've done wrong. I haven't hashtagged anything except the first photo.

That's why only the lonely have found me.

And I'm just about to add #space #neildegrassetyson #science #harrypotter #prisonerofazkaban #tonightshow #redcarpet #photobomb and anything else I can think of, when I realize . . . no. That's not me, and it's not Vicurious, either.

I leave them all the way they are, the way I am. Alone and unseen. I turn off my computer, slip on my pajamas, and crawl into bed. The phone on my nightstand won't be bothering me tonight.

7

I FUMBLE TO TURN OFF the alarm on my phone Monday morning and immediately wonder what Jenna posted for me, out of habit. I see an Instagram notification and assume that's her as well, until I wake up to the reality. No Jenna here, but Vicurious has a whole bunch of new followers. They found me, somehow, without any hashtags at all.

On the *Cosmos* image, one of my original #alone users has left a comment tagging people, and those people have left comments tagging others with spacey identities. Someone left a comment on the Buckbeak image and tagged someone named dumbledorefanatic, who then left a comment tagging five other people. They're talking to each other in the comments, throwing hashtags around like crazy.

But even more unbelievable is how many new followers there are: seventy-three, who appeared overnight and . . . wait, make that seventy-four. I haven't counted the comments on all of the images, but *Cosmos* has twenty-seven, and Buckbeak has eighteen.

I start hyperventilating a little, excited but also a bit terrified. People are actually watching my account, interested in what I'm doing. I swing my legs to the floor and bend forward, head between my knees. *Breathe, Vicky. Breathe.* I hold my phone in front of my upside-down face, staring at the screen in disbelief. Another follower pops up. And another. I scroll through them to make sure I don't recognize any names from school. As far as I can tell, they're complete strangers. Still, it takes a while for my breathing to calm. I watch my follower number tick up as the morning light slowly brightens my room.

Seventy-six . . . seventy-seven . . . seventy-eight . . .

It's unbelievable. I can't help wondering: Would Jenna like me better if she knew I was this girl?

I get ready for school and head out to the bus, my phone turned off and shoved in the bottom of my book bag. Knowing it's there, that Vicurious is out in the world making "friends," puts my heart in an unnerving state of hiccup. I head to class, worrying someone has seen her and will recognize me.

Lipton smiles at me as I walk into world history and I can't help thinking, *he knows.* Why else would he be smiling at me? As I sit down, about to launch into a full-on panic attack, he leans over and says, "How's the Siege of Jerusalem coming?"

"Great!" I blurt. "Very siege-y."

He laughs, and I want to crawl into a hole. I don't know how people manage to control both their thoughts and emotions at the same time. One or the other of mine is always escaping.

"Sure you don't want to join Team Thermopylae?" He makes a thumbing motion toward Adam. "It's a lot of work to do all by yourself. And we could use the help."

Adam narrows his eyes in a decidedly not-interested-in-your-help sort of way. He hates me. I'm pretty sure.

"Sorry. I did my research already." I quickly avert my eyes and start flipping through my textbook.

"No way," says Lipton. "Adam and I haven't even gotten ours half done, and we've both been working on it for like two hours every night."

I lift my eyes to his face, which is open and kind, then glance at Adam, who continues to scowl at me. My brain locks up. All I can do is blink at him.

Adam snorts. "Told you, dude."

Told him what? My gaze drops to the space between my desk and Lipton's, a distance that feels too close and too far at the same time.

He shrugs and hands me a neatly torn-off corner of notebook paper. "In case you change your mind."

I take the note. He's put his name and phone number on it. He notices me staring at the paper like I've never seen paper before, and reaches out to touch my arm. "You okay?"

And then all of a sudden I'm really *not* okay. My eyes start filling with tears. My throat tightens around the knot of emotion that's trying to push its way out of my chest. I want to pretend everything is fine, but there's too much everything: Jenna leaving, Jenna thinking I'm pathetic, Jenna making new friends and rubbing it in my face, the hope that Vicurious will make people see me differently, but the ever-present fear of being seen *at all*. I'm like a bottle of fizzy soda that's been shaken too hard. I could explode at any moment. And here's Lipton trying to unscrew the cap.

"Why are you being nice to me?" I practically bark the words at him, then clamp my mouth shut before anything else comes out.

Lipton's eyes widen. He withdraws his hand from my arm. "I, uh . . . sorry?"

I blink rapidly to keep tears from spilling. "It's allergies. I'm just . . . I'm trying not to sneeze."

I press my fist to my lips and concentrate on holding in whatever is trying to force itself out—which is feeling more like a scream than a sneeze.

Lipton looks at me funny, then leaves me alone, which is the best thing he could do. I concentrate on my breathing, try to get myself under control. It's ludicrous how easily and without warning I can be sent spinning. Every emotion, every fear, hovers dangerously close to the surface. I'm so focused on protecting myself from hurt, I have no idea what to do with kindness.

I make it through the rest of my morning classes and practically dive into the yearbook office, so relieved to have made it to lunch period without exploding. No one else is there, so I snag the computer in the corner. Marissa has attached a sticky note to the top of it. "V, Pull homecoming pics."

I open the folder marked "homecoming" and start to click through the images. There are hundreds. The football game, the dance, the parade, the float carrying all the homecoming-queen candidates waving their dainty hands like they're Queen Elizabeth.

There's Marissa again, hair in a sophisticated updo. She's beautiful, and she's everywhere. Does everything. I choose a picture of her being crowned queen, with Adrian as her king. They're not looking at the camera, but at each other. Laughing. It's the kind of photo that makes you want to *be* them.

I search for other photos that make me feel that way. Images of the people I can never be, the moments I will never have. A cheerleader teetering at the top of a pyramid. A line of girls sitting hip to hip and arm in arm in the stadium stands. A row of pep band members, trumpets raised. I throw a requisite touchdown shot into the mix, choosing one that captures that moment of pure joy on the player's face when he reaches the end zone.

I can't help imagining where Vicurious might appear in each photo. Locking arms with a row of friends, high-fiving the touchdown. I'm nervous Marissa will hate what I've picked, but Marvo said I have a good eye and I cling to his praise like it's a life raft—a tiny one that's losing air, and sharks are circling. But still, it's keeping me afloat.

That's how I feel most of the time, like I need to stay calm and still so the sharks won't notice me and attack. I make a mental note to check Instagram for hashtags like #dontnoticeme and #saveme. Because, after what I saw on #alone, I'm starting to think that I'm not.

Studying the photos, I spot the people who are alone in the crowd. I zoom in on them. Find another, and another. Soon my monitor is filled with close-ups of people hiding in plain sight— the people who watch, but don't participate. My people.

The door behind me creaks and I spin around. Marvo and Beth Ann walk in. He's smiling. She's not. I scramble to close the images, but knock the mouse off the desk instead. If I bend to pick it up, they'll definitely see the collage of lurkers on my screen.

I leap up and turn to face them, blocking the monitor from view. "Hi! Hey! How's it going? Here to work on yearbook? Of course you are. Stupid question. I mean, why else would you be here. Right?"

Oh, God.

Their eyes go wide. My heart nearly pounds through my chest and smacks them in the face. Marvo glances at Beth Ann and back at me. "She speaks."

I laugh in a desperate, it's-really-not-that-funny-oh-kill-me sort of way.

Beth Ann scowls and starts searching for something in the pile of papers on her desk. "Of course she speaks."

"I mean, like, full sentences," says Marvo.

"Stop picking on her."

"I'm not—"

"Yes, you are," Beth Ann snaps at him, flipping through her papers more frantically.

"You don't have to be such a—"

Her hand shoots out, a stop sign in his face, paired with an incinerating glare. "If you *ever* say that word to me . . ."

"What word?" Marvo grins. "Meanie?"

"That's not what you were going to say. And if you want to keep your balls, you better not say what we both know you were going to say."

Marvo crosses his hands over his private parts and backs toward the door. "My balls and I will just be going now."

"Wait!" Beth Ann stalks over to him, grabs his shirt, and kisses him. Right in front of me. And he kisses her back, and she puts her arms around him, and he puts his arms around her, and . . . I am staring at them like a weirdo.

Before they can catch me, I spin around to face my computer again and grab the mouse that's dangling off the edge of the table. I put the computer to sleep so the screen darkens, and drop to the chair. Not because I want to stay here another minute—but because the room is spinning and I don't want to embarrass myself further by passing out in front of Marvo and Beth Ann's make-out session.

Besides, they're blocking the door.

I sit very still in hopes they'll forget I exist, though I can still see them in my peripheral vision.

"Knock it off," says Beth Ann, slipping out of Marvo's embrace and rushing back to her desk.

He laughs. "You started it."

"I just . . ." She growls. "I need to find that stupid essay. I swear I left it in here."

Marvo helps her search, rifling through the stacks of folders and loose papers on her desk. The bell rings. Beth Ann starts whimpering.

"We'll find it," he says. "Calm down."

"Don't tell me to calm down!"

"Okay!" Marvo's hands are pressed to the sides of his head.

I slide my backpack on and stand to leave. I don't want to be late for class. I don't want to get in the way. I avert my eyes and slowly head toward the door. That's when I see what's pinned to the bulletin board. "The Refugee Crisis of 1939" by Beth Ann Price.

I stop. Point to it. Clear my throat. "Is this it?"

Beth Ann spins, runs to the board. "Ohmygod. Yes!"

She grabs me by the shoulders and says, "I could kiss you," then unpins her paper and hugs it to her chest. Marvo twirls her around, her red sneakers flying through the air. Red Converse. High-tops. I stare at them spinning and then bouncing up and down.

They've got yin-yang symbols on the toes.

Beth Ann . . . she's the girl from the bathroom who asked if I was okay. No wonder she was staring at my shoes the other day. I dash out and am halfway down the hall when I think I hear someone calling "Vic!" But I don't look back. I probably heard wrong, anyway, or they're shouting for Victoria Ewing or Victor Santos or even someone named Nick or Rick. There is nothing more humiliating than turning when it's not you they're calling.

And it's *never* me they're calling.

8

IT'S NOT UNTIL LAST PERIOD that I realize I put my yearbook computer monitor to sleep but never closed the photos. If anyone sits down to use that workstation, they'll see the way I zoomed in on random loners and think I'm really strange. The moment the bell rings, I head there instead of toward the buses.

I'm out of breath when I open the door and, in a rare show of mercy from the universe, the room is empty. But there's a soda can next to the keyboard, and when I touch the mouse, a blank screen comes up.

Someone's already closed all the photos, which means they've seen what I was doing. I push my chair away from the desk and leap up to race for the bus, slamming right into Marvo.

He clutches my upper arms to steady me. "Whoa there."

"Sorry. Didn't hear you come in," I pant, stepping out of his grasp.

"You staying after?"

I shake my head, eyes darting to the clock above the door.

"You ran off before. Didn't you hear me calling you?"

"No, I . . . bus," I say. "I have to catch the bus."

He waves off the urgency of my transportation needs. "I can take you—"

"No. I mean, thanks. But, no. It's okay. I can make it." I scoot to the door.

"Hey, Beth Ann and I meant to tell you before. There's a party at Marissa's house on Saturday," he says. "All the yearbook staff is invited. You should go. It'll be fun."

"Oh, yeah. Okay. I'll try," I say, knowing full well that "walking into parties alone" is at the very top of a list even more terrifying than the Terror List. "Sorry, I have to go."

"Go! Go!" He holds his hands up like he's surrendering. "I'll see you later, Vi."

I fly out the door. *Vi?*

He called me "Vic" before. Now he's suddenly calling me Vi? Pronounced vie, as in lie, pie, sigh, oh my, I'm gonna die. *Vi as in Vicurious.* I swallow the dread that's creeping up my throat.

Has Marvo seen Vicurious? The very irrational, paranoid part of my brain starts worrying that my log-in for the yearbook computer is somehow linked to my Instagram and anyone could hack into it and see what I've been doing.

But I must quickly dismiss those thoughts, because the buses leave in about two minutes, which means I have to run. Like, full-out sprint. Which I can't do. I mean, I know how to run, and I do have a modicum of athletic ability, but I can't race down the halls that way. It draws too much attention.

So, I fast-walk as calmly as possible. When I reach the front of the school, the buses are closing their doors. The first in line is starting to drive away. I stutter to a halt, chest heaving. It's an excruciating moment of indecision. Do I approach my bus, and risk that the driver won't notice me and I'll have to bang on the door or stand there looking ridiculous as he drives away? Or do I stand here looking ridiculous right now and risk that he *does* notice me and honks until I get on the bus?

It's a no-win situation, so I'm considering a third option, which involves ducking behind a nearby shrubbery or sitting on the ledge by the school entrance as if I'm staying after on purpose.

Unfortunately, or fortunately—I'm not sure which—I don't have to make any decision, because Lipton comes tearing out of the school shouting, "Wait! Hold the buses!"

He sprints past me, skids to a stop, and spins around. "Are you missing your bus, too?"

I nod feebly.

Lipton lunges for me, grabs my hand, and starts dragging me toward the departing line of buses. "What number?"

"Th . . . thirteen," I sputter.

He tears toward bus thirteen, dragging me behind him and waving frantically. Also shouting. "Hold up!"

The bus in front of mine starts pulling out, but we reach bus thirteen before it moves. Lipton slaps his hand against the door.

The driver sees us and pulls the lever that swings it open.

I want to disappear, slide right under the bus. I remember once a kid slipped on ice and fell beneath the bus and it ran right over his legs. Even that sounds slightly more appealing than boarding the bus right now with everyone staring.

Lipton beams at me like he's just climbed Mount Everest, and the driver says, "You getting on or what?"

So I get on and slide to the window of the first seat that's empty. Lipton takes off for one of the buses behind me, and someone shouts, "Go Tea Bag!" out the window. Everyone laughs. I concentrate on calming my gasping breath, making it shallow and quiet.

More than anything I want to text Jenna right now. Sinking low in my seat, I pull out my phone and log into Instagram instead, curious to see what Vicurious and her seventy-eight followers have been up to today. Except Vicurious doesn't have seventy-eight followers anymore.

She's got 1,723.

I blink at the screen. One thousand, seven hundred, twenty-three people are watching me? That's more than the entire student body of Edgar H. Richardson High School. I try to imagine them all seated in the gym for a pep rally, filling the bleachers and the floor. *I have that many followers?*

I turn my phone off. Press my forehead to the cool window. Close my eyes.

How is this happening? All I did was Photoshop myself into

a few images, which takes a certain skill, but not exactly the sort that people on the internet get excited about. I have no special talent. I'm not funny or clever. *Why are they following me?* I can't believe I'm not hyperventilating yet. In fact, the feeling seizing my chest is something else entirely. It's . . . glee?

No, it can't be that. I'm not even sure what that feels like. Yet I'm having a hard time stopping myself from smiling. Vicurious is a hit! And the fact that I'm more psyched than scared about that is so foreign to me. A burst of laughter—a really loud one— is hovering at the base of my throat, and I'm tempted to get up and skip down the bus aisle. But Vicky doesn't skip down aisles, or laugh out loud.

Only Vicurious does that.

9

ONCE I'M HOME AND HAVE shared an acceptable amount of information about my day with my mother, I retreat to my room with the cucumber-mango-cilantro-lime smoothie she prepared for me and plop down in front of my computer. I click through all the activity on my Vicurious account, trying to figure out how it blew up so fast. There are hundreds of likes and dozens of comments. I scour my feed for clues. I mean, even if you're a fan of Neil deGrasse Tyson or Jimmy Fallon, you don't follow every single person who posts a picture of them.

People seem to be responding to the *vicariosity* of it, if that's even a word, which I'm pretty sure it's not. They're writing stuff like:

OMG I LOVE THIS! I'm vicurious too.

and

When watching everyone else have fun is not enough.

I open my followers list and start clicking on them one by one. Their posts are mostly the usual stuff. Selfies. Cats. Books. Shoes. Quotes. Drawings. Food. Every now and then there's a feed that's filled with nearly naked shots. It makes me uncomfortable, like I've just walked in on someone while they're getting dressed. I click away as fast as I can.

After checking out about forty of my followers' feeds, I realize there are just too many to study them all. So I scan the list for familiar names. I'm on the lookout for jennaelizabethtanner, of course, but also marvolicious, which is Marvo's username. If he's following Vicurious, I'll know that calling me "Vi" was not a coincidence.

My eyes are bleary by the time I get to the bottom of the list, which thankfully does not contain Marvo. No Jenna, either. New followers have popped up while I was checking, though. I still haven't figured out why, or how, Vicurious is attracting so many, so I go back to the comments.

Then, I see.

Someone's tagged my Academy Awards photobomb of Jennifer Lawrence with #jenniferlawrence and then a user whose name is Jennifer Lawrence has written:

Photobombing on the red carpet. Looks like something I would do.

I switch over to her page, and she's actually reposted my post, and told her 58,472 followers to follow me, too. My heart starts racing at the thought of the actress Jennifer Lawrence following me, but then I notice three other Jennifer Lawrences have commented on my photo, too.

I do a Google search for "Jennifer Lawrence Instagram," hoping to find an official website or something. A bunch of Jennifer Lawrences show up. But right underneath them is an article titled, "Jennifer Lawrence Scorns Social Media," and it reports that Jennifer Lawrence has said, "If you ever see a Facebook, Instagram, or Twitter that says it's me, it most certainly is not me."

I'm kind of relieved. Also impressed. Jennifer Lawrence may be the only person on the planet not using social media and she couldn't care in the least. I wonder what it must feel like to be so utterly unconcerned about what anybody else thinks. I guess that's part of what Vicurious is about—capturing that feeling, that confidence.

I log out, delete my browser history, and push away from my desk. The smoothie Mom made for me after school is still sitting there. All melty. I stir it with the straw and stare into its depths.

"Vicky, are you in there?" A pounding on my door jolts me from my smoothie reverie.

"What?" I run stocking-footed across the room to open the door a crack and peer at my mother.

"I've been calling you!" Her face is all exasperated. "Jenna's on the phone."

"Jenna?" I glance at my backpack, where my cell phone has been safely tucked away since I got home. "What phone?"

Mom rolls her eyes. "The home phone, silly. Come talk to her."

"I . . ." My mind freezes for a second. The only thing I can think of is—*why are we the only ones with an actual landline?* And then, *What will I say?* "I . . ."

Mom pushes my door open and grabs my arm, dragging me toward the kitchen. "What is wrong with you? You've been holed up in your room like a hermit for days. Your best friend wants to talk to you. So talk to her."

She picks the phone up off the counter and shoves it into my hands.

It feels like I've just been pushed onto a stage in front of a thousand people. My mother's glaring at me, fists on her hips, as I bring the phone to my ear. I open my mouth but nothing comes out.

Mom grabs the phone back from me. "Jenna? Just hang on a second, sweetheart. Vicky will be right with you." She presses the mute button and her voice, which was all sugar with Jenna, turns back to a snarl for me.

"What is the problem? I'm trying to be patient and under-standing with you, Vicky. Truly, I am. But now you can't even talk to your only friend?"

"Not with you staring at me like that," I say.

"Fine!" She throws her arms in the air. "I'll leave the room. But you're going to have to get over this . . . this . . . absurd shyness.

Self-consciousness. Whatever it is. If you expect to function in the real world—"

The zombie vacuums start to roar to life in my head. I press my hands to my ears and turn away from her, away from the phone and Jenna, and start walking to my room.

Mom grabs my arm and pulls me back to the kitchen. When we reach the counter she maneuvers me around to sit on a stool. She pries my hands away from my ears and presses them to my lap.

"I will leave you alone now." Her voice is low and really calm. Too calm. "You will pick up the phone and talk to your friend. You think you can do that?"

I nod slowly.

"Terrific." She lifts the phone from the counter and hands it to me. "I'll just be in the living room. And we can talk about this after."

I wait until she's gone, take a deep breath, and push the button to unmute the phone. But I'm not ready. I haven't figured out what to say. Everything that comes to my head is wrong. Does she realize how jealous it makes me to see her hanging out with those girls in their matching outfits? And why is she dressing to please some boy she hardly knows? What's up with that? The worst, though: How could she have said what she said about me? I can't bear to hear her deny it, to try to convince me she doesn't *really* think I'm pathetic, when she obviously does.

As I slowly lift the phone to my ear, I hear her voice on the other end. "Hello? Vicky? Are you there? I can't believe you're not even going to talk to me. You'd rather just sit around in your room and mope? You're being so . . . aargh. Tristan was right." There's a pause. A sigh. "Are you even there?"

I take a deep breath. I say, "I'm here," just as she hangs up.

She hung up on me.

I listen to the dead line for a moment. Maybe she put me on hold like Mom put her on hold. But the dial tone is soon blaring in my ear so I know we're disconnected. I also know my mother is eavesdropping. She'll make me call back if I don't talk.

So I talk.

"I'm sorry. I keep forgetting to charge my phone," I say. "Is everything okay?"

I pause for her answer. Pretend she's telling me something not okay.

"That sounds awful."

I pause again, listen to the floor creaking in the next room.

"I'm fine. I got invited to a party at Marissa DiMarco's this weekend. Adrian Ahn is going to be there."

I imagine her reaction. I laugh. It doesn't even sound that fake.

"I should go," I say. "I've got homework."

It hits me what she said a moment ago, right before she hung up. *Tristan was right.* And it feels like I've actually been hit. Punched. What was he right about? That I'm pathetic?

"Okay, bye," I whisper.

The phone is still pressed to my ear when Mom comes

bounding in. She pets a hand down my hair. "Now, that wasn't so hard, was it?" Her voice is all sweetness and light again.

Which makes me want to scream.

"What is going on with you? What was that all about?"

"I—"

"It's just Jenna. I know you're shy, but really."

I don't say anything. What is there to say? That I'm afraid to talk to the one person I've always been able to talk to, because I'm trying to pretend I'm someone she might actually want to talk to? I try to put words together to explain this, but Mom's already on to the next thing.

"And I couldn't help overhearing . . . that you mentioned Marissa's party . . ."

I just sit here, trying not to let my head explode, while my mother talks at me. About me.

" . . . which is just terrific. You can wear your new skirt . . ."

The new skirt I've cut to shreds. I reach my fingers slowly to my hair. Comb through it so it hangs in front of my face.

" . . . and the black top. And those earrings I got you . . ."

She keeps stroking the back of my hair, oblivious to what I've done to the front of it.

" . . . I'm so happy to see you getting out . . ."

Except she doesn't see me. She's absently petting the back of my head, looking out the window, where the Vicky of her dreams apparently resides.

" . . . your father will be so pleased."

She says this whenever something pleases *her*. So it doesn't sound so much like it's all about *her*. My father really doesn't care if I go to parties or not. He hates parties himself.

Mom gives the back of my head a final pat and moves to the refrigerator. I can't really see her through my hair veil, but I can hear her taking stuff out and putting it on the counter.

"So, how's Jenna?" she says.

I consider the various truthful answers to this question. *Jenna has a boyfriend. Jenna thinks I'm pathetic. Jenna is clearly better off without me.*

"She changed her hair," I finally say. "Her mother didn't even notice."

10

I TRY TO DO HOMEWORK, but mostly end up reading the same paragraph over and over until it's time for dinner, which is torture. Mom keeps talking about Marissa's party. Dad tries to change the subject, but news of the fancy coffee machine they got at his office is no match for my mother.

"It makes all these flavors," he says. "Caramel mocha. French vanilla."

Mom gives him a patient smile, then turns back to me. "Do you think any of the parents will be staying?"

I stop midbite and pull the fork from my mouth. "At the party?"

"Yes, at the party." She gives a breathy laugh-snort.

"Uhhh, no. This is a high school party, not a third-grade play-date."

"I should at least pop in and say hello to Roberta."

I glare. Dad eyeballs her over the top of his glasses.

She sighs. "It just seems a little rude to shove you out the door and speed off. Am I allowed to at least stop the car?"

Dad laughs. I do not.

"Maybe I'll just stay home," I say. "I don't really want—"

"N-n-n-n-no." She wags her finger. "Don't even think about it. You're going to that party."

I blink at the uneaten food on my plate. How many parents force their children to go to parties? Is this normal? I take my dish to the sink and retreat to my room.

Mom calls after me when I'm halfway down the hall. "It'll be fun! You'll see!"

I shut my door a little harder than usual, pressing the lock with a forceful thrust of my thumb.

Jenna would laugh. She'd say, "Geez, get control of yourself."

I never could throw a proper tantrum, storm out of a room like she could, ranting about the injustice of whatever it was— not being allowed to order pizza or getting a bad grade on a perfectly brilliant essay. She'd vent on my behalf, too, whenever I was left out of something or teased. She'd fume and stomp. I always felt better after, even if I never did the venting myself.

But she's not here to vent for me now. So, I coil up with the tension of it, a spring that can't be sprung, and lie on my bed and stare at the ceiling. I deserve this ceiling. Dull white. They could put that on my grave when I die. "She was dull white." I am moping, just like Jenna said I would. Moping and contemplating the dull-whiteness of my ceiling.

How can I be mad at Jenna for calling me pathetic? I *am*

pathetic. I'd rather hide in my room than go to a party, which is probably the definition of pathetic. But Jenna and I had plenty of fun *not* going to parties.

I spring up and go to the bottom drawer of my dresser, where I keep most of the clothes my mother buys for me. It's like a rainbow in there; she's always trying to convince me to dress more colorfully. I root through and pluck out a red-and-white-striped shirt. She thought it looked cute and French. I thought it looked a little *Where's Waldo.*

I try it on with the neon-yellow skirt and the black-and-white zigzag tights, add the two-tone wig and red swirly X-ray-vision glasses, and . . . it's absolutely hideous.

But definitely not dull.

I look like Waldo on crack. See, Jenna? *Not moping.* It's time for Vicurious to do some Waldoing of her own.

The baby-powder-and-hair-spray trick worked pretty well on the yin-yang tattoo, which has hardly faded. I set up my bedroom like a photo studio with a sheet draped along the wall and down the floor. The white background will make it easier to cut around my form and place myself in different photos. I take a few shots where I'm standing straight on, then walking toward the left and right, à la Waldo. The process is tiring, because I have to run back and forth to the Photo Booth application on my computer to start the timer for each one. I'm getting better, though, at knowing how to hold a pose and set the lighting just right.

I click through them all and save my favorites, then search the internet for the perfect image to disappear into. I end up choosing a crowd scene at a huge outdoor music festival. There are hundreds of people in a muddy field. I don't even know which band is on the stage, but Vicurious fits beautifully into the sea of people, walking toward the stage with her red-and-white shirt clearly visible. I tweak and save the image and email it to myself, then go digging in my backpack for my phone so I can post to Instagram. The phone is alive, lighting up with new followers, likes, and comments as I take it in my hand. I give the screen an upward swipe, and another, and the notifications keep rolling. With each swipe I think, *This will be the last of them*, but they won't stop coming. I open Instagram, afraid to look but dying to know, and when I see the number, I can't believe it.

Vicurious has 3,755 followers.

I expected to gain a few, but more than double what it was before? It's more than Hallie Bryce has! I laugh out loud, because I don't know what else to do. I can only stare at that number and watch it tick upward right before my eyes.

Still not moping, Jenna!

I remember that I'm meant to be posting the *Where's Waldo* image, so I save it from email and pull it up in Instagram. I write a short message, and since I'm feeling adventurous, throw on some hashtags, too:

Can you #seeme? #notalone #whereswaldo

The first like comes in less than five seconds. Then three more, then ten. Within a few minutes, people are leaving "I see you!" comments. It makes me feel better. I put on my pajamas and hide my Vicurious costume in the back of my closet, then watch my Instagram feed until my mother knocks on my door and says good night. I quickly log out and crawl into bed.

I lie awake for a really long time, trying to convince myself that gaining thousands of followers who *see me* makes up for losing the only person who ever really did.

I oversleep because I was awake until four a.m. and don't even remember turning my alarm off. My mother discovers me still zonked out about ten minutes before the school bus arrives. She hands me a granola bar and a juice box (I swear she still thinks I'm eight) as I race out the door. I spend most of the bus ride worrying that someone will laugh at my stupid juice box.

When I get to world history, I'm just hoping I can put my head down and do my work and be left alone. So, of course there's a note on my desk, a folded paper with my name emblazoned on the side.

I pull it to my lap as I slide into my seat. Lipton is squinting at the Smart Board as if trying to puzzle out the homework assignment that's written up there. He's very studiously pretending to be busy with that.

I open the note. It's a photocopy, actually, from a book about the Crusades. Several paragraphs subtitled "The Siege of Jerusalem" are highlighted in yellow. There's a note written in the margin:

Saw this when I was doing my research. Thought maybe you could use it. —L

I glance up, and Lipton grins and gives me a thumbs-up. My eyes dart around to see if anyone just saw that, but nobody's paying attention. So I smile back at him. I mouth the word "thanks" and he smiles wider.

My face gets hot. Because I'm ridiculous.

I look down to put the paper in my backpack and notice that he's got his pant leg tucked into his sock, which is bright red. It reminds me of the time I left the house with a dryer sheet clinging to my back. At least Jenna told me before I got on the bus.

I should tell him.

But that could be just as embarrassing. Instead, I push my pencil off my desk so it drops and rolls near his foot. Normally I would never do this because everyone would stare and think I'm a klutz, but they're all busy talking and nobody will notice but him. He immediately leans down to pick it up, hesitating for the briefest moment before sitting back up and handing it to me with a wobbly smile.

I wobbly smile back at him, and notice a blotchy flush rise to his cheeks. He faces front again, but his arm drops to his side and his fingers find his pant leg and he tugs it out of his sock.

I am the first to arrive at the yearbook office for lunch period, and have just taken a bite of ham and cheese on rye when Marissa blusters in.

"Oh, good. You got my text," she says. "Now, where's Beth-vo?"

I freeze, holding my sandwich to my mouth. I threw my phone in my backpack when I raced out the door this morning and haven't looked at it since.

"Marv-ann?" she tries, crinkling her nose. "Are they coming?"

I blink. Lift my shoulders in a slow shrug.

She flounces into her rolly chair. "Nobody pays attention to me, I swear."

This statement surprises me. Marissa has to be the most attention-paid student at Richardson High. I put my sandwich down.

"We'll start without them." She swivels to face me, opening a spiral notebook in her lap and holding her pen at the ready. "Any ideas?"

"Uh..."

"I just don't want this yearbook to be an exact replica of every other yearbook that came before. I want something different."

I nod.

"Something besides the usual clubs and sports and class

pictures and candid hallway shots, you know?"

I nod again.

"Maybe feature some student artwork or something?" She writes the idea in her notebook.

I don't nod, because I'm starting to feel like a bobblehead doll. I put on a serious-thinking face instead. Bite my lip. Furrow my brows. One-on-one conversations are less terrifying than talking in front of a class, but Marissa makes me nervous. And I'm afraid one of my Vicurious ideas will pop out of my mouth.

The door opens then, and Marvo and Beth Ann come in laughing. I exhale.

"Finally," says Marissa. "Did you get my text?"

Marvo pulls his phone from his pocket and reads the text, obviously for the first time. "Yep. Got it."

"My battery died," says Beth Ann. "What are we doing?"

"Brainstorming." Marissa clicks her pen. "I want this to be the yearbook everyone will remember. Like nothing anyone's ever seen before."

They plop into chairs and put their own thinking faces on. Then Marvo hops up and starts pacing.

"How about this. We Photoshop naked people into the crowd at a football game, the choir concert, different photos all through the yearbook," he says. "Nobody will even notice until it's published and then, whoa. It'll be like *Where's Waldo*. Only, naked."

My head snaps up.

Beth Ann laughs. "Who's the naked guy? You?"

He shrugs. "Why not?"

"Because you'll get suspended? We'll all get suspended," says Marissa.

"I'll wear a wig or a hat or something. A mustache. Nobody will know who it is." He winks. At *me*.

I hold my breath. What are the chances Marvo just happened to think of Photoshopping someone into a *Where's Waldo* scene, in a disguise?

But he moves on, striking every possible pose his Naked Dude could be photographed in for the yearbook. The Statue of Liberty. The Incredible Hulk. *The Thinker.*

Beth Ann is cracking up.

"Don't forget this one." She does the clichéd John Travolta *Saturday Night Fever* pose. I took a Vicurious photo like that but I don't think I've used it yet. Or ever will, now.

"Naturally." Marvo mimics the pose. Then does another that vaguely resembles *Washington Crossing the Delaware*. "And this."

"You could wear a tricornered hat. Nothing else."

Marvo laughs, tips an imaginary hat, and waggles his eyebrows at Beth Ann. "At your service, ma'am."

"Great. And we'll all be expelled." Marissa huffs. "Or arrested."

"We can deny any knowledge," says Marvo. "Someone snuck into the yearbook office and Photoshopped naked people into the pictures. We had no idea. Nobody has to know we have a Photoshop genius in our midst."

They *all* turn and look at me.

"You're a Photoshop genius?" asks Marissa.

"Uhh . . ." I shake my head, face burning.

"She vanquished an obscene gesture from one of your hockey photos in like five seconds flat," says Marvo.

Beth Ann laughs. "Doesn't mean she wants to Photoshop your naked ass into every yearbook photo. Maybe it's not such a great idea, after all."

"You think?" Marissa rolls her eyes, repositions her notebook on her knee. "Any suggestions that won't ruin our chances of getting into college?"

Marvo slumps into his chair again, and gives me a weak smile.

Beth Ann lifts her feet, tapping the yin and yang tips of her red Converse high-tops together. "How about this. No head shots. Only feet. Everyone will be identified and remembered by the fabulousness of their shoes."

I tuck my slightly scuffed tan oxfords under my chair.

Marvo holds a boat-sized foot aloft. "Size thirteen, baby. And you know what they say about—"

"Please," says Marissa. "This is a yearbook meeting, not a presidential debate."

Marvo groans.

Beth Ann steps on his feet and they start walking around the room like that, her Converse on top of his.

I observe from my corner desk, nervous to be this close to the action. Vicurious belongs here, not me. And if they've discovered we are one and the same, then she is lost.

I don't think I can bear to lose her, too.

Marissa closes her notebook and shoves it into her backpack. "Never mind. We'll just do the same boring stuff."

"Aw, come on. We'll think of something." Marvo extricates himself from Beth Ann. "Give us a day or two."

"Fine," says Marissa. "Just let me know if anyone has an idea that doesn't suck."

I do have an idea, which probably sucks, and it would lead them dangerously close to Vicurious. So I keep it to myself. I quietly gather my things, and when they aren't paying attention, I slip out of the room.

The bell hasn't rung yet, so the hall is nearly empty. The stillness of it only magnifies the roar that almost constantly fills my ears, my brain, my chest when I'm at school and danger seems to lurk behind every corner. The harried start of my day has only made it louder. I steer for the nearest girls' bathroom, passing Mrs. Greene's office on the way. Her door is open. She's in there, but the overhead fluorescents are off. Only the twinkly lights she has strung along the walls are illuminated. It seems peaceful, and I am tempted to go in. She looks up and sees me and smiles.

I drop my eyes to the floor and hurry to the bathroom.

My usual stall is empty. I lock myself in and try to catch my breath. When Jenna was here, this hardly ever happened. She'd see me in the hall and nudge my arm and say "hey" and that's all it took. She was my own personal reset button.

Now, every little thing piles up until I'm buried under it and can hardly breathe. And it's so completely ridiculous and I *know* it is. My mother gave me a juice box, people spoke to me and smiled at me, and you'd think I was being chased by a pack of slobbering hyenas.

Why does every single thing have to feel like a pack of slobbering hyenas?

The bell rings and the bathroom fills, and people are waiting so I can't stay in here or they'll start banging or wondering what's wrong with me. I flush the toilet and go to the sink to wash my hands.

There are two girls fixing their hair and makeup at the mirror. If they notice me, they don't acknowledge it.

"Ugh. I'm breaking out. Do you have concealer?" says the one standing nearest to me. Her name is Mallory. She sits in front of me in biology.

The other girl digs around in her makeup bag and hands a tube to Mallory. "Don't use it all."

I'm drying my hands when one of the other stall doors opens and Hallie Bryce comes out. She glides to the only empty sink. Mallory and her friend stop in mid-makeup-application to stare at her. Even in this dingy bathroom, the sight of Hallie is breathtaking.

She dries her hands and glides out. Mallory and her friend watch her go. The minute she's through the door they turn to each other and say, in unison, "Oh my God."

Then they laugh and turn back to the mirror.

"Is she even human?" says Mallory.

Her friend shakes her head. "Impossible. Nobody is that perfect."

Mallory dabs concealer on a blemish. "I bet she never gets zits."

"I hate her."

"So do I."

I find myself wanting to defend Hallie—*Hallie Bryce who is beautiful and graceful and talented and* . . . absolutely does not need me to defend her. She's got thousands of followers online, and not like my followers, who aren't actually following *me* but a fictional character. Hallie is a human work of art and obviously doesn't care what a couple of girls sharing zit concealer in the bathroom at Richardson High School think of her.

Mallory and her friend giggle some more and leave, not the least bit concerned that I heard the whole conversation. I look at myself in the mirror, at my gray oversized sweater and my mousy hair that is neither blond nor brown but somewhere in between. I am concrete and linoleum.

Invisible.

No one will ever guess that I'm Vicurious. They don't even see me.

11

I SLOUCH LOW ON THE bus ride home, knees pressed to the seat in front of me, eyes level with the bottom of the window. The urge to text Jenna is strong. An ache, almost. I check her Instagram instead. It doesn't make the ache go away, just shifts it from my chest to my stomach. New selfies with Tristan pop up on the screen. Laughing, smiling, kissing. Her hair is perfect. Her makeup is perfect. Her eyes are even lined.

Since when does she wear eyeliner?

I click back to Vicurious. She's up to 4,121 followers. The *Where's Waldo* post has 237 likes. I scroll through them, look for Marvo. If he's following, then I'll know where he got the whole naked *Where's Waldo* idea. There's no Marvolicious, but plenty of other interesting names. One girl, invisiblemimi, posts selfies where she crops most of herself out of the photo. She shows only her shoulder, or part of her face, or her hand. She adds the #seeme tag on everything. But she also uses #dontseeme and #ignored and #lonely and #talktome and #donttalktome.

I know exactly how she feels.

I tap on the hashtags to see who else feels this way. Some of the posts are kind of disturbing—nude photos and spam-level weird—which isn't supposed to be allowed on Instagram, but I guess their porn checkers are too busy to catch it all. I skip around them, and what's left are people just sharing their pain, hoping that somebody—anybody—is paying attention.

I cringe at the pictures of cut marks, of blood dripping down pale arms or thighs slashed and raw. Of too-thin bodies, and mascara-stained cheeks.

People are *liking* their photos, which feels wrong. Is that what they want—positive reinforcement of their suffering? Or maybe it's just the acknowledgment. To be seen. They expose their deepest pain for a handful of little red hearts.

I feel almost guilty that my silly posts are getting so much attention while the people who desperately need it receive so little. It's not fair that followers flock to Vicurious and flee those who are hurting. But I understand it.

Joy attracts and misery repels.

Isn't that why Jenna prefers her new friends over me? Heck, that's why I prefer Vicurious to myself. Aside from that first post, Vicurious is never alone. She's fun, fearless, energetic . . . happy. She's everything that I am not. She's an escape from the misery.

But it's not enough. They need somebody to care about them, to do more than "like" their pain. I want to wave my arms at Instagram and say, "Hey! Can't you see? Over there! They need you!" Maybe that's what we're all doing—waiting for someone else to step in. Like there's a magical Instagram fairy who will appear out of nowhere and make it all better.

Then it strikes me. Maybe *I'm* the magical Instagram fairy.

I let the idea settle for a few minutes, my brain wrapping around it like curls of smoke from a pipe. Can I do that? Can I be that person? I don't know, so I flip the question. Can I *not* do that? Can I just look away?

The answer is, *I can't.*

So, I take a deep breath, and start clicking in comment windows of these people who are suffering. I write:

I care.

I see you.

I'm here for you.

I understand.

You are not alone.

I do it all the way home on the bus, on their pages, not mine. My follower number ticks up and up anyway. I want to tell them, *You don't have to follow me!* It makes me feel dirty, somehow. That there's a reward attached to caring. But I can't ignore them. Some start asking me to follow back. I guess that's how they measure their worth.

Is that how we *all* measure our worth now?

There are too many, though. And I don't want to follow

anyone if I can't follow *everyone*. I don't want any of them to feel left out or overlooked or not good enough. If they leave a comment, though, I reply. I give hearts and smileys.

It's not enough, but it's something.

I continue after dinner and late into the night. Vicurious adds a thousand followers. One in three is #alone or #ignored or #depressed. I try to reach out to them all, but their numbers keep growing and I can't keep up.

I pay for the effort on Wednesday morning, nearly falling asleep in world history. Lipton whispers to me a couple of times, alerting me to the page number we're supposed to be on, or that Mr. Braxley has told us to write something down. He smiles and I want to smile back, but it's taking all my energy to stay awake *and* balance the extra weight of #loneliness I'm carrying today.

The bell rings and I start to gather my stuff.

Lipton says, "Wait. I, uh, wanted to ask you . . ." He pauses. Swallows. "Just a second."

He starts digging around in his backpack and I wonder if he's got another page of Siege of Jerusalem notes, which is nice of him except I should probably do my own research. He glances up at me nervously and keeps searching.

Finally, he produces a small bag of peanut M&M's. He holds it out to me. "Do you want these? Mr. Patton gave them to every-one in English, but I'm allergic to peanuts, so . . ."

I stare at the yellow bag of M&M's. It's kind of random and a little weird. But he's standing there, hopeful, smiling. "Uh . . ."

"Unless you're allergic, too?" The smile drops from his face and he starts to draw his hand away.

Suddenly, I want those peanut M&M's more than anything else in the world. I want the smile back on Lipton's face. I thrust my hand out. "I'm not allergic."

"Great." He presses the bag into my palm. His smile returns.

I realize I haven't said thank you after he walks away, and then I feel bad about it. But mostly I feel tired.

Mrs. Greene's office door is open again when I walk past, but I keep going, wishing with every step I take that I had the nerve to go in. Just to rest. She said I could. I could eat my M&M's in there instead of the bathroom. I could share them with her and we wouldn't have to talk at all, just sit in her comfy chairs under her twinkly lights and eat Lipton's peanut M&M's in the quiet.

I surprise myself by pivoting to walk back toward her office. But someone has beaten me to it. The door is closing, and through the opening I see her slender legs, her perfect bun. Hallie Bryce isn't gliding, for once. She slumps into the comfy chair, head sagging to her chest. Mrs. Greene slips a "Do Not Disturb" sign over the doorknob and pulls it shut.

I stare at the closed door. Why would Hallie Bryce possibly need to talk to Mrs. Greene?

For the rest of the day, it's all I can think about. I look for Hallie in the hall, in classes we share. When I spot her, she's as tall and poised and confident as ever. Not showing the slightest sign of distress, and oblivious to the jealous murmurings of classmates like Mallory and her friend from the bathroom. But always alone.

I never noticed that before.

I end up saving the M&M's to eat on the bus ride home, and when I finish them I press the empty wrapper flat so I can save it. I don't know why. Maybe to make sure I didn't imagine that Lipton really did give me his peanut M&M's. Sometimes Vicurious feels more real than my real life, and it's good to know my existence—Vicky's, that is—has not gone unnoticed.

When I get home, my mother is waiting for me in the driveway. I tuck the M&M's wrapper into my pocket as I approach the car. She rolls down the window.

"Are you going somewhere?" I ask.

"Hair salon," she says. "And you're coming with me. I made you an appointment."

I groan and get in the car. There's no use arguing. This is a torment my mother inflicts upon me every few months, usually coinciding with occasions like Marissa's party that she deems momentous enough for additional grooming. It definitely belongs on the list. Having to sit in a chair and be subjected to random questions by a complete stranger who also happens to be wielding a pair of scissors is not my idea of a good time.

Mom hands me a small pile of torn magazine pages. They're hairstyles. "I thought you might like to try something new."

Translation: she'd really like me to try something new.

I flip through the pictures of gorgeous models and celebrities and their fabulous hair—short wavy bobs and flowy tendrils and pixie cuts.

"Have you met me?" I say.

She gives me a side-eye. "Yes, and I think you'd look great with one of those hairstyles."

"Because I look terrible the way I am."

"I didn't say that."

"You implied it."

She sighs. "I just think you'd be happier with a hairstyle that doesn't weigh you down so much."

We arrive at the salon and go inside. I follow behind her, because walking into any place where you're expected to answer questions about your intentions upon arrival always stresses me out.

Mom is happy to speak for me, though, so I let her do her thing. It's not until I'm in a chair with a red cape tied around my neck and my mother sitting in the waiting area that I tell my stylist, Rachel, "Just a trim, please."

"An inch? Two inches?"

"I was thinking more like a quarter inch."

She smiles. "You won't even be able to tell—"

I nod. "Perfect."

Rachel leads me to the sink for a wash, then sets about trimming. "I won't try to make you look like someone else," she says. "That's what people want, sometimes. But they're never happy with how it turns out."

I mumble "thanks," and she gets to work. She doesn't talk incessantly or ask me questions about school. She just trims, and when she's done, she runs her fingers through the thickness of it. "I could thin it out a bit if you like. Nobody but you will notice the difference. It won't be so heavy."

I consider this for a minute and say, "Okay."

She takes out a different pair of scissors and cuts some more, and afterward my head does feel lighter. Like the fabric that frames my face has changed from corduroy to chiffon. She dries it and styles it just the way I normally do, then holds a mirror so I can see the back.

I hardly ever look at the back of my head, and am surprised at how much it resembles Hallie Bryce's hair when she's not wearing a bun. I tilt my head to the left and right and my hair sways softly, just the way Hallie's does.

"Everything okay?" Rachel says.

I don't tell her she *did* make me look like someone else, because it's too late to stop her. I press my lips tight. Nod my approval even though I'm not sure I approve. She removes the cape and all the extra hair falls to the floor. Then she gestures toward my hands clasped in my lap. "You want me to throw that away?"

I look down and see the yellow M&M's wrapper pressed between my fingers like I'm clinging to it for dear life. I hadn't even realized I was holding it. "No," I say, quickly shoving it back in my pocket. "That's okay."

I hold my breath as I walk out to the waiting area, steeling myself for the fuss my mother will make about how different I look.

She doesn't, though. Make a fuss. She rolls her eyes when she sees me, pays the bill, and gives Rachel a tip. It's not until we're walking back to the car that she says, "I'm so glad I paid forty dollars for you to look exactly the same as when we walked in."

I gape at her. "What?"

"Did she even cut it, or was that a very expensive wash and blow-dry?"

"She cut a ton," I say.

Mom snorts. Shakes her head.

We get into the car and I flip down the visor to look in the mirror. It's completely different. But maybe Rachel was true to her word and nobody will notice the difference except me.

I'm a little worried the M&M's wrapper is going to turn into some kind of security blanket, because I pull it out again on the bus the next morning and hold it in my palm all the way to school. I'm nervous walking the halls with my new haircut, but quickly realize that nobody's looking at my hair. Nobody sees me at all.

I shove my coat into my locker as the warning bell rings, and hurry to class. Mr. Braxley is already standing in the front of the room, and the bell rings a few seconds later. I sit and try to calm my breathing.

"Okay, people," he says. "You should be pretty well into your research by now, but if anyone has questions or issues with the project, or with their group, or their lack of group, see me after class."

He looks straight at me.

Everyone turns to stare. Okay, maybe not everyone. But Lipton's gaze is practically searing a hole through the side of my head. I can feel it.

I glance over. He beams at me with his thousand-watt smile.

"Your hair looks really nice today," he says.

I blink at him.

He has the warmest eyes, and his smile is really wide, and there's that adorable gap between his two front teeth. But what I really like about him is that he sees me even when I'm invisible. Tingles shoot all the way from my toes and fingertips and kneecaps and elbows straight to my chest. My heart starts pounding like I've just sprinted a marathon.

So of course I act like he's got a contagious skin condition and say nothing.

"Did you get it cut?" he asks.

I shake my head. Eyes bulging.

"Huh. Looks different." He shrugs, then beams at me again. "Last chance to join Team Thermopylae. Adam and I are meeting at my house Saturday if you want to join us."

"I, um, can't," I say.

His smile droops. "Oh well."

Mr. Braxley starts teaching, and I focus on taking notes. My hair falls gently over my shoulders every time I lean forward, not the stiff curtain it usually is. I can still hide behind it, but I don't. I tuck it behind my ear so I can see Lipton in my peripheral vision.

I'm pretty sure he's watching me, too. And it feels good to be seen. I wonder if this is how all those people on Instagram feel, when they write #seeme and someone finally does.

12

I'M FEELING KIND OF OKAY on Friday night, thinking about Lipton and trying to come up with ideas for a new Vicurious post. Surfing, maybe. Or meditating with the Dalai Lama. Anything to take my mind off Marissa's party tomorrow night, and the fact that I haven't told my mother I will not be attending. Mom and Dad went out to see a movie, so I'm listening to music and doing a pretty good job of drowning out the roar in my ears.

Then I make the mistake of checking Jenna's Instagram page. She's posted a picture at a concert, where all you can see is the purple glow of stage lights and the silhouettes of so many arms raised and waving in the air. She doesn't even say where she is or which band, but I can tell it's someone huge.

Way bigger than the East 48 concert I "went" to.

So I ditch the Dalai Lama and start searching for the biggest concert I can find. I've got my neon-yellow skirt and tights and black top and clunky sandals on, and my wig and bracelets and sunglasses. My lips are red. My yin-yang tattoo is freshly drawn.

I take new photos against the white sheet, jumping around with an air guitar.

In less than an hour, I'm breathless, but I'm also on stage with the Foo Fighters at Wembley Stadium. Never mind that I was a little kid when they played that gig. What good is living vicariously if you can't go back in time? I choose an image where lead singer Dave Grohl's face is turned to the side, and position myself so it looks like we're making eye contact. Jamming together. I blast their song "The Pretender" and post the image, writing:

In which I time travel to the #foofighters
2008 Wembley Stadium concert.

I watch the notifications as they start to come in. Foo fans are noting which concerts they wish they'd been at and they're tagging their friends and tagging *me* on their own photos from concerts they attended. They even start a new hashtag:

#vicurious

And I'm so excited, I squeal. When I created my account, I thought the name was something Jenna might recognize because of how I always said "vicuriously" when I meant "vicariously." But to see it as a hashtag and know that people are using it and . . . I started that? It's weird. And wonderful.

I laugh at myself and continue to watch my feed as the

comments come in and new followers show up. I click on the #vicurious tag every now and then to see new posts, and when I like them, people get all "OMG THANK YOU," and "vicurious just liked my photo I can die happy now."

I posted one picture with the Foo Fighters and now it's like they're carrying me around on their shoulders.

The last time something like this happened—on my post with Neil deGrasse Tyson—I backed away from it. The attention kind of scared me. This time, I decide to see how far it can go. I take a bunch of photos of myself lying on the floor—arms and legs outstretched at various angles. I find a more recent concert picture online of some shirtless guy crowd surfing atop a Foo Fighters audience that's going totally bonkers. You can see the band onstage, hair and sweat flying. It's perfect.

I do a little precision Photoshopping to put myself in place of the shirtless guy in the photo. The volume of my skirt and sticking-outedness of my wig help hide the gaps between our different-shaped silhouettes. I use the airbrush tool to feather around the hard edges of my shape so they blend into the picture.

Satisfied with the results, I post the new image. I write:

Feeling the love, Foo fans! #foofighters #vicurious

I lie back in bed, raising my phone to my face every few minutes to see how many likes the post is getting. Foo fans are all over it. Someone comments:

I was there! For realz!

Others chime in:

Me too!

And maybe I shouldn't feel like I was really there, but I do. I turn the music up even louder and close my eyes, and I can feel their hands holding me up. After a while, my purple-and-orange wig is no longer a wig, but real hair. Strands of it stick to my sweaty face and neck. I can see Dave Grohl thrashing around onstage, and feel the pounding of the bass from the speakers.

Boom. Boom. Boom. Boom.

"Vicky!"

Bang. Bang. Bang. Bang.

"Wake up!"

I lift my head, disoriented. I must've fallen half-asleep because it takes a moment of looking around my room to realize I'm not at the concert. I swing my feet to the floor and reach to turn down the volume on my speakers.

"Vicky! For Christ's sake, answer me!" It's Mom. She's pounding on the door.

"I'm up! I'm awake." I stumble from my bed to the door and fling it open, panting.

My mother reels backward when she sees me. "What the—"

I look down at myself. Reach a hand to my hair.

Oh, no. I forgot I was dressed as Vicurious.

"Mom, I—"

"What have you done to your new skirt?"

"I, uh . . . was just—"

"You've ruined it."

I'm too panicked to form words, to make something up that explains my current state of bizarre.

"Now what will you wear to the party?" Mom's eyes jump to my hair. "Please tell me that's a wig."

I tear the wig off, exposing my panty hose head wrap with all my hair shoved inside. I peel that off, too, mind racing for an explanation as my real hair spills out around my face. "It's . . . I was . . . it's for Halloween," I stammer. "For a party. Marvo's. It's a punk rock theme. I was just trying to put together something . . ."

She sighs. "It's great that you're getting invited to parties. But did you have to ruin a perfectly good skirt? Couldn't you have cut up your thrift store clothes instead?"

I drop my gaze to the shredded neon that hangs from my waist. I feel like a little girl caught dressing up in her mother's clothes and playing with her makeup.

"Well, it's . . . cute, I guess. For a punk rock party," says Mom.

"Thanks."

She reaches for the colored wig in my hand. Inspects it. "Thrift?"

I nod.

"And you're actually going to wear this in public?"

I shrug. Of course I'm not, and she knows it.

"Are you sure everything is okay? This is a little . . . odd, even for you." She hands me the wig.

"Yeah, thanks."

I shuffle back into my room and sink to my bed again. Half my brain is still with Vicurious. The rest wants to go back there. It's scary how quickly I immersed myself in the fantasy. It felt like a dream, crowd surfing at the Foo Fighters concert, but it didn't disappear the way dreams normally do. It's like there's a muscle memory of it. The sensation of my body floating on a sea of hands—I can feel where they touched me. It made me feel powerful.

As Vicurious, I'm invincible. As Vicky?

Invisible.

I lie in bed with my phone and open Instagram again. Instead of seeking the energy of Foo Fighters fans, though, I find my way to those who feel #invisible, too.

They're right where I left them. All #ignored and #lonely and hoping someone will #talktome #donttalktome #seeme #dontseeme. I start leaving comments again.

I see you.

You are not invisible.

Are you okay?

They send me smiles and thanks. They ask if I'm okay, too. And I don't know how to answer. Vicurious is fine. She's great. And she's who they came for, who makes them feel special.

But me? I'm not so fine. I don't say anything, though, because I'm afraid they won't want her attention if they know she is someone like me.

13

BY FOUR O'CLOCK ON SATURDAY afternoon my followers have grown to 8,523, and I should be excited about that, but mostly I'm just trying not to throw up. The mere thought of knocking on Marissa DiMarco's door or walking into a house full of people—*her people*—is making me ill.

I'm not going. There's no way.

I kept meaning to tell my mother, but she was so excited about it. I didn't want to get her upset or angry. And now it's time to go. The party started a few minutes ago and the designated hour of leaving (so as to arrive fashionably late but not too late) is upon us. Mom is waiting for me in the living room and I am standing in front of my full-length mirror in the least party-going clothes imaginable. Baggy sweater, loose jeans, slightly scuffed shoes. The usual.

"You ready?" she calls down the hall.

I take a deep breath and open my door. I've already imagined the conversation. She'll take one look at me and say "You can't go to the party like that" and I'll say "Okay, I guess I'm not going" and she'll say "Change your clothes" and I'll return to my room and lie on my bed until she figures out I'm not changing my clothes, that I'm not going to the party. She'll be disappointed in me. But there will be no point in arguing because by that time, the party will already be half over.

Except when I step into the living room, all she says is, "Great, let's go." She picks up the keys and walks out to the driveway.

"Did you see what I'm wearing?" I ask, following her to the car. "I can't go to the party."

"Yes, you can, Vicky. You're going to this party."

"I can't."

Her face softens. "Look, sweetie. I understand it's been hard since Jenna left, and I blame myself for letting you become so dependent on her. But you can't hide in your room forever. There are people other than Jenna who I'm sure would love to be your friend. You just need to give yourself the opportunity to meet them. It's only going to get harder the longer you wait."

I swallow. "I'm not going."

She slumps against the car door. I wait for her to double down on her position, give me an ultimatum or something. But she doesn't. She just sighs.

"Let's get some pizza, then," she says, forcing a smile.

"All right." I pour myself into the car, my body limp with relief that she didn't turn that into more of an ordeal. It's not like her to give up so easily.

We back out of the driveway and I turn on the radio. Mom taps the steering wheel and hums along.

After we're driving for a couple of minutes, I notice we're not headed in the direction of our favorite pizza shop. "Aren't we going to Pietro's?"

"I thought we'd try something new," she says.

We drive some more, and not toward any shopping center I can think of. "Where is it?"

"Not much farther."

I start sweating, my body sensing the danger before my brain fully realizes what's happening, that we are not driving toward any pizza place. We are driving into Marissa DiMarco's neighborhood.

"Mom. What are you doing?"

"I'm taking you to the party," she says.

I clutch the edge of my seat, fingernails digging into the fabric. A wave of nausea hits. I try to focus on the horizon, like it's just a little motion sickness and not my mother trying to throw me to the sharks.

"You have to face your fears, Vicky," she says calmly. "That's the only way to overcome them. Just walk in there and smile and say hello. I know you're shy, but you can do this. It's not a big deal."

My mother has been telling people I'm "just shy" my entire life, and maybe that excused a lot of my awkward behavior growing up. But I don't think it explains whatever's wrong with me now. This isn't the same as hiding behind her skirt when I was little or being timid around strangers. This is me feeling like I'm going to die if I have to walk into that house. And I don't understand why she doesn't see that.

I inhale a ragged breath. "I'm not doing this, Mom. I can't."

She pulls up in front of the DiMarcos' house. "Then I guess we're going to sit here in the car for three hours."

"Oh my God." I start to hyperventilate.

"Don't get yourself all worked up," says Mom.

Other cars are stopping, too. Kids are getting out; they're walking past our car and toward the house. I bend over as far as I can so they can't see me.

"God, Vicky. It's just a party."

I slowly suck in air, blow it out, suck in air, blow it out. I focus on my breathing, try to block everything else out . . . until Mom shifts the car into gear and tears away from the curb. The blood returns to my head almost immediately. The danger is gone. I wait until she turns the corner before I sit up.

"You're being ridiculous," she says. "The way to overcome fear is to just face it."

Mom turns the next corner, and we're circling the block, heading right back to Marissa's house.

"You're going to this party," says Mom. "If I have to circle the block all night. This is for your own good. I'm just trying to help." But she doesn't realize this is making it all worse. It's like she'll do anything not to have to admit there's something really wrong with me.

I drop my head between my knees again. My ears fill with the vacuum cleaner roar.

Mom stops in front of the house. Taps her fingers on the wheel. I duck lower. Gasp for air.

She pulls away again and rounds the corner. This time I know the danger isn't over.

"Please take me home," I whisper between my knees. "I'm not feeling well."

"It's all in your head." She continues to the corner and we're circling the block again.

I want to shout, "OF COURSE IT'S IN MY HEAD!" I mean, where else would it be? Except it's not in my head the way my mother means. I'm not imagining things. My heart is, in fact, racing. My skin is sweating, my lungs are gasping, my stomach is twisting. My brain is telling them to do all that, and I'm pretty sure my brain is IN MY HEAD.

We're almost around the block again. I have to figure out a way to make this stop because people will start noticing the car that keeps pulling up and leaving without dropping anyone off. They'll recognize my mother. They'll know I'm in here.

I unbuckle my seat belt as we approach the corner.

"Wait until we—"

"Just drop me here," I say.

She pulls to a stop, and I throw open my door.

"Vicky—" Mom starts to object, but I'm out. I'm standing on the street. And she's smiling. "What time should I pick you up?"

"I'll get a ride." I slam the car door and step onto the sidewalk and wait for her to drive away. She hesitates, but there are cars behind her. So she turns and drives off. I wait until she's turned the corner before I spin on my heel and start walking in the opposite direction.

It's a miracle I'm walking at all. I can't even feel my legs. I search for a place to hide, because my mother is probably circling the block to check on me. The trees that line the street are large. I could plaster myself to the trunk of one and scoot around to the other side when she drives past. That wouldn't look ridiculous at all.

I notice a gap in a row of hedges, and before I can think twice about it, I slip through and sink to the grass on the other side. I bring my knees to my chest and pull my mossy-green sweater over them, so I'm as small and hedge-like as possible. I'm afraid to look toward the house to which this hedge belongs, as any movement will only draw attention. So I rest my forehead on my knees, let my hair fall around me, and try to get my breathing under control.

I think about what my mom said, about facing the fear, but I just don't know how. I've never known. Avoiding things like parties or groups is what I've always done and I wouldn't begin to know how to change that. Especially all by myself, without Jenna to speak for me when I can't find the words.

I'm not sure how long I sit here before someone passes on the sidewalk with a tiny little dog that's sniffing at the hedge. It barks at me, but the owner yanks its leash and says, "Jasmine!"

The dog makes a whimpering sound and scampers away.

I exhale.

Then something furry rubs up against my wrist and I spring backward.

"Mawrr!" It's a cat, gray with white markings, now with its back arched and fur fluffed out in fright.

"Sorry. Sorry," I whisper, extending my hand for it to sniff.

The cat slowly un-freaks itself, pacing in front of me, eventually approaching my hand and rubbing against my wrist. God, what I wouldn't give to be a cat. Nobody thinks it's weird how skittish they are. Or that they rub their face all over you, or knead their paws into your lap and circle three times before sitting down. Cats are gloriously odd, and people still love them.

The cat is now rubbing its full body on my legs, practically lying on me. I unhook my sweater from around my knees and sit cross-legged. The cat makes itself right at home in my lap and I pet it until it is purring so loud I'm afraid someone in the house might hear.

The house.

I kind of forgot it was there. I glance toward it, scanning the windows to see if anyone's looking out at me, then lower my gaze to the back patio. There's a grill, a table with an umbrella, some reclining lawn chairs, and . . . a guy.

He's sitting in one of the lawn chairs, reading a book. Maybe if I slink away quietly, he'll . . . oh, no. He raises his arm, palm facing me like he's hailing a cab. He slowly rises and starts walking toward me.

I'm too terrified to run. Also, the cat is now nestled and sleeping in my lap. I focus my gaze on the guy's feet, and when he's about halfway across the lawn, I see it.

His left pant leg is tucked into his sock. A bright blue sock.

"It *is* you," Lipton says as he comes within a few paces of my kneecaps. "I was just sitting there reading, minding my own business, and I looked up and thought, *Is that Vicky Decker in my backyard?* And it is. It's you."

His face is all incredulous delight. "What are you doing here?"

"I was just, uh . . . petting this cat. Your cat, I guess?"

Lipton nods slowly. "Yeah. That's my cat." He gestures toward the house behind him. "That's my house."

I keep petting the cat, because I'm not sure what else to do.

"Are you . . ." Lipton's eyebrows go all squiggly as he tries to figure out why I'm sitting in his yard. "Did you . . . um . . ."

"I came for the party." I nod in the direction of Marissa's house. "But I couldn't . . . I, you know." My face contorts and my hands wave around my head in what my screwed-up brain apparently thinks is an acceptable form of communication.

Remarkably, Lipton seems to understand. "Ah," he says, nodding. "Parties are not my thing, either. I'd much rather, uh . . . sit on my patio. Read a book. Talk to cat-petting girls who appear in my yard."

I smile. "Were you invited?"

He shoves his hands into his pockets. "Nah."

"Would you go if you were?"

"I don't know." He shrugs. "Probably not."

It suddenly occurs to me that I'm having an actual conversation. And not completely sucking at it. He spoke, I spoke, he spoke. I didn't blurt out anything strange. I should be knocking on wood this very moment, since I obviously just jinxed myself.

The cat seems to sense it, too, because it stretches, rolls off my lap, and saunters off. It pauses about ten paces away to look over its shoulder at me and lick its paw.

I brush the fur from my lap. Lipton extends a hand to help me up. And I panic. Because he's about to touch me and hardly anybody ever touches me and he's smiling his adorable smile and I'm *sweating* and what if he can smell me?

So, instead of taking his hand, as any normal person would, I push myself backward. Into a somersault. A backward somersault. Then spring to my feet. Like a lunatic.

Lipton steps away, scratching his chin. "That's, uh, quite a dismount you've got there."

"Yep! I like to keep myself nimble." I groan inwardly while brushing off the leaves that are now stuck to my back and hair.

"You want to come in?" Lipton's chin scratch moves to a back-of-head scratch, and he doesn't look all that certain it's a good idea to invite me into his house. "Play *Minecraft*, maybe?"

I blink at him. Playing a video game sounds strangely appealing, even though I don't know the first thing about *Minecraft*. But it would also involve going inside his house. Meeting his parents, probably. Maybe a sibling or two. Cue sweat glands.

"I can't," I say, arms swinging at my sides like I'm about to do the standing long jump. "But thanks for letting me pet your cat. And hide behind your shrubbery. It's very nice shrubbery you have. I would definitely recommend it highly to anyone seeking shrubbery to hide behind. Or . . . behind which to hide, rather. Yes. Yours would definitely be the shrubbery of choice for grammatically correct shrubbery hiders."

Lipton bites his lower lip, nodding. "Okay, then."

"Okay. Bye!" I make my escape before my mouth can spew anything more ridiculous, slipping through the gap in the hedge and walking toward home. Or in the general direction of home, because I was not paying attention on the drive here. Anyplace that is not Marissa's house or Lipton's backyard should suffice.

Just get me out of here.

14

I'VE WALKED ABOUT A HALF mile before my vital signs have calmed enough for my brain to start functioning properly and remember that I have a phone in my pocket that has a map app. Which might be useful at the moment, because I have no idea where I am.

My phone screen is alive with messages for Vicurious. Every time I see one I think it's a text from Jenna. I open my Instagram settings as I'm walking and turn off the notifications. Then I punch in my address and get directions for walking home.

It's 4.7 miles. I haven't walked that far since ... ever? My phone says it'll take an hour and forty-two minutes.

I trudge along, checking the map app every few minutes to make sure I haven't wandered off course. I wish there was a life app for that. Instead of "turn left" and "turn right" it could remind me to "breathe" and "walk" and "speak" and "shut up" and "please, seriously, stop talking."

My phone bleeps a notification, and now I really think it's

Jenna, because who else would it be since I shut off the messages from Instagram?

Are you having a good time?

Ugh, Mom. I ignore it and keep walking.

Are you sure you don't need me to pick you up later?

I check the next few directions on the app and shove the phone into my pocket so I can ignore my mother properly.

It buzzes.

And buzzes again.

And again.

When I've walked far enough that I don't know where to turn next, I pull it out to look at the map. The screen is full of more texts from Mom.

Who is bringing you home?

I want to know who you're getting a ride with, Vicky.

I don't want you driving home with someone who's been drinking.

It says I'll be home in forty-six minutes, and I recognize the way now. So I shove the phone into my pocket and let it bleep away. It's completely dark at this point, and the road I'm walking on doesn't have streetlights. Or sidewalks. Cars come up on me fast, not seeing my olive-green drabness at the side of the road. Some swerve and honk; others fly by without even spotting me.

By the time I reach my neighborhood, I'm sweaty from both the exertion and the anxiety of nearly being run over a few times. I'm so tired and thirsty I push the front door open without pausing to think what I'll say. I just want to crawl into my bed.

Dad's sitting on the couch, watching TV. He looks up. "Hey, kiddo. You're home early. And all in one piece."

I nod. "Imagine that."

He lowers the volume on the TV. "Your mother will be relieved."

"She expected me to be torn to shreds or something?"

"She worries," he says. "You know how protective she gets."

"Is that what you call it?"

My father frowns at me. "What do *you* call it?"

"Oh, I don't know, emotional manipulation? Aggravated menacing? Something like that?"

"Vicky."

"Seriously, Dad. She forced me to go to a party against my will. She *tricked* me. What kind of mother—"

"She means well," he interrupts. "Maybe she doesn't always get it right, but she's trying. You should give her a break."

"Yeah, well, she doesn't trick you into going to parties, does she?"

He chuckles under his breath. "She has."

"And you're taking her side?"

"You have to understand." He glances toward the kitchen, voice low. "Your mother is a social creature. We're like aliens to her. She's just trying to help us adapt to her world, to fit in."

I shake my head. "I'd rather phone home, E.T."

Dad laughs.

She blusters into the room then, nose glued to her cell phone, not even realizing I'm here. "She's not answering me, Gary. Do you think she's okay? Should I go over and get her? I never should've—"

Dad clears his throat and she looks up and sees me. "Oh. You're home."

"Indeed."

She lowers her phone. "You didn't answer my texts."

"I was at a party."

She nods. "Right. Of course. But I didn't see you go into the house, and—"

"Nora." My father reaches a hand out to her. "She's fine."

Mom slips her fingers into his and lets him pull her to sit on the couch next to him. "Of course she's fine," she says. "She's perfectly fine."

No, I'm not.

I want to say it, tell my mother I'm not fine at all. That I didn't go to the party because I physically couldn't face it. That maybe I need help. And I almost do. The words are on my tongue, waiting to pass my lips.

Then Mom's smiling at me and asking, "Did you have a good time?"

And I'm nodding, and telling her what she wants to hear, because she so desperately wants to believe there's nothing wrong with me.

"I'm tired from dancing," I say. "I think I'll go to bed."

I'm halfway to my room when Mom calls out, "Who brought you home?"

I hesitate for a moment, then say, "Lipton Gregory."

"Oh! He's driving already?"

"His mom dropped me off." I hurry to my room so I can put a closed door between us and avoid any more questions that make me tell lies.

I flop onto my bed, sweaty and thirsty and hungry, but I don't want to go back out there. I find a half-full water bottle in my backpack, slurp it down, and scrounge a piece of gum from my desk drawer. Maybe if I Photoshop Vicurious into a feast somewhere, it'll feel as if I've actually eaten. The thought of it makes me hungrier.

I swipe my phone open to see a stream of notifications— Mom's frantic texts, and . . .

Jenna?

She's been texting me like crazy. All those beeps my phone

was making from my back pocket, which I thought were my mom, were actually Jenna. I quickly scroll back to the first one and read through them.

Hey. It's me.

Earth to Vicky! Come in!

You there?

Come on, I know you have your phone. I really need to talk to you.

The time stamp on the first several texts is forty-five minutes ago. Then nothing for about ten minutes until they start up again.

I know why you're mad at me.

I butt dialed you, didn't I?

I saw the call on my phone log. Outgoing call, four minutes. After school last week. I was with Tristan. You heard us talking?

Whatever I said, I didn't mean it. I was just trying to be cool.

I'm sorry.

My throat tightens. I want to laugh or shout or cheer or cry. I'm not sure which. But here is the truth in front of me and my best friend apologizing and all I have to do is text her and say, "It's okay." And everything will be okay. We'll go back to the way it was, and I can even tell her about Vicurious! She will *die*.

I scroll a bit farther down so I can text her back, and there's more. Fifteen minutes ago, she texted again.

So that's it?

We're done?

Make new friends, forget the old?

Nice, Vicky. Thanks a lot.

Hope you and Marissa and Adrian will be very happy together.

Can't believe I wasted 12 years on you.

You know how many parties I missed because of you? How many friends I could've had? And this is what I get in return?

Have a nice life.

The air goes completely out of my lungs. I double over. Drop to my knees on the floor. *You know how many parties I missed because of you? How many friends I could've had?* The memories come back to me like a tsunami, laying me flat in a giant wave.

All those times at lunch, Jenna and me together, alone, when girls would come by and say to her, "Want to sit with us?" And she'd look longingly toward their table with its one empty seat, and shake her head. When they walked away, she'd say to me, "Too crowded" or "I'd *much* rather sit with you."

And all those party invitations slipped into her hand so I wouldn't see? I saw. But Jenna never wanted to go. "It's more fun just the two of us," she always said. And I believed her.

How could I have ever believed such a thing?

I would sob if I could get some air, but all I can manage is the shallowest of breaths. I am slowly submerging into quicksand, and any sudden movements will only speed my demise.

My eyes move around the room from where I now lie on the floor. It's a perspective I haven't tried before. Every flaw is exposed down here. The spots where the strip of wood molding has pulled away from the wall. The dust bunnies trapped under the bed. A balled-up sock. The banged-up rungs of my desk chair. A tiny earring back, made all the more mysterious because I hardly ever wear earrings and don't remember dropping it. A spot low on the wall that missed its second coat of paint.

At full height, standing tall, everything seems perfect. It's not until you sink down low that you can see the flaws. From my perspective, it's hard to see anything *but* the flaws.

I take it all in until my gaze finally comes to rest on the crack of light below my door, where I can see into the hallway.

I blink once every hour, or so it seems. A pair of shoes appears outside my door. My mother. She doesn't knock, though. Just stands there for a minute. My light is off, so she must assume I'm asleep. Her shoes linger a minute, then tiptoe away. The hall light goes off.

It's completely dark now. It occurs to me that I must be uncomfortable, lying here on the hard floor for so long. But the only pain is the ache in my chest.

My eyes adjust to the darkness. I scan the room for my phone, for any sign of life. But I've turned off the notifications from Instagram. Mom's asleep. And Jenna?

She's really gone this time.

15

I WAKE TO A POUNDING, but it's not at my door. The noise is coming from inside my own head, and my mouth feels like I slept with it wide open in front of a fan. The piece of gum I was chewing last night is a hard ball wedged against my teeth. I sit up and spit it into my hand. The pounding turns into more of a howl, as every aching part of my body lets out its own cry of pain.

I crawl to my door and stumble down the hall to the bathroom, gulping water from the sink faucet. It helps, but not much. Also, I can smell myself. I peel off my clothes, leaving them in a heap on the floor, and climb into the shower. The water is too hot, but I leave it that way. It makes me feel less numb. The steam is so thick, I can barely see my feet.

I let the water pour over me until it runs cold, then wrap a towel around myself and pad to my room. The house is quiet. It's still early, and Sunday.

I towel off, put on some clean clothes, including my fuzzy socks. I rub my hand over my freshly socked feet. They're so soft and fluffy. I want a suit made of these socks. A big sock suit with armholes. No, forget the armholes. It could be more of a cocoon. A big, fuzzy sock cocoon.

My phone sits in the middle of my unslept-in bed. Seeing it reminds me why I spent the night on the floor. It hurts to think those thoughts again. I don't even want to think her name. The girl whose name shall not be spoken. The girl who pitied me. The girl who lied to me for almost twelve years.

The girl who erased me from her life with a single text.

Not thinking about her is making me want to cry. And I try to never cry about myself. If I cried about myself I'd be bawling all day, every day.

I sit at my computer and open my Instagram and I cry, instead, for my new friends who are #depressed and #lonely and #sad. They are legion. I want to wrap fuzzy sock cocoons around them all, and myself, too.

I Google "fuzzy sock cocoon."

Surprisingly, there are some images of sweaters and coats that pop up, but it's the babies that draw my attention. Tiny, newborn babies snuggled in cozy little knit cocoons with matching hats or miniature hoodies.

They look so safe and warm. I change my search to "babies in cocoons" and hit the jackpot of fuzzy sock-like cuteness. God, I want to be one of those babies. Go back to a time when contentment came from sleep and swaddling, from being warm and dry and fed.

I glance at my bed, consider rolling myself in the comforter for the rest of the day. Would my mother lovingly feed me if she found me like that? Doubtful. She'd more likely tear the blankets off and expose me to the cold.

The way to overcome your fear is to just face it.

I open Photoshop. In less than an hour, I am snuggly in a cocoon . . . only my head showing, with my orange-and-purple hair and the peace sign sunglasses, which seem most suitable for the occasion. I'm tucked in there with the sweetly sleeping babies, all nestled together like a row of spoons. I pull the photo up on my Instagram, and write:

In which I disappear. #safe #warm #fuzzysockcocoon

I will die if someone else has used that hashtag. So I check. As expected, "No tags found." And I'm glad. One of my followers inaugurated #vicurious, so this is my first original.

There are more than one million of #safe, though, and more than eleven million of #warm.

Vicurious is up to 9,202 users. I can't believe I'm so close to 10,000, or that adding 800 followers would ever seem "close."

I go to the kitchen. Eat cereal. Drink orange juice. Mom comes in, all chipper. "What shall we do today?" She starts filling the kettle to boil water for tea. "Go shopping? Have a nice lunch out, maybe?"

It really is astonishing how determined the woman is to ignore the fact that I hate things like shopping and nice lunches out.

"I have homework," I say.

Her smile falls. "Of course."

I sit with her until the tea is ready, then take a cup to my room. Today's mission: 10,000 followers or bust.

Several hours later, I can't even remember all the places I've sent Vicurious. To a World Cup soccer match. The inauguration of Pope Francis. Wimbledon. Hang gliding. Bungee jumping. Line dancing. Cattle herding. And I am no longer hashtag-averse. It's #score #praisegod #game #set #match #whee #ahhh #foottapping #yeehah #saddleup and anything else I can think of.

My number of followers ticks up and up and up. By three o'clock I've reached my goal of 10,000. It's not enough. I still feel empty, so I keep posting. Vicurious at the Tony Awards. The Golden Globes. The Emmys. I tag celebrities. I crash my favorite PBS series, inserting myself in place of the lead female actress.

When my eyes are swimming from staring at the computer for so long, I lie on my bed with my phone, checking it every few minutes as my follower count bumps higher and higher. By dinnertime it's 12,800. By nine o'clock it's 14,200. I've added something like 5,000 followers in a single day. Instagram doesn't even write out the full number anymore; it's too big. They put "k" for thousand now.

That should make me happy, right?

And it does, for a while. But if the rate of followers slows down, even for a few minutes, it feels like rejection. I'm Vicky again, walking the halls alone. Huddling in the corner bathroom stall, eating my lunch on a toilet. Texting and texting and texting a friend who has better things to do, who thinks I'm pathetic, who can't believe she wasted her life on me.

I scroll through the comments on my posts, looking for someone who understands. It's not until I see a follower named Jenna that I realize I'm really looking for *her*. Hoping she'll find me here and see me differently. But the Jenna I find isn't *my* Jenna, whose Instagram was simply her name, jennaelizabethtanner. This Jenna is justjennafied. We start chatting back and forth on the picture I posted of the fuzzy sock cocoons.

justjennafied Why are you so #vicurious?

vicurious To get away.

justjennafied From what?

vicurious Myself.

justjennafied What's wrong with you?

vicurious LOL. Everything.

justjennafied You're so popular. And funny. Alive.

vicurious That's not me.

justjennafied Who are you?

vicurious #nobody

justjennafied Not true. Who are you really?

vicurious #alone #lonely #sad #scared

justjennafied Me too.

I pause here, and wonder if she really feels this way, or if she's just saying that to make me feel better. And then I start to see an echo of "me toos" pop up.

tanyazeebee Me too.

fauxfriendella Me too.

kookiestkimberly Me too.

ambivalentlessly Me too.

shriekingshackup Me too.

It goes on and on. So many, and yet we've found one another. I watch their names blip up with every new comment, their not-real names. Until I see one I recognize.

radhakrishnanraj Me too.

Selfie Raj? I click on his name to get to his page, and there he is. He follows me. Someone from my school has found me, and follows. I sit back in my chair, amazed.

I want to follow him back. Let him know he's not #alone.

But I haven't followed anyone yet, and for Raj to be my first? It could give me away. If someone connects me to Richardson High School, they might recognize me.

Has Raj recognized me?

My heart starts thumping. I search my posts to see if he's left any other comments, any sign that he knows who I am. But all I find is that single, lonely "me too."

It hits me harder than all the rest, somehow. Raj is *real*. I know my other followers are, too. But they are anonymous names and hidden faces. I see Raj every day. He walks the same halls, breathes the same air. I could touch him, if I wanted. Talk to him.

Except I can't. I'm starting to sweat just thinking about it. But knowing someone as lonely as I am is right there, so close, makes me feel a little bit less alone.

16

MAKING IT THROUGH SCHOOL THE next day is like swimming upstream in a river of mud. Jenna's texts are weighing me down, and every time I see Raj in the hall I stop breathing for a few seconds, worried he'll recognize me. But he keeps moving along in his rhythmic, steady way, oblivious to the "me too" I am sending him telepathically. The fact that I can't work up the nerve to speak to him only makes it worse. It takes all my energy to press forward, unable to focus on more than what's directly in front of me. I keep stopping to duck into doorways and bathrooms and stairwells to catch my breath and steel myself for the next stretch of hallway.

I almost make it to world history but have to kneel down in an alcove and pretend to tie my shoe. That's when I hear them. Lipton and Adam. They've stopped at Adam's locker, which is just around the corner from where I'm crouched.

"... so I asked her if she wanted to come in and play *Minecraft*," says Lipton.

"Dude," says Adam. "You didn't."

"What's wrong with that?"

"That's so . . . Are you, like, twelve?"

"You play *Minecraft*. You're not twelve."

"Yeah, but I would never ask a girl to come over and play. What were you thinking?"

"I was thinking she might like *Minecraft*!"

"Yeah, well. Maybe wait until you know for sure."

"So, what should I ask her?"

Adam snorts and pushes his locker closed. "I don't know. But not that. Something you're sure she's interested in."

"I think maybe she likes my socks? She's always looking at my ankles."

"Oh, God. No."

"I was joking," says Lipton. Unconvincingly.

"Just try not to say anything stupid, okay?"

"I'll try," Lipton mumbles. "No *Minecraft*, no socks . . ."

They walk off toward class, and I am now paralyzed by the realization that Lipton maybe . . . likes me? Unless he asked more than one girl to play *Minecraft* this weekend. What are the chances of that?

I force myself to continue my swim upstream to Mr. Braxley's classroom before the bell rings. Against all better judgment, I glance at Lipton as I sit down. He disarms me with his smile. I mean, literally. My arms stop working and I drop all my books. He leans over to help me. The perspiration is flowing down my sides like waterfalls.

"Hey." He hands me the book that fell near his feet.

Speak to him speak to him speak to him speak to him. "Thanks!" I blurt, taking the book. "Thank you," I say again, because once is apparently not enough. "Thank you very much." Okay, *stop.*

"You're welcome," says Lipton. "You're welcome. You're welcome very much."

My eyes widen at his reply.

He laughs.

I swallow. Gulp, really.

He smiles. Pushes the hair off his forehead. It flops back down.

Smile, Vicky. Smile. I pull my lips into a shape that reveals my teeth, but isn't exactly a smile. It likely resembles the face I make in the dentist's chair when the hygienist is taking X-rays. My eyes are watering, too. Because I keep forgetting to blink.

Blink. Blink. Blink.

Lipton clears his throat, then leans toward my desk. "So, I was wondering if you'd like to come over to my house after school," he says. "To, uh, pet my cat?"

On the other side of Lipton, Adam tips slowly forward, his head landing square on his desk with a loud thunk. He groans.

"I mean, we could do other things, too, of course," Lipton stammers. "Whatever interests you."

Say yes say yes say yes say yes. My brain is blaring the correct answer in my head! But do I listen?

"I can't," I whisper. "I'm, um, busy."

Adam groans some more.

"It doesn't have to be tonight." Lipton shifts his weight from one foot to the other. "It could be, you know . . . whenever."

My heart is pounding so hard now, and the roar in my ears is so loud, I'm not even sure what he just said or if I heard him right. I start flipping the words around in my head to make sense of them, until I'm fairly certain they went something like, "It's tonight or never." Which can't be right.

He's staring at me, waiting for my answer. His cheeks are getting blotchy. *Oh, no.* I'm embarrassing him. He's starting to look like he might throw up. That's not what I want.

"That's not what I want at all." It comes out almost a hiss. I smack my hand to my mouth.

"Oh." Lipton looks like I just slapped him across the face. "Never mind."

"Okay, class." Mr. Braxley starts teaching. I would sincerely like to concentrate on what he's saying, but I'm too busy trying to calm my heart rate and figure out what just happened.

Lipton asked me out.

Breathe.

He asked me to come to his house.

Breathe.

To pet his cat.

Breathe.

I panicked and said I was busy.

The rest is a blur. But it can't be good, because Adam's eyes are shooting death lasers at me. Lipton keeps glancing my way and jiggling his knee. Just like I do! Except his pant leg is tucked into his sock AGAIN. It wouldn't be so obvious if he didn't have such colorful taste in socks. Today he's wearing bright yellow.

I do like his socks. Should I tell him? *I like your socks, Lipton.* Maybe it would fix whatever I've messed up. I wait until class is over and I start packing up my things. I watch him do the same, hoping he'll look up at me again so I can smile and deliver the compliment.

But he doesn't look at me. And then he's leaving. I'm missing my chance!

In a panic, I blurt out, "Nice socks!" Which isn't how I meant to say it.

He spins around, looks down at his ankles.

Jeremy Everling laughs, points at Lipton's socks. The pant leg is tucked in. "Nice," he says. "Very stylish."

Lipton doesn't reach down to fix his pant leg. He just gapes at me. His expression is even worse now than if I'd slapped him. It looks like I killed his dog or something.

"Cold," says Adam, shaking his head.

I watch them go. The classroom empties. The roar of the vacuums quiets to a hum and I realize what I've done. It's like I was trying to drive through a dense fog and couldn't see which way to go. Now the fog's lifted and I can see where I made a wrong turn, but it's too late. I've gone off a cliff.

I'll never find my way back to Lipton, or to Jenna, or anybody. I'm stuck here at the bottom of a ravine—alone again.

17

FOR THE REST OF THE week, I go to yearbook, select photos, remove obscene gestures and nose pickers and crotch scratchers. I crop, file, nod, smile. I listen to Marvo and Beth Ann and Marissa brainstorm ideas to make this yearbook the most memorable ever.

I don't care if the yearbook is memorable.

Lipton doesn't offer any more peanut M&M's. He doesn't nudge me when I zone out, or tell me what page we're on. He doesn't even glance at me in class anymore. I stop carrying the candy wrapper I saved because it only reminds me of what I've ruined.

I go to school. I go home. I do my homework. I eat. I sleep. I repeat.

I don't check in on Vicurious. Don't log in to Instagram at all. Adrian Ahn tosses a drumstick at me on purpose in the hall one day, and I don't even realize until it's too late. It hits me on the shoulder and clatters to the floor.

"Sorry," I mumble, and keep walking. I should be embarrassed, but I'm not.

He calls after me, "Vicky! Hey!"

Huh. Adrian knows my name. He's shouting it in the hall, and I feel . . . nothing. Nothing at all.

At first, it's kind of nice, this numbness. Nothing fazes me. If people stare, I don't care. If they laugh or think I'm weird or stupid or ugly, I haven't noticed.

And then I find myself standing in front of Mrs. Greene's office one day, not entirely sure how I got there or why. Before I can shuffle off, she looks up from her desk and smiles. "Hi, Vicky. Do you want to come in?"

It's easier to stay than to come up with an excuse not to, so I shrug and sit down in one of her comfy chairs.

She gets up and shuts the door, but doesn't say anything right away.

We sit in the quiet. My eyes follow the string of twinkly lights draped across the room. Back and forth, back and forth. It's almost hypnotic. I wonder if she did that on purpose.

"I get the sense you're having some trouble," she says after a while. "Would you like to talk about it?"

I pause. This is my opening. I could tell her everything right now. Maybe it would help. But all I say is, "No, thank you."

I prepare for a pep talk, like something my mom would say. But Mrs. Greene is true to her word, and doesn't make me talk.

She works at her computer while I sit there with my eyes closed, just breathing.

I am breathing.

Some days, it feels like that's enough. I'm just so tired. It takes all my energy to make sure my mom thinks I'm fine, to sit upright in class all day when I really want to rest my head on the desk and close my eyes, to go through the motions of every-thing, to not cry when Lipton pretends he doesn't see me.

When I finally leave Mrs. Greene's room, Hallie Bryce is wait-ing outside. She says hi to me, and I stare at her, waiting for my usual panic to ensue. When it doesn't, I say hi back, and she glides past me through the doorway but crumples into the chair as if she simply cannot carry herself erect for a single second more. And I totally understand how she feels.

Mrs. Greene gently closes the door.

I don't move. Not right away. Because for the first time all week, I let myself really feel something. And it's not even my own pain.

I feel bad for Hallie Bryce.

I start to feel like my old self. Not my best self, from before Jenna left, but my week-ago self, before I ruined everything with Lipton. The result is that I remember how horrible I felt before everything went numb. The pain Mrs. Greene was sensing? It's not so raw as before, but it's there. I'm still at the bottom of the ravine but no longer wanting to lie on the jagged rocks and suffer. I want to climb out.

I'm just not sure how to do it.

On the Saturday morning before Halloween, my mother says, "Don't you have a party to go to tonight?"

I blink at her.

"The one you ripped your skirt apart for? Marco's?"

And then I remember the other lie I told my mother.

"Marvo," I say. "He canceled."

She narrows her eyes at me. "Or you just don't want to go."

Last week, I overheard her telling my dad that she ran into Roberta DiMarco and told her I'd had a nice time at Marissa's party. The woman gave her a funny look and said, "Vicky was there?" And Mom said, "Yes, I dropped her off myself!" And Mrs. DiMarco apologized and said, "It was so crowded. I'm sorry I missed her." My father said, "You know how Vicky is. She was probably standing in a corner and Roberta just didn't notice her."

"There's no party," I tell her now. Which is the truth, since I made it up in the first place.

"Then you ruined a perfectly good skirt for nothing." She sighs. "You can wear it for the trick-or-treaters, I guess. Though I doubt the neighborhood kids will know who you're meant to be."

"They won't get that I'm a punk girl? It's generic enough—"

"No. That . . . What's her name? She's all over the internet."

168

I freeze.

"Orange-and-purple hair, bright yellow skirt."

I blink. Blink again.

"Oh, you know who I'm talking about. She calls herself Vicarious or something." Mom goes to the computer in our kitchen and opens a browser to her Facebook page, scrolling down and then leaning back so I can see it from where I'm sitting at the kitchen island. "Just add some crazy sunglasses and an armful of bracelets and you're a dead ringer."

I slide off my stool and walk closer, peering over her shoulder. There's Vicurious riding the hippogriff with Harry. One of my mother's friends posted a link to my Instagram on her Facebook page, adding:

I've always wanted to do this! Go Vicurious!

Mom turns back to the picture, clicking to enlarge it. She studies it a minute, looks up at me, then back at the screen. "You know . . . ," she says, turning to face me again.

She recognizes me. I lean to brace myself against the back of a chair, wait for the dizziness that usually comes in moments like this. But, oddly, I don't feel it. I feel relieved, like I can finally let my guard down.

"I'm . . ." I start to say it, *I'm Vicurious*, but I can't. I need her to say it, to see me. To finally #SEEME.

Mom's eyebrows crunch together as she studies my face. She's visualizing me with the wig and the sunglasses, the lipstick. I'm sure of it. Vicurious almost always smiles, so I smile for my mother. So she'll know it's me. Mom, it's *me*.

But she just smiles softly, then turns back to the computer. "You really pegged her. It's a shame you can't wear that costume to a party."

"Yeah. Shame," I mumble. "Guess I'll never be her."

Mom shrugs. "Maybe next year."

I retreat to my room, my whole body trembling now. It's exactly what I wanted, right? To disappear. Lose myself. Leave Vicky behind and experience life as someone else entirely. And I've done it. I've *really* done it.

Yet I haven't been online in days. I've ignored Vicurious completely, haven't even charged my phone.

I sit at my desk. Open my computer. Log in to Instagram. And with a few clicks, I find my way back to her. I don't care how many followers she has. I'm not going to chase followers again. I just need a place to escape myself. A place . . .

My eyes don't seek it out, but the number of followers is right at the top of the page and . . .

I can't even . . .

I lower my head between my knees to stop from hyperventilating. And hallucinating. Because I'm pretty sure I'm seeing things now. I catch my breath and the blood returns to my head. I sit up again. Open my eyes. And there it is.

264k

followers

That's . . . not possible. It has to be some kind of glitch. I click through all my posts, scan the comments, try to figure out what's happening. How did I go from 14,000 followers to more than a quarter million in six days?

A quarter million.

I Google "Vicurious," and what comes up is crazy. There's so much. First is my Instagram. Then a Twitter account, which I never set up. I click on it, and see that someone has posted a screenshot of my user photo as their icon, and is tweeting all my Instagram posts. She has 23,420 followers.

I click back to the Google search window. Next is a link to a YouTube video titled, "OMG Best Instagram Ever." It has 437,258 views. It's posted by . . . oh my God. It's Rhyming Rhea! I've been watching her channel for years, since she started it when she was fifteen and I was twelve. She's this wild, redheaded girl from England who does everything in rhyme. Sometimes she gets all Shakespeare-like, and other times she raps or makes really simplistic poems about whatever is on her mind. She has 2.1 million followers now. The description for the video says, simply, "Vicurious!"

I press a trembling finger to the play arrow and hold my breath.

She's wearing footie pajamas. She says, "Hello, sweeties!" in her British accent, sounding just like that lady from *Doctor Who*. Then a beatbox track starts, and her head is jutting side to side to the beat.

"Today I'm in my jim-jams,
hanging with the Instagrams,
saw this girl, said what is THIS?
She calls herself Vicurious . . ."

A little picture box pops up in the bottom right corner with posts from my Instagram.

"Check out her fuzzy sock cocoon,
hey baby do you want to spoon?
Or ride a spaceship to the moon
with Neil deGrasse Tyson. Swoon!"

She tips her head back like she's fainting. I watch, mesmerized, as she raps her way through almost all of my posts, rhyming "*Where's Waldo*" with "crazy hairdo" and "hippogriff" with "Pope Francis." When the rhyming ends, she does a little bow. But it's not over. The video cuts to her, still in pajamas, sitting in front of the camera and talking right into the lens. No rhyming.

"If you've been watching my videos for a while," she says, "you know I suffer from depression sometimes. I talk about it, probably too much. Sorry 'bout that. You understand, though.

Right?" She pauses as if waiting for her audience to answer. And I guess we do, because she says, "Thanks, loves. You're the best. I take medicine that helps, and you guys help me a lot, too. But sometimes I just want to escape my life and be someone else, go somewhere else."

She raises her hands in a calming gesture. "Not permanently, loves. Just for an hour or an afternoon. That's why I like this girl so much. I mean, how many times have you seen a photo and thought, Aw, man, I wish I could do that. I'm so jealous. I want to be there. I want to feel that. So, she does! She does all this crazy stuff and, spoiler alert, it's not real. We all know it's not real. But it's soooo fun to pretend and imagine, and I love it. I just love it.

"But that's not even the best part," she continues. "The best part is, if her followers tell her they're depressed or alone, she's there for them. She's like, Hey, I see you. You're not alone. I'm here for you. It's really great. I'm a fan. Check her out."

She puts her fingertips to her lips and blows another kiss to the camera, and says, "Love you, Vicurious."

I watch the whole thing again. And again. My heart is pounding. I keep looking over my shoulder, thinking it must be some kind of prank. Half a million people have watched this video, and half of those people have followed me. It's insane. All I'm doing is Photoshopping myself into pictures! Anybody could do it with a few tutorials and a little practice. It's not that special.

I read the comments below the video, of which there are hundreds. They say things like:

OMG I LOVE HER.

Thanks. I needed this.

Sometimes the fantasy is all I have to get through the day.

Glad I'm not alone. Or am I? Damn. I am.

And then a dozen people leave comments telling that last person she's not alone. It's like a big group hug.

I spend an hour catching up on some of Rhyming Rhea's videos that I've missed in the last couple of weeks, and rewatching my old favorites. She raps about books and music and her favorite shows, but also everyday stuff like doing homework or her "mum" driving her crazy. She raps about depression, too. "Don't believe the lies it tells, that no one loves you, no one cares . . ."

I can't believe she likes me, *loves* me.

Well, not *me*. She loves Vicurious. She loves the girl I'm pretending to be; she loves the pretending itself. She loves that I answer the followers who say they're #lonely and #depressed, but Vicky would never do that. Vicky watches Raj at school every day and *knows* he's lonely. Vicky is too chicken to say anything to him.

I suck.

Vicurious, though. She's got 264,000 followers and growing. I search for Rhyming Rhea on Instagram, and click on the follow button for the first time. She doesn't have as many followers on Instagram as she does on YouTube, only 37,000. I laugh, because how ridiculous is it that I would ever think 37,000 is not that many? I scroll through the images she's posted, which are mostly screen grabs from her videos that say, "Posted a new video today. Follow the link in my bio."

Also pictures of her cat.

As if on cue, Kat comes meowing at my door. I let her in. She perches on my bed, then starts batting at something on my comforter. It's a stray Vicurious bracelet.

I pick it up and rest it on Kat's head, like a miniature tiara. She bats it away and paws at it some more. Like she wants me to put it on or something. Instead, I pull my costume out of the closet, take the two-tone wig, and drape it over Kat's head.

She quickly backs out of the wig and hisses at it. "Come on, Kat," I soothe.

She gives me a go-away glare, and stretches. It's one of those glorious cat stretches, tail and butt sticking up in the air, front paws forward, big yawning mouth upward. Like a yoga position. Then she reverses it, rear legs outstretched like a kitty plank pose, but with one back paw sticking out in the air. I grab my phone and take a photo. When she goes for a third stretch, I hold the wig at her head so her yawning face is visible and snap a photo with my other hand. She looks hilarious. And pissed.

"Aww, poor kitty." I take her in my arms and try to pet her, but she is all skittish now. She hides under the bed.

I know exactly how she feels.

I crawl to the floor. I make kissy and cooing sounds. Kat eventually gets close enough that I can scratch her head, then comes out and lets me pick her up. I show her the photos of herself as I upload them from my phone to my computer. She purrs.

Vicurious hasn't posted anything in days, but there are dozens of comments on the latest post asking if I'm okay. Some of them are blaming the new followers for chasing me away. They're arguing among themselves, making all sorts of assumptions about where I've disappeared to and why. It's too much attention, some say. It was only meant to be for my friends, one suggests. A dozen others pile up on her, asking if she knows me personally. Several claim to go to school with me. But they live in the UK or Canada or Singapore and can't possibly.

A few devotees seem to know me better than I know myself, though.

reallllaubrey She's just taking a break.

owntherabbithole She'll be back when she's ready.

donuts4every1 Probably has homework like the rest of us wankers.

I give my Siege of Jerusalem homework a side-eye and drag the last image of Kat into Photoshop. About twenty minutes later, she is dancing a hula on a Hawaiian beach, wearing my wig and the Photoshopped additions of the shredded yellow skirt, bracelets, and sunglasses. The white cat-eyed ones, of course.

She looks fabulous.

I post it with the caption:

Sorry I've been away. Took a little cat nap.
Better now.

And I do feel better. I don't know if it's the crazy number of followers, or the love from Rhyming Rhea, or maybe just letting myself go numb these past few days. There's still a weight on my chest, but it's not as heavy.

I stare at my Instagram page, the number 1 above the following tab, and wonder if Rhea noticed she's the only person I'm following. Which probably looks weird. But following people like Raj and Hallie and Adrian would give me away. I hit the search window and look up some of the people Vicurious has featured instead. There's Neil deGrasse Tyson, even though his account never posts anything and I'm not sure it's really him. I follow it anyway. And Jimmy Fallon, who has over 8.5 million followers, which puts my measly fandom into perspective. There's an official page for *Poldark* on PBS, so I follow that, too. And the Foo Fighters. I throw in Neil Patrick Harris and Will Smith for good measure.

None of them will follow me back and that's okay. Rhyming

Rhea follows me, and a quarter million people I don't know. Also Raj. I search for his Instagram and there he is, with his daily selfie. Pale blue button-down shirt today. Almost time for a haircut, Raj. I click back through his posts, really fast. It's like a stop-motion film. Then I return to the most recent photo.

He's added the #alone hashtag this time. He's never done that before.

I stare at it until it stops looking like a real word. I move the cursor to the comment window and hover there for a moment.

Then I hold my breath and I write:

vicurious You are not alone, Raj. I see you.

18

AT SCHOOL ON MONDAY I make sure Raj doesn't spot me, but observe him from afar. He does seem to have an extra spring in his step today, and I wouldn't call it a smile, but the shape of his mouth is definitely on the brighter side of neutral.

I go to my locker, even though Hallie's there. She says, "Hey," and smiles.

I smile back. "Hi."

We get our things from our respective lockers and put our coats and lunches away and all the while my heart is pounding and I'm sweating. But still. I did it. I said hi to Hallie Bryce, twice now, and I did not die.

I get to world history early so I can leave a note on Lipton's desk. I tear off a tiny strip of paper, about two inches wide and the height of a single line of college-ruled notebook paper. I scrawl my message:

I'm sorry.

And I leave it on his desk. But when he gets to class, he drops his books right on top of it. Adam scowls at me as he always does, but Lipton continues to pretend I don't exist. He hasn't looked at me since that awful day.

After class, the note is no longer on his desk. I imagine it stuck to his notebook, or to his arm, and the ink will leave a mark, like a tattoo, only in reverse. He'll spend the rest of the day wondering how he got "yrros m'I" written on his skin, and what it means. Or he'll see it in the mirror when he's brushing his teeth before bed tonight.

On Tuesday I try again. Only this time I've carved "I'm sorry" into the side of a pencil, using one of my mother's kitchen knives. I get to class and I leave the pencil on his desk.

He arrives, picks it up, glances around . . . even, I'm pretty sure, at me. He lays his book on the desk and gently places the pencil in the little vertical ridge along the binding. He doesn't hold the pencil sideways and read it.

Mr. Braxley walks to the front of the room and tapes a paper to the wall. "This is the sign-up sheet for your presentations," he says. "We'll do two per week until we get through them all. And since the due date was always Monday, this shouldn't put anyone at a disadvantage. Because you all should be ready to give your presentation on Monday. Right?"

A weak nod goes around the room. Nobody's anywhere near ready, obviously. "Still," says Mr. Braxley, "I'll give a bonus ten points to the first group to make their presentation."

People start getting out of their chairs to sign up, but Braxley shoos them all back to their seats. "I should mention," he says, grinning, "that the opportunity to sign this sheet must be earned. By answering questions. Correctly."

The class moans. All except for Lipton. He sits up straighter. If this were a quiz show and there was a glowing red button to be pushed when you knew the answer, his hand would be hovering over it. Twitching.

Meanwhile, I am paralyzed by the dueling fears of raising my hand to answer a question in class, and being left with the dreaded first slot on the schedule. Giving a presentation at all is terrifying. Going first? Just kill me now.

Mr. Braxley starts a review for our upcoming test. Every now and then he shoots out a question. "First Christian emperor?"

Lipton is caught off guard and doesn't get his hand in the air fast enough, so Renee Prusso takes the first stab. "Constantine," she says.

Mr. Braxley points to the schedule. She gives a squeal and briefly consults with her project team members, then skips up front and writes on the sheet. She takes the last slot, and everyone whines because they wanted to go last. I'm happy, though. Going last is almost as bad as going first. It means waiting and watching everyone else and realizing how bad your presentation will be in comparison.

I pull my attention back to Mr. Braxley, who is talking about a period of peace and prosperity that lasted two hundred years, around the first couple of centuries AD. "Anyone know what this period was called?"

Lipton's hand is in the air before anyone else's. Mr. Braxley gives him a nod.

"Pax Romana," says Lipton, all breathless.

"Which means?"

"Roman peace." He breaks into a grin and bolts to the front of the room, ignoring Jeremy Everling's coughed utterance of "Socks!" Lipton pencils his project name into a slot somewhere in the middle.

The torturous process continues. Sometimes I know the answers before anyone else, but I can't bring myself to raise my hand. By the end of class, I'm the only one who hasn't signed up. Mr. Braxley eyes me and says, "If you aren't on the schedule . . ." and points his pencil toward the paper.

I gather my things, and make my way to the front of the room as everyone files out. The emptiness of that first slot on the sign-up sheet taunts me. *Monday.* First presentation. For a project I haven't even started.

My hand trembles as I raise my pencil and start to scrawl my project title onto the paper. But before I can spell out the word "Siege," another hand, holding its own pencil, reaches over my arm.

It's the pencil I etched "I'm sorry" into. It erases "Battle of Thermopylae" from the third to the last slot and writes "Siege of Jerusalem" in its place. I step back, stunned, as Lipton puts his own project into the first slot. Adam hovers in the doorway, shaking his head.

We are standing so close, Lipton and I. Closer than I've been to another human being in a long time. Lipton has the faintest beginnings of facial hair on his upper lip, but it's blond. And there's a dimple in his right cheek that is tweaked upward in a close-lipped, sideways smile. A side smirk.

I mouth the words "thank you" because that's all I can manage in such close proximity to that dimple.

He shrugs, tucks the "I'm sorry" pencil behind his ear, and walks out.

19

I FLOAT THROUGH THE REST of the morning on that moment with Lipton, and the hope of his forgiveness. It's almost like crowd surfing at a Foo Fighters concert, being lifted up that way. Or saved, at least, from falling flat on my face.

I know I don't deserve it.

In the yearbook office at lunch, the brainstorming on "how to make the yearbook not suck" continues. Marissa wants something groundbreaking. She wants to write about it in her college applications. She wants to win awards.

"Could we *not* have eight pages of football?" says Marvo, flipping through last year's book. "And why do the cheerleaders get two pages when the LGBTQ Club only gets one lousy photo? I guarantee there are more LGBTQ kids at this school than cheerleaders."

"Yeah, but they don't build pyramids wearing miniskirts," Beth Ann says with a fake smile.

Marvo shakes his head. "Some kids aren't in here at all. I was in five photos last year. How many were you in?"

Beth Ann says, "Three."

Marissa cringes. "Sixteen."

They all turn to me.

I shrug, as if I don't remember that I was in zero yearbook pictures. I purposely hid in the bathroom when they took the freshman class photo.

Marvo turns to the index in the back of the yearbook where every student is listed alphabetically, along with pages on which they are pictured. My name is there, but no page numbers.

He looks up. "You weren't in the yearbook at all?"

I shake my head.

"That's just wrong."

"It's okay," I say quietly.

"No, it's not." He flips through the book, stops at a two-page collage of the most popular kids with their friends—hugging, smiling, laughing. Marissa is in at least three of the pictures. The spread is titled "Friends!" but the obvious subtext is, "Don't you wish you were us?"

Marvo points to an unsmiling kid caught in the background of one. "I want to know who that guy is." He points to another. "And her." He's basically pointing out all the people I zoomed in on that day when I left the images open at my workstation.

The three of them argue for a while over how to identify the kids who are "hiding in plain sight" and "diamonds in the rough" and "the best-kept secrets." Beth Ann suggests we cliché them to death until they come out. She glances at me and says, "Anyway, some people don't like being the center of attention."

Marvo chuckles.

"What?" She scowls at him. "Not everyone is as starved for attention as you are."

He leans back in his chair again and smiles at her. "You'd be surprised."

And I am officially freaking out.

"So, who do we feature in this not-the-usual-overachievers section?" Marissa opens her spiral notebook to a fresh page and writes a number one on the first line. "I need names."

"Vicky Decker," says Marvo.

I hold my breath expecting "Vicurious" to be the next word out of his mouth. Instead, he grins and says, "Secret weapon of the yearbook staff. And I bet she has some great ideas. Don't you, Vicky?"

Marissa looks over at me, her pen poised to write. If Marvo knows about Vicurious, he's not outing me. *Yet*. I swallow and slowly raise my hand.

"You don't have to raise your hand, Vicky," says Marissa.

I pull it back down. Hug it to my stomach. "Sorry."

"You don't have to apologize."

I almost say sorry again but manage to stop myself.

"Just . . . what?" says Marissa. "Do you want to be featured?"

"No," I say. "No, thank you." I drop my gaze to my knees,

which are bouncing. I press my hands to steady them. "I was thinking we could focus on kids who do stuff outside of school. Like Hallie Bryce is a dancer. And . . ." I dart a glance at Marissa. "And Adrian Ahn has his band."

She smiles. Writes their names on her list.

I think of a dozen other kids I've discovered online just by clicking on who follows who follows who.

"Elizabeth Gaffey makes the most amazing cupcakes," I say. "And Darla McMann is a dog walker. She must walk ten miles a day with different dogs. Also there's Becca Eliason. She paints her fingernails to match the books she's reading. And Geoffrey Phillips is helping his grandfather build a race car. It's pretty cool."

Marissa keeps writing and I keep talking, faster as I go. "There's a girl, Felicity, who's a yarn bomber. She knits scarves around trees. And Joshua Devon is really good at skateboarding. He does these amazing flips." I pause, but only for a second. "Lindy Johannsen makes jewelry out of soda tabs and safety pins. It sounds like they would look cheap but they're really beautiful and delicate. And, uh . . . Raj Radhakrishnan, he, um . . ."

I glance up. Marissa has stopped writing. I've probably said too much, but I can't seem to stop. "Raj, he, uh, takes these really interesting selfies. He stands in exactly the same spot every day and he changes his clothes, of course, and gets his hair cut every few weeks. Objects in the room move around sometimes. It's uh, it's kind of . . ." My voice drops to a whisper. "Fascinating."

Marvo tips his chair back and lets out a low whistle. Beth Ann says, "Wow." And Marissa closes her notebook.

I can't think of the last time I've spoken that many words at once, even in one of my unintended word vomits, and it's left me breathless. Also strangely invigorated.

The bell rings, and Marissa smiles, but as if someone's holding a gun to her head and forcing her to read a ransom note. "Great ideas, Vicky. We'll, uh . . . keep brainstorming. It's a good start, though. Really good."

She backs away from me and out of the room. Beth Ann follows, but Marvo holds the door.

"You coming, Vic?"

I gather my things and hurry out. I feel like a cat whose fur has been brushed the wrong way. I'm poised to skitter to one of my hiding spots, but I hesitate, estimating how long it will take to reach the bathroom versus Mrs. Greene's office, except someone else might be in there so it would be quicker to just go straight to the bathroom, except if all the stalls are taken and then—

"Walk with me," says Marvo.

I didn't even realize he was still there. He hooks his arm through mine and we are walking. *Ohmygod, I am walking down the hall with Marvo.* I have never walked down the hall with anyone other than Jenna. Not on purpose, at least. Other people have walked near me or next to me for a few paces, but not *with me*. I always slow down or speed up to leave a respectable gap.

But Marvo is walking *with* me, our elbows linked, his stride slowing to match my stuttering steps.

"So, how do you know all those people?" he says. "I never see you talking to anyone."

"I, uh . . . don't really . . ."

"Because they do sound fascinating. Yarn bombing!"

We keep walking, and Marvo's friends say "hey" and look at me funny. They're putting us together and *we don't belong together* and I really need to find the nearest bathroom.

". . . much better than eight pages of football," says Marvo. "Or cheerleader pyramids. Which are great, I mean no offense to cheerleaders, but it's the same every year . . ."

I'm really trying to listen to him, but my brain can focus on only one thing at a time, and right now I am conscious of how much I am sweating and worried he'll start to feel a little damp.

Then Lipton is walking toward us and he sees me and his eyes get brighter. He smiles and flashes his dimple, but then his gaze flits to my arm, which is still hooked into Marvo's, and the light dims. The dimple disappears.

Marvo is still talking merrily away, but Lipton is *getting* away. And I can't let that happen again. I push toward him, dragging Marvo along. I reach for Lipton. I catch him by the wrist.

He turns, surprised.

"Lipton. Hi! Hey," I say, breathless. "This is Marvo. We work on the yearbook together. That's, uh. That's who he is." I awkwardly extricate myself from Marvo's arm.

After his initial startled expression and a brief moment of confusion, Lipton's eyes are shining again. He nods to Marvo. "Hey."

And Marvo nods back at him. "Hi."

"So, uh, Lipton might be someone we could feature in the yearbook," I say to Marvo.

They both crinkle their eyebrows at me.

"He plays *Minecraft!*" I declare. "He's also very smart. And nice. And, you know, different. Than the usual. Like we were talking about."

Marvo appears on the verge of bursting out laughing, which I actually hope is at *me* and how idiotic I'm acting, not at Lipton. But he doesn't laugh. He just nods again and says, "Cool."

Lipton, meanwhile, has turned an interesting shade of red.

"Nice meeting you, dude," says Marvo. "Later, Vic." He walks away, glancing back once to give us a casual salute.

I swallow. "Sorry, that was, I didn't want you to—"

"It's okay," Lipton says quickly, his gaze dropping to his feet, where a sliver of sock is exposed. It's a plain old white athletic sock, not his signature red or blue or yellow. It makes me sad that I did that to him, took the joy out of his socks.

"I'm so sorry about that day in class," I murmur. "When you asked me . . . you know, if I wanted—"

"To pet my cat?" He cringes. "I'm such an idiot."

"No, you're not. I am. I get so nervous in front of people . . . and then I, with your socks, and Jeremy . . ." I close my eyes for

190

a second, frustrated at my inability to complete a sentence, my own words as jumbled as my thoughts were that day.

"It wasn't your fault," he says softly. "I shouldn't have asked you in front of everybody. That was stupid."

"I'm stupid." I shake my head. "Jeremy is stupid."

Lipton snorts. "Don't blame yourself for that. Jeremy has pretty much been bullying me since kindergarten. You could've said you loved my socks and really meant it, and he still would've made fun of me."

"I *do* love your socks." I glance down at the white. "The colorful ones."

"Really?"

I nod. Smile.

He laughs. The sound of it lifts the tension from my shoulders.

"So, I'll see you in class tomorrow?"

"Yeah," says Lipton. "See you in class."

We nearly collide in the process of trying to walk away from each other. Lipton steps aside then and gestures for me to go first.

I head straight to Mrs. Greene's office, because I'm feeling good and I don't want to lose it. The door is open. The twinkly lights are on. Mrs. Greene looks up and motions for me to come in.

I sit. And I breathe. She lets me. I almost feel like talking. *Almost.*

After a while, she says, "You look happy today."

I nod and pinch a smile between my lips.

For the first time in a long time, I can't wait for tomorrow.

* * *

The rest of the week is marked by small moments of happiness that make me wonder if I'm imagining things, or slipping into a truly vicarious state. When Lipton's hand brushes against mine while passing out worksheets in class, I dig my fingernails into my palm to make sure I'm not dreaming.

Five minutes later, I catch myself absently stroking the little spot where he touched me. Like a weirdo.

I keep finding notes on my desk when I get to class, too. Another photocopy of information on the Siege of Jerusalem. The tiniest piece of paper imaginable folded into an even tinier square, with "hi" written on it. A picture of his cat, autographed:

Missing you. —K

I tear off a slightly larger piece of paper and write a note back to him:

Your cat's name starts with K?

He turns it over and writes something. Slips it to me.

Yes.

But he fails to provide the name. I write back:

Are you going to tell me what it is?

He studies my note a minute, tapping the end of his pencil on his chin. He finally writes back, then folds and folds and folds the note until it's super tiny.

I unfold and unfold and unfold it to reach his message:

Kitty

I smile. It's too perfect. He puts his head down and writes again, then flips the page up for me to see.

Yours?

I frown. How does he know I have a cat? For one panicked minute I am sure he's seen my cat photo on Vicurious and knows that she is me. When I don't respond right away, he tears off another piece of paper, scribbles what appears to be a really long message, and tosses it into my lap.

What's your cat's name? You are obviously a cat person. So I assumed you have a cat. Unless it died? Oh, God, please tell me your cat didn't die. I'm such a jerk.

I bite my lip to keep from smiling, though it sneaks out the corners of my mouth. His note sounds kind of like one of my own word vomits. Is it possible that another human brain functions even a little bit like mine?

I write on the back of Lipton's note:

> You are not a jerk.
> My cat's name is Kat.

Lipton reads it and laughs out loud, one barking burst of joy. Everyone turns to stare, including Mr. Braxley. I stop breathing. Lipton pops the note in his mouth, as if we were trading world secrets.

Adam expresses his dismay with his signature head-desk move. Mr. Braxley simply points to the trash bin next to his desk. Lipton rolls his eyes, strides up there, pulls the note from his mouth, and drops it in the trash. Everyone's snickering.

I am *mortified*.

But Lipton smiles at me as he returns to his desk, and it makes me forget everyone else. I smile back. It reminds me of the way Jenna could set everything right with just a nudge and a "hey." I didn't think anyone else would ever wield such powers again. And yet here is Lipton.

He waits for me after class. He walks me part of the way to my next one. Neither of us says anything for a while. Then he stops. And I stop. "I could text you," he says softly. "If I had your number."

I stare at his left elbow. That's as close as I can get to eye contact as I consider his offer. Texts from Lipton would surely add countless happy moments to my life. But it would also put him in the realm of Vicurious, which is all I use my phone for anymore. And I don't know why. I just don't want him there.

I want him *here*. With me. Vicky.

"I don't want you to text me," I say.

Before I can explain further, his whole body slumps. "Okay. Fine. I—"

My eyes leap to his, which are all achy and confused.

"Because I like your notes better," I quickly add. "On paper. They're, I don't know . . ."

"Real," he says.

I nod. "Exactly."

"Okay."

We start walking again, the fabric of his jacket touching the knit of my sweater. That slight bit of contact gets me through the rest of the morning, somehow.

When lunch period arrives, I open the door to yearbook and glance at the list of people I suggested for the special section, which has been taped to the wall for two whole days now. I keep expecting to find that Marissa has crumpled it up and thrown it away. I won't even be upset if she does. But it's still there.

Marvo isn't here today. Just us girls. I go to my corner desk and start clicking through photos.

"Have you seen this?" Marissa says to Beth Ann, who leans

over to look at her computer screen.

"Yeah. She's cool. Good taste in tattoo art." She lifts her red Converse and waggles the yin-yang toe in front of Marissa. "Marvo loves her. He says she's the only person who understands him, which, thanks a lot, but whatever. She cheers him up when he's in one of his funks. I hope she posts something today so he can get his butt back to school."

I stop clicking the second I realize they are talking about Vicurious, and now I'm trying not to gawk. *Marvo has funks?* I can hardly believe it. He's always laughing, talking. It's like he's standing in a perpetual spotlight, always performing. But I don't see him every day, come to think of it. I don't see him *lots* of days.

"Adrian is totally obsessed with her," Marissa says. "He wants to dye his hair purple *and* orange next time."

I stop breathing.

"It's cool, I guess," says Marissa. "But anybody with a wig and Photoshop could do it. I don't see what all the fuss is about."

Beth Ann laughs. "Yeah, and I could've written a kick-ass book about a boy wizard, but I didn't think of it first, did I?"

Marissa sighs. "I just can't believe she has so many followers. For basically crashing everybody else's party."

"It's more than that," says Beth Ann. "Have you read the comments?"

"Yeah, I get it. She *sees* me." Marissa rolls her eyes. "Now if I can just get Adrian to see me. He wouldn't shut up the other night about how cool it would be if she Vicurious-ed one of his gigs."

I'm trying very hard not to let the freak-out that's happening inside me show on the outside. Adrian wants Vicurious to feature his band? He wants to dye his hair to match hers? I turn back to my computer and pretend to be working but am just zooming in and out on the same photo and trying not to hyperventilate.

Marissa rolls her chair over to where I'm sitting, and watches from the side of my desk. I quickly find some teeth to whiten, some shadows to brighten. I remove a stop sign that looks like it's growing out of someone's head.

"Vicky could do it. Couldn't you?" She nods toward my monitor. "Photoshop someone into a crowd?"

"What?" I swallow. "I don't—"

"But you *could*. If you wanted to. Right?"

"I wouldn't—"

"Oh my God, Vicky. I didn't say you would. Just that you could." She turns to Beth Ann. "I mean, who knows who this girl is? It could be anyone. It could be *Vicky*. And half a million people are following her like she's some kind of messiah?"

I'm tempted to correct her on the number of followers. Rhyming Rhea's fans are still flocking to my site, but I'm only up to about 327,000 at last count.

"I'm not even on Instagram," I say.

She snaps her head to face me. "I was speaking hypothetically."

"Dude," Beth Ann cuts in. "You're pissed at your boyfriend. Don't take it out on Vicky."

Marissa inhales deeply and holds it for a few seconds, then

blows it out. She smiles at me. "I'm sorry. That was rude. I just meant that anyone halfway proficient at Photoshop could be Vicurious. *You* could be Vicurious."

"Still rude," says Beth Ann, shaking her head. "You're suggesting that someone like Vicky couldn't possibly have a half million followers. That she'd only deserve it if she were famous. Or popular, like you."

Marissa clenches her teeth. "That's not what I'm suggesting at all. I just—"

"You totally slammed our girl Vicky here because your boyfriend has the hots for someone on the internet, and you can't say 'I'm better than her' because you don't know who she is," says Beth Ann. "And that's super frustrating because you're used to being better than *everybody*."

Marissa's face goes red, and she looks like she's going to cry. "I don't think I'm better than everybody. Or anybody." She grabs her book bag and storms out.

We watch her go. Beth Ann groans, then folds her arms across her desk and drops her head into them. "I am such a bitch."

I'm not sure what to say, so I don't say anything. I know she hates being called a bitch, but does that count when she calls herself one? She *was* kind of hard on Marissa.

Beth Ann snorts and sits up. "Great. Even the nicest person on the planet thinks I'm a bitch."

"I don't . . ."

"Please. At least you're honest. It's good to know there's one person around here who isn't a total fake." She grabs her book bag and leaves the room.

I pull my lunch out and eat in the quiet, a new list forming in my head. For once, it's not the things that terrify me. It's not about me at all. It's a list of everybody I know who is suffering, or struggling in their own way.

Hallie
Raj
Lipton
Marissa
Marvo
Beth Ann

They are names I would never have expected to find on the same list, people I've always thought were either perfect or happy or didn't care. It's a list I can mentally add one more name to:

Vicky

Which makes me happy, I'm ashamed to admit. I don't mean to revel in anyone else's pain. But I've existed on a list of one for so long. It feels good to have others I can count myself among, even if they have no idea. They're not alone, and neither am I.

20

AT HOME ON SATURDAY, I pull out my Siege of Jerusalem assignment and try to do some research online. I'm way behind, even with Lipton giving me notes and offering up his presentation slot. I last only about fifteen minutes before switching over to Instagram—just to check how many followers I have this morning.

I note my new total, 349,000, then decide to take a quick peek at some of the comments on my last few posts.

An hour later, I'm in deep, and instead of lifting me up today, Vicurious followers are dragging me down. I should've known to expect trolls, but I fooled myself into thinking I had created a place where no one would ridicule me or criticize. Behind the wig and sunglasses and crazy clothes and jewelry, I would be safe.

Silly me.

It seems when you reach a certain level of popularity, the haters come out of the woodwork to take you down. Some even have the word "hater" in their usernames. I can ignore the generic negativity in comments like "I don't get it" or "This is stupid" or "Why? Just why?"

It's the ones that hone in on *me*, on who I am and the decisions I've made. Those are the ones that really bother me, make me question and second-guess and worry that I've done something terribly wrong.

hipstrh8er that yin yang tat is kinda lame

I lift my shirt to look at the Sharpied symbol on my side. It's obviously not a real tattoo. Or maybe he takes exception to using the yin-yang symbol at all? Someone else writes:

zzaakkattack yah a little cliché

I start stressing over it, because is it totally not cool? I never heard that before, but where would I hear that? Beth Ann is much cooler than I am and she drew the yin-yang on the toes of her shoes. It's entirely possible, though, that Richardson High School itself is not the pinnacle of cool.

Then I start worrying that it's offensive or something, that I've accidentally insulted someone. I start Googling and finding all these discussions of whether or not people who aren't Chinese or Buddhist or Taoist should wear the yin-yang symbol at all, or if it's cultural appropriation, and I'm not even sure what that means and my head is going to explode.

I take deep breaths. I scan the comments to see if anyone's saying that, if anyone's offended. But they're not. Some chime in to defend me, to say it's a positive thing, it's universal. Anyone can use it if it means something to them.

And it does mean something to me. It's the symbol of my friendship with Jenna, of the balance between us, the strengths and weaknesses, the ups and downs. Seeing it still gives me the tiniest hope that it's not completely over, that our friendship will right itself in the end. So I try to push the yin-yang haters out of my mind. But that's not the only thing people are complaining about.

One of my very first followers writes:

tanyazeebee Why don't you follow anyone back? Only following 8, only 1 woman? That's bullshit.

I frown. Did I only follow men? It wasn't on purpose. My first was a girl—Rhyming Rhea. And I would've followed Jennifer Lawrence if she had an Instagram. Or Demelza Poldark. Still, the criticism stings. So I find some of my favorite women on social media. There's Amanda Palmer, singer-songwriter-ukulele player. She's so cool and different and completely unafraid. She once let a mob of fans autograph her body. I wouldn't mind living vicariously through her for a day or two.

I click the follow button.

I try to follow J. K. Rowling, but it's a fake account. So I follow Emma Watson instead. If Hermione had an account, I'd follow her, too. But the only ones I find are fan sites. I follow the Malala Fund and Oprah and Zooey Deschanel. And finally, Ellen. *The Ellen Show*. She's got more than forty-two million followers. A single one of her posts gets 350,000 likes.

I haven't posted a photo today, so I quickly pop Vicurious onto the set of *The Ellen Show*, making it look like we're dancing together. I didn't even have to Photoshop anyone out, because Ellen is *always* dancing. I post it with #ellen and #keepdancing tags.

It's comforting to know there's someone out there with a following so huge, it makes mine seem tiny. She's got to be bigger than most states, population wise. I look it up. And I'm right. Ellen's fan base is greater than the population of California, which is the largest state in the country. It makes the target on my back feel slightly smaller.

But not for long.

machomike33 Are you a lesbo?
eeemojijen You only follow famous people. Not nobodies like me.

I block machomike33, then I nod at eeemojijen's comment because it's true. I've only followed famous people, and it's not because I think they're the only ones worthy of my attention.

It's more because I can disappear into their massive numbers of followers. They won't even notice me there. I realize that doesn't make sense for someone with 350,000 followers, but making sense is clearly not my strong suit.

If I could start this all over, I'd follow back every single person who followed me. I didn't do it at the beginning because of my preexisting condition (the irrational fear of following people on social media). Now there are so many, it would take me weeks to click the follow button on them all, and I don't want to leave anyone out accidentally.

Still, I don't want anyone to feel like a nobody. Knowing the can of worms I'm about to unleash, I follow eeemojijen. Maybe it's the "jen" in her name that makes me do it, which gives me an idea. I open my list of followers and search for anyone with "jen" or "jenna" in their username. A little voice inside my head asks me, *Why are you doing this?* It says, *She's not Jenna and neither is that girl or that one or that one.* It tells me to *give up already, she doesn't want you anymore.* But I do it anyway. Sometimes I do things without understanding why, and this is one of those times.

I find seventy-eight and follow them all. The last I click on is one of the first who followed me, and the first I ever replied to: justjennafied. When I'm done following Jens and Jennas, I wait.

I watch for new Jennas to show up, and they do. I follow them. *Look,* I tell my little voice, *there are people on social media who follow only Justin Bieber. If I want to follow people named Jen and Jenna, what's the big deal? It doesn't have to mean anything.*

Yet when none of the Jens or Jennas are jennaelizabethtanner, I'm disappointed, so I guess that means something.

Monday morning is Lipton's presentation on the Battle of Thermopylae, and I'm nervous for him. You'd think I was the one about to stand in front of the class. Usually, I'm just glad everyone's attention is focused on someone other than me.

But it's Lipton. And I'm afraid for him. Or something. At least I anticipated this possibility and put on a second T-shirt beneath my sweater before I left the house, in case I soak through the first.

Mr. Braxley prolongs the agony by teaching through most of the period, saving the presentation for the end of class. Lipton looks like he might vomit. I notice he's wearing purple socks, so I point to them when no one else is looking and give him a thumbs-up. He barely manages a weak smile, he's so nervous. And Adam isn't helping. He's tapping his foot like he's seriously overcaffeinated.

For once, I'm not the one trying to hold it together. This could've been me, though. And oh, so much worse.

Finally Mr. Braxley tells Adam and Lipton to start. Instead of plugging a thumb drive into the classroom computer, Lipton has brought his own laptop. He was worried his presentation software wouldn't be compatible with Mr. Braxley's and didn't want to risk it. Still, he practically slumps with relief when his "Battle of Thermopylae" title page appears on the Smart Board in really huge letters. Adam starts talking, shuffling through his notecards. He gives an introduction, which is presumably leading us to the battle in question. It's going fine until the title page dims, goes black, and a screen saver pops up. It's a photograph of Taylor Swift wearing a bright pink miniskirt and matching crop top with silver sequins.

The class ROARS with laughter.

Lipton lunges for the computer. "It's not mine! It's my sister's. I swear!" He hits the keyboard and the image goes away. "My sister did it. We share the computer!"

The class is absolutely howling. Adam walks away from the podium toward the windows. I'm afraid he's going to thunk his head against the glass and hurt himself, but he just stands there looking out.

Mr. Braxley, chuckling, tries to calm the class. "All right, all right. Quiet down." He coaxes Adam back toward the desktop podium to resume his remarks. Mr. Braxley bites his lip, pats Adam on the shoulder, and says, "Shake it off."

Which starts the uproar all over again.

Mr. Braxley quiets the room a second time. He looks sheepish, having made the joke that set everyone off. "I'm sorry," he says. "Adam, Lipton, we're laughing with you, not at you."

I really, *really* hate when people say that.

Adam reads the rest of his introduction in a weak monotone. "Now we have a video we created to illustrate the battle."

Lipton manages to say, "Could someone turn down the lights?"

And the video begins.

They've reenacted the Battle of Thermopylae on *Minecraft*. There's one huge army (the Persians) and one small one (the Greeks) at the foot of the huge cliffs by the sea—all constructed with bitmappy blocks. The soldiers have cubed, bearded heads with rectangular bodies and limbs. They're holding shields and swords.

The battle commences with ominous music in the background, dramatically narrated in a deep voice that is clearly Lipton trying to sound intimidating. The soldiers start attacking, their little swords clanking against one another. It sounds like several dozen people clicking their pens. Each time a soldier is struck and killed, red chunks of body parts fall to the ground.

"'Tis but a scratch," Jeremy says in a high-pitched voice.

His friends start laughing. "It's just a flesh wound!" They're shouting out lines from *Monty Python and the Holy Grail*, and Mr. Braxley makes Lipton stop the video until everyone settles down again. "I've got a nice stack of detention slips for anyone who talks for the rest of the presentation. Everling? You hear me?"

Jeremy nods, smirking.

I don't even want to turn around to see Lipton's face. I'm pretty good at imagining worst-case scenarios, but even I couldn't have dreamed this nightmare.

The video resumes, and Lipton's deep narrator voice says, "The Greeks fought valiantly, holding off the much larger Persian army for two days, until . . ."

I do my best to ignore the fact that everyone is squirming visibly, trying to keep from laughing. The video is actually really impressive once you get past the funny sounds of the swords clashing and the chunks of body parts flying around. It must've taken hours to create a geographically accurate landscape around Thermopylae, and generate all those little soldiers and swords and arrows.

The whole thing comes to a dramatic conclusion when a traitor to the Greeks reveals a secret passage, allowing the Persians to enter the city. Lipton's voice gets more and more animated. Our classmates wrap arms and hands around their mouths to keep from laughing as Leonidas and the last few Spartans are slaughtered by tiny arrows that hail down on them from the cliffs above.

The video ends. The bell rings. The class rushes out so they can release the laughter they've been holding in. I remain at my desk, Lipton somewhere behind me. Silent. Adam lifts his head from the podium.

"Told you," he says.

Lipton doesn't try to catch my eye as he packs up his computer. I shuffle out. That's what I would want, if it were me. To be left alone. To not have to speak of it, or have it spoken of, or even share facial expressions that acknowledge its existence at all.

Kids are still making fun of the presentation in the hall, and I'm almost overtaken by an urge to run at them, bring my arms down on theirs and make them stop. It's a new feeling, wanting to confront the humiliation. To stop it. When it happens to me, I only want to hide.

I make it through my next two classes, then slip into the girls' bathroom at the beginning of lunch period instead of heading directly to yearbook. My usual stall in the corner is empty, so I lock myself in and pull out my phone. Even before opening the screen, I can see Vicurious has been busy today. I navigate to my notifications and scroll through them.

Half are people named Jen or Jenna thanking me for following them. The other half are people not named Jen or Jenna, begging me to follow them.

And there's one from justjennafied, a comment on the image of Kat in the Vicurious wig, which says, simply:

Nice cat.

It makes me catch my breath, because that's what Jenna—my Jenna—always used to say whenever Kat would hiss at her or refuse to be petted by anyone but me. I click over to justjennafied's page to see if there's any sign she's my former best friend. But she's only been there for a couple of weeks, and hasn't posted much. No selfies. There's a view out a dirty bus window, the scenery blurred. A photo looking straight up at the sky through a canopy of trees. Another pointing down at a leaf-clogged gutter. She puts a single tag on her photos: #lost or #sad or #dirty.

It can't be her.

Just in case, though, I comment to justjennafied the way I always used to reply to Jenna.

She knows who feeds her.

I tag justjennafied to make sure she sees it among the hundreds of comments on that post, and am about to leave my bathroom stall when two girls walk in. I hug my backpack to my chest and lean against the wall to wait them out.

It's excruciating. They're talking about what they're going to wear to a friend's party on Saturday. It's a strange dance in which one girl's wardrobe must not outshine the other's. They must complement each other, but without being matchy-matchy. In the end, they pick essentially the same outfit in slightly different colors.

I hope they're done because I *really* have to leave for class, and I've been quiet way too long to all of a sudden walk out of the stall.

"Let me just check my Instagram," one says.

I suppress a groan.

"How many followers are you up to?" the other asks.

"Two hundred fifteen."

"Following?"

"Three twenty-eight."

"I'm two thirty-seven, and four eighty-five. I need to stop following people who don't follow me back."

"Like Vicurious?"

I suck in my breath, but the sound is covered by the other girl's laughter. "Yeah," she says. "Or change my name to Jen."

"Maybe call yourself JenJennaJennyJenniferJenniest."

"It wouldn't work. She hasn't followed anyone new since the weekend. Not even the ones who changed their names."

"Whatever. I still love her."

"Me too."

"Me too. Me too. Me too!"

My eyes widen at their repetition of "me too." Like it's a *thing*.

I am so focused on their conversation that I forget I'm holding my backpack, and it slips. It doesn't hit the floor, but the sound of me struggling with it is enough to stop the girls from talking.

"I didn't know anyone was in there," one says quietly.

"Me either."

"Who's in there?"

I want so badly to say, "It's me, Vicurious!" But I gather my things and unlock the stall instead. I shuffle out to a sink.

"Eavesdrop much?" It's Mallory, from biology. The one who thinks Hallie Bryce isn't human.

I close my eyes. Pretend I'm three years old again and if I can't see them, they can't see me.

The other girl says, "It doesn't matter. She's ..."

I can't hear what she says I am, or if she says anything. But it's easy enough to fill in the blank. Maybe she made the international crazy gesture, twirling her finger at the side of her head.

Or mouthed something, like "nobody."

They leave, and I stare at myself in the mirror.

How can they love Vicurious and be so dismissive of me? Of anyone? They're just like the kids in class who took Lipton down without a thought as to how that made him feel. Knowing I have followers like that makes me want to hurl. Or shout "YOU SUCK!" really loud.

Instead, I swallow it down, like I always do. Take a deep breath. And stomp (as quietly as possible) to class.

21

ON THE BUS, I CHECK Jenna's Instagram. My Jenna, jennaeliza-bethtanner. She hasn't posted anything in more than two weeks. Nothing since that last photo of her with Tristan. I switch to justjennafied's page. Her first post was a little over two weeks ago. I toggle between them. Jennaelizabethtanner stopped posting about the same day that justjennafied started.

The annoying little voice in my head says *Why do you even care what Jenna does after the way she treated you?* And I don't have an answer, except that I've tried to stop caring about Jenna and obviously, I can't. It's not a switch that turns off that easily. She was my best friend for twelve years.

Mom is waiting with a smoothie when I get home. "Apple, strawberry, mango, and a little spinach," she says.

I sit. Stare at it. The spinach and strawberry combo does not make for a particularly pleasing color.

"You're not hungry?" my mother asks when I don't pop the straw in my mouth immediately.

The thing is, I'm never hungry when I get home. My stomach is still unclenching from the day. But Mom always insists I eat something, and I do it so she won't think something's wrong.

But not today. I'm smoothied out.

"Actually, I hate smoothies," I say.

"Since when?"

"Since you make them for me every single day and if I have to drink another one I'm going to scream."

She jerks her chin back. "Why didn't you say so? I thought you loved smoothies."

"I did."

She glares at me. "But not anymore."

"Nope." I realize too late how rude I'm being. I can never seem to find the correct balance between sharing my feelings and keeping them to myself. "Sorry."

She whisks the offending smoothie away from me and starts scurrying around the kitchen, pulling things out of the fridge and trying to come up with an alternative snack. "I could put some cheese and crackers out, or—"

"I'm really not hungry." I stand and push the chair in. "I think I'll just have a nap."

Her face goes all knotty. My mother has two gears—either she's totally ignoring me, or she's obsessing over me. "Are you sick? Is anything the matter?" She reaches to put a hand to my forehead.

I gently push it away. "Just tired."

"You rest, then," she says, like it was her idea. "I'll let you know when dinner's ready."

I get to my room and pet Kat for a while. *Nice cat.* Lots of people say that, probably. It doesn't mean justjennafied is Jenna. It just means she likes the photo of my cat. Still, I log in to see if she left another comment. There are so many in my notifications, it's almost impossible to identify ones sent by a specific person. There's no way to search by name. I go to the Kat photo and scroll down to the comment I left, and continue from there. Other people like my cat, too. They ask what her name is. They say, "Our cats should totally hang out!" They try to direct me to the link on their profile pages where I can find a photo of their cat.

"You're famous," I say to Kat.

She licks my pinkie knuckle with her sandpapery tongue. I poke around my Instagram for a few more minutes. Almost all of my photos now have comments like that. "Come to my concert, Vi!" or "Hang out with us!" or *"Seamos amigos,* Vicurious!" which I think means they want to be friends. I click on links from a few profile pages to see what sort of fun Vicurious may be missing.

Most of the photos they share are selfies with two or three or ten friends smashed together in a group hug, all grinning their super-cute faces at the camera. These are people who would never be draping their arms over my shoulders in real life. Like the girls in the bathroom. Or the "Friends!" section of the yearbook.

I scan the backgrounds. Every now and then, I notice someone like me, standing alone. Watching from the edges. I save those to a file on my computer. When I have a dozen or so, I set up my little photo studio and get into my Vicurious costume. Then I pose. Arm out from the shoulder, bent a bit at the elbow, and hand hanging from the wrist as if someone's standing there, and my arm is draped around their shoulders. I do a bunch like that, then try some where my head is tipped to the side, like I'm leaning on someone. I even take a few with my arm hanging close to my side, my fingers cupped as if I'm holding someone's hand.

Then one by one, I go through the photos people sent me, and I find the person lingering in the background. The girl looking wistfully toward the kids featured in the photo. The boy pretending he's waiting for friends. The guy with his hands shoved in his pockets, leaning against a fence. The girl peeking around her hair.

All these people deserve to be noticed. But I also know how terrifying it is to receive unwanted attention. Thrusting them into the public eye, in front of almost a half-million Instagram followers? That would be ten times worse than my mother's attempts to force me into social situations. I can't do that to them.

But I want to let them know that *I* see. I want my followers to look for people like them—the unseen and ignored.

So, I drape my arm around them. I hold their hands. I lean

my head on their shoulders. Then, to protect their privacy, I turn them into simple silhouettes, each a different solid color but shaded so they seem almost ghostly. *Invisible.* And completely unrecognizable to anyone but themselves.

I crop the photos so they're square, but otherwise leave them alone. I don't zoom in or anything. I want people to have to work a little to find us, like *Where's Waldo.*

Then I post them. All twelve photos. I tag them:

#hiding #seeme #sayhi #lookaround #bekind

I quickly turn off my notifications, because the reaction to twelve photos at once might be a little crazy. And the followers who asked me to use their photos might be upset that I'm hugging the wrong person. I take a last look at my page, the ridiculous number of followers, which is now up to 423,000.

I shut off my phone for the night and write a note to Lipton on paper. I tell him how great his presentation was, how sorry I am that everyone laughed, how sure I am that he got an A, how I wanted to stay and talk to him afterward but thought he probably didn't feel like talking. I tell him his purple socks made me smile.

The next day, I get to world history early so I can leave my note on Lipton's seat. I'm afraid to place it on his desk, in case someone notices and snatches it up. So I put it on his chair. I side-eye the note as people file into class and the bell rings.

But no Lipton.

Adam comes in and sits down. He looks smaller today. His neck isn't as long; his arms are shorter. He's all pulled in on himself, trying to avoid being noticed.

Welcome to the club, Adam.

"We'll have our presentation first today, and then some time to discuss what we've learned," Mr. Braxley announces, shutting down the snickers that follow with a raised handful of detention slips. "Prusso, Hudson, Fenimore. You're up."

Renee Prusso and her friends Maggie and Laura scurry around getting ready for a few minutes. They keep giggling nervously. They've brought a USB drive, and Mr. Braxley pops it into his own computer, which is connected to the Smart Board.

I make a mental note to do the same. I don't use a screen saver, but with my luck, a photo of Vicurious would randomly pop up. For Renee and company, a PowerPoint title page comes on-screen.

It reads "The Black Death."

In Comic Sans.

That wouldn't be my first choice of font for a presentation on the most deadly plague known to humankind.

I glance around to see if anyone else noticed, but they're all just slouching in their seats as usual. Adam turns his head ever so slightly toward Lipton's desk, as if to commiserate but forgetting that his friend is not there.

The girls begin their presentation. And it is SO boring.

I really wish Lipton were here to exchange notes. And then I remember that he gave me his phone number that day when the projects were assigned. *In case you change your mind,* he said. I slowly pull my world history textbook from my backpack and find the note neatly pressed between its pages.

Phone in my lap, volume turned off, I type his number into a text window and write my first message.

Are you okay?

There's a "..." on his side of the screen for a while, and then:

Who is this?

Oh, God. Right. I'm such an idiot. He has no idea it's me.

It's Vicky.
Vicky Decker?

I am mortified, and normally I would give up, but I take a deep breath and type:

Yes. Sorry. Vicky Decker.

. . .

There's an unreasonably long pause on his end, and now I am really wishing I had not identified myself by name. Maybe he was sleeping. Or really doesn't want to text with me. And now I've basically forced myself on him.

If you don't want to text I understand.

. . .

Sorry to bother you.

No, it's not that. I'm just surprised.

In a good way.

I am not sure how to respond to that, so I open the emoji window and choose from among the smiley faces, making sure I don't accidentally select one of the kissy ones.

☺

Did you stay home today?

No. I'm in class.

Don't let Braxley see you texting.

Renee & Laura & Maggie are giving their presentation.

. . .

There's another really long pause on his end, and I realize I've just forced him to think about his presentation. Which is probably the last thing he wants to do. So I quickly type:

It's soooooooo boring. Yours was 100x better.
Thanks.
They are seriously giving the Worst. PowerPoint. Ever.
Boring pictures?
No pictures at all.
???

I look around me to make sure nobody is watching, and I lift my phone just enough to take a photo over the top of my desk of one of their text-filled screens. They have simply put their entire report into bullet points and are clicking through it as they read aloud. In monotone.

I text the photo to Lipton.

Is that Comic Sans?
Yeah.
cringing
Me too.

I realize after writing "me too" that it's a Vicurious thing, and get a brief pang of anxiety that it will give me away, but it's not like my Instagram is the only place anyone ever said "me too." Lipton's typing again.

Is everyone laughing?

No. Sleeping.

Jeremy Everling fidgets in his chair then, and glances back toward Lipton's desk. He shakes his head at Adam. Adam shrugs. I have no idea what that exchange meant, and Adam probably doesn't, either. But he regains a bit of his height.

Jeremy just looked wistfully at your empty desk.

Really?

He and Adam are commiserating over how much better your presentation was.

No they're not.

Jeremy is making faces. He is so bored. Everyone is slumped over.

Which is worse, boring people to death or having them laugh hysterically at you?

I know my answer. The fear of being laughed at is number one on my list. I've been boring people my whole life because I'm so terrified of being laughed at. But I can't say that to Lipton.

Equally painful.

If you say so.

Your presentation was great. I learned a lot.
You're just being nice.
I'm serious.

. . .

I try to think of something that will make him feel better.
Make him understand that I really mean it.

It made me want to learn Minecraft.
LOL. I think I love you.

. . .

I blink at the screen. Did he actually just text that he loved
me? He was kidding. Obviously. Thus the LOL. Right? Before I
can think of a non-awkward reply, he texts again:

I mean I love that you want to try Minecraft.
Or go to a Taylor Swift concert.
Ouch.
Kidding.
I know. It really was my sister's screen saver.
I believe you.

I sigh. Disaster averted.
The presentation drones on until the bell rings and they

can't even finish. As everyone's packing up to leave, Mr. Braxley says, "Your presentation is not meant to be a recitation of your entire written report, people. Please refer to the directions I gave you, or talk to Adam and Lipton."

Renee, Maggie, and Laura slink out, while Adam starts texting as he goes. It makes me smile, knowing the message he's probably sending Lipton right now.

I'm mentally writing my own message to Lipton as I walk down the hall, and don't notice Adrian Ahn sidling up to me until he rubs right against my arm.

"I see you," he says.

I nearly jump out of my skin. "Excuse me?"

"I just wanted to say hi. Let you know that I see you." He leans his lips close to my ear. "You're not invisible."

I blink up at him, nervous I might say something ridiculous in front of Adrian's cadre of adoring fans, which today consists of three freshmen—two girls and a guy.

Adrian gives my arm a friendly nudge. "See you later."

He strides off, his groupies staring at me. And I know what they're thinking. Why is Adrian Ahn talking to *her*?

Because it's exactly what I'm thinking.

My breath starts coming in short gasps, my eyes darting around. Does he know about Vicurious? Do they *all* know?

I stumble down the hall and around the corner, toward the ladies' room. I'll hide there, just to calm down. I'll wait and see if anyone comes in talking about me. But just as I'm about to push the door open, I spot Adrian with his arm draped around Raj Radhakrishnan's shoulder. They're walking down the hall together. I let go of the bathroom door and move toward them.

"How's it going, Raj?"

"Great, it's . . . okay." Raj attempts a smile, but his mouth doesn't quite make it.

Adrian stops walking and glares at the kids lingering around him so they scatter. I look down and pretend to be searching for something in my backpack. He pulls Raj to the side of the hall. "Talk to me, man. You seem a little down."

Raj shakes his head. "It's nothing."

"Come on, dude. It's not nothing. What's going on?"

He stares at Adrian, clearly as confused as I am, but whereas I'd just shrug and look away, Raj actually responds. "My parents are getting a divorce. It's not going that well."

"Fighting a lot?"

"They're not even talking. Nobody on my dad's side of the family is speaking to either one of us, actually. My cousins, their friends and families . . . everybody blames my mom for leaving. So, we're kind of on our own now, my mom and I."

"That sucks. I'm really sorry." Adrian squeezes Raj's shoulders. "You ever need someone to talk to, let me know."

He nods, smiles faintly. "Thanks for, uh . . . asking." The whole conversation has got to be a total shock. Adrian has probably never even spoken to Raj before.

But he pulls something out of his pocket, a little card. "Why don't you come to our next show? I'd love to see you there."

Raj's smile gets wider. I think it's the first time I've seen him look genuinely happy. "Sure. Thanks," he says. "I'll be there. For sure."

"Excellent." Adrian drops his arm from Raj's shoulder and reaches his other hand out to give him a fist bump, which Raj totally fumbles. Adrian laughs and claps him on the back. "Take care, man. It'll be okay. See you."

Raj says, "Yeah, see you, Adrian." He shakes his head a bit, like he's just woken from a dream. But I could swear he's grown about two inches, and he was already tall.

Raj sees *me* standing there and says, "Hi, Vicky." He smiles. I almost fall over.

"Uh, hi, Raj."

"See ya," he says, and gives me an awkward little wave with his long hand.

I wave back and follow after Adrian, keeping enough distance that I don't look like one of the groupies, but close enough to observe him noticing kids that nobody else ever seems to notice. He says "I see you" to half a dozen more before the one-minute warning bell rings for the next period.

I hurry to class, stunned by what I just witnessed. I can't believe Adrian took my Vicurious posts to heart like that. It makes me feel like a superhero. *Of kindness.* Which has got to be the dorkiest kind of superhero there is.

Still, I can't help but wonder if this is happening anywhere else. Are people being nice in high schools all over the country? The world?

Because that's just crazy.

22

MY INSTAGRAM IS GOING BERSERK after school with thousands of new followers and a steady stream of comments. I see you, I see you, *I see you*! When I get home, my mother is sitting at the kitchen computer as I walk in. There's no smoothie waiting. She points to the cupboard and says, "Get yourself a snack if you want."

I'm not hungry, but I pour myself a glass of juice.

Mom barely looks up from the computer. "That girl with the purple-and-orange hair is really blowing up. She's on *The Ellen Show* and everything."

"That wasn't real," I say, trying to keep my voice that of a casual observer. "She just Photoshopped it."

"Yeah, but now Ellen wants her on the show. Look."

Mom brings up a YouTube video from *The Ellen Show*, and leans back so I can see over her shoulder. Ellen's sitting on the set where she gives interviews. There's a picture of my Instagram avatar on the screen next to her. She's saying, "Have you seen this girl? Vicurious? She's all over the internet. My followers have been talking about her all week, about how she's reaching out to kids who feel invisible and ignored, and encouraging others to do the same."

The image switches to the one of me dancing with her. "She posted this picture of herself standing right over there, dancing with me. And I thought, great, now I don't even remember who I've danced with." The audience laughs. "And my producer said, 'Ellen, she wasn't really here. It's Photoshopped.' And then I was kind of bummed out, because she looks like a lot of fun." More laughing. The whole time Ellen's talking, they're flashing my Instagram posts. With Neil and Jimmy and Jennifer and the Foo Fighters. "I thought, why don't we invite her for real? So, Vicurious, if you're out there, we'd love to have you on the show."

I stand there staring at the screen, no longer breathing. Mom doesn't notice.

"I bet they'll get all kinds of imposters saying they're her," she says.

"Yeah," I say. "Because the real Vicurious would never go on TV in a million years."

Mom gives me a funny look. "Why not?"

"Because she's anonymous. Then she wouldn't be anonymous anymore."

"She'd be famous," says Mom.

"She already is famous," I point out.

"But nobody knows who she is."

"She's Vicurious."

Mom gives an exasperated sigh. "Who she *really* is. Nobody knows."

"Maybe she likes it that way."

Mom turns and studies me for a minute, and I think, *This is it. Finally. She sees me.* But she just shakes her head and turns away with a sigh.

I retreat to my room, shakily, and rewatch the video a dozen times.

I never thought I'd have to add "Appearing on the *Ellen Show*" to my Terror List.

Two hours later, Mom calls me for dinner and I grab my phone from the dresser, which is a huge mistake. The notifications are coming in like lightning. I keep the phone in my lap under the table and glance at it once too often.

"Vicky," Mom says sternly. "Who's texting you?"

For one panicked second I expect her to ask if it's Ellen. I shove the phone under my leg. "Nobody."

"Is it Jenna? Tell her we're eating, sweetie."

I pretend to text Jenna but instead open Instagram, turn off the notifications, and log out completely.

"Or is it those friends from the bus?" Mom says. "The ones in that photo you showed me? You never did tell me their names ..."

"It's not them."

Mom finishes chewing the food she just scooped into her

mouth and dabs her lips with her napkin. "I'd like to know who you're communicating with online."

"Nobody," I say. "It was just a game. It sends all these notifications. I turned it off."

"What game?"

"Um . . . I, uh . . . *Candy Crush?*" I never play games on my phone, and she knows it.

She reaches her hand out. "Give me your phone."

"What? Why?"

"As your mother, it's my right. No, it's my *duty* to make sure you are using this device responsibly and safely. Let me see the phone."

I roll my eyes and hand it to her.

She swipes the screen.

"Password?"

I shake my head.

"Give me the password, Vicky."

She'll see the text exchange with Jenna. And Lipton. She'll see my pictures of Vicurious. The one of Jenna and her new friends on the bus. She'll know I faked them as my own.

"That's invasion of privacy. I'm not giving you the password."

She stares at me. "Well, since I pay for the phone, I'll keep it until you do. Obviously, there's someone on there you don't want me to know about. And that concerns me."

"There's nothing for you to be concerned about. I just want my privacy."

"Nora," Dad says. "Come on . . ."

"No," Mom snaps at him. "This is exactly how kids get into trouble. Into drugs or . . . or . . . trouble with boys or with friends. They keep it secret. And parents are supposed to ask questions. That's our job. So don't tell me—"

"Okay, okay." Dad shakes his head and turns to me. "Vicky, could you please give your mother your password?"

"I'm not using drugs." I speak as calmly as possible. "I just don't want Mom reading my stuff."

"I won't read it. I just want to see who you're corresponding *with*."

I clench my jaw and put out my hand so she'll pass me the phone. But instead of keying in the password, I go to my message settings and turn off "show preview." That way, if Lipton texts me, it won't appear on the closed screen for all the world to see. I close my phone and hand it to her.

"I thought you were putting in the password."

"Nope."

Dad sighs. "Then it looks like you'll be losing your phone, kiddo."

I shrug.

Mom disappears into her bedroom with my phone.

"You really can't just tell her your password?" says Dad.

"No," I say. "I really can't."

He sighs. "You've gotta pick your battles, sweetie. Is this the one you want to fight?"

232

"She's the one picking fights," I say. "I was just trying to eat my dinner."

Mom walks back in. "What's that?"

"Nothing." I stand to take my plate to the sink. "I'm not hungry."

"Shame," she says, stabbing a tortellini with her fork and popping it into her mouth. "Just let me know when you want your phone back."

I go to my room and turn on my computer. When I open Instagram, I nearly pass out. I have 827,000 followers. And growing fast. I sit there staring at it long enough to see the number tick up to 828,000.

At this rate, I could reach a million by morning. *One. Million. Followers.* It's too many to fathom. What does that many people even look like? I search, "What does one million people look like?" Images come up. Outdoor events where the masses have gathered. A million people meditating with the Dalai Lama. The mall in Washington, DC, transformed into a sea of humanity.

I imagine them all turning to look at me . . . and stare . . . and . . . *breathe, Vicky.*

My pulse pounds in my ears. WHAT WAS I THINKING? I never meant for Vicurious to get this big. All I really wanted was to show Jenna that I wasn't a nobody. That I could be fun and daring and interesting. *To Jenna,* not a million total strangers.

I'll just delete the account. Simple as that. I'll put this all behind me, and nobody will ever know. I frantically search the

Instagram menu on my computer for a delete button. But there isn't one. There's only "temporarily disable my account."

Click it, Vicky.

I move the cursor over the link, my hand trembling on the mouse. Everything will be so much easier if I just step away, go back to my simple, quiet existence. Be myself again, just Vicky. All by myself.

But I can't stop thinking of the soon-to-be-a-million people who've come to me, and not because I wear a crazy wig and sunglasses and Photoshop myself into stupid pictures. It's because they want to be seen. And because I saw them, people like Adrian Ahn and Ellen are seeing them, too.

What message would it send if I erased them, even temporarily? That I don't want to see them anymore? That I never really cared in the first place?

I know how that feels.

I don't want anyone else to feel it.

I move my cursor up to the corner instead, and click on the icon that takes me out to my home page. I toggle through my images. I stop to read comments, and reply to my followers.

I tag them, I thank them, I let them know that I see them. And I'm not leaving.

23

AT LUNCH PERIOD ON FRIDAY I'm relieved, as usual, that the weekend is near and I can get away from everything that makes me nervous. But I'm also realizing I'm going to miss Lipton, and the yearbook staff, too. I haven't missed anyone since Jenna, or before, so it feels strange.

Beth Ann and Marvo and I are sitting there working and eating our lunches when Marissa bursts through the door crying. At first we all just stare at her, completely shocked and not sure what to do. Then Marvo holds his hands up like he's under arrest, in case anybody was planning to blame him.

I try to work up the nerve to say something comforting. Beth Ann sighs and spins her chair to face Marissa's. "What's the matter? Adrian still ignoring you to save the world from all the lonely people?"

"Where do they all come from?" Marvo mutters.

Beth Ann tips her chin toward the door. "Beat it. It's females-only day."

"Since when?"

"Since I said so." She glares at him, and he is gone in about three seconds.

Marissa sniffles. "We always eat lunch together on Fridays. It's the one day, the *only* day."

"And he blew you off."

She nods. "He's completely ignoring me, and if I get upset about it I'm being selfish and uncaring because he's hanging out with some kid who doesn't have any friends."

"Yeah. Sucks that your boyfriend is a super-nice guy."

Marissa scowls at Beth Ann. "Does he have to do it every single day? Can't one day be for me?"

"There are lots of kids with no friends, I guess."

"I just want him back," says Marissa. "Preferably without Raj Radhakrishnan attached to his hip."

Beth Ann laughs. "Hey, Raj is not so bad. And soon to be featured in the yearbook!" She points to the list on the wall.

Marissa moans.

"Gotta love it when the loners win the day though, am I right?" Beth Ann rolls her chair over to where I sit and puts a hand up to high-five me.

I can't remember the last time I was high-fived, if ever. I lift my hand to meet hers. She slaps it hard, and I wasn't holding it firm enough. Our hands bang against my forehead.

"Ow."

"Oh, shit." Beth Ann has a concerned look on her face, but is also giggling. Because who can't high-five without getting bonked in the head?

"My bad," I say.

"Are you okay?"

I nod. "I'm prone to high-fiving accidents, apparently."

"You are so weird," she says.

I blanch. What was I thinking, trying to act like I fit in here?

Beth Ann nudges my shoulder. "I meant that in a good way. You know that, right?"

I swallow. "Right. I knew that."

Marissa watches the whole thing, pouting. Then starts crying again. Or is she laughing? "I should be having lunch with my boyfriend but instead I'm here, watching you two idiots."

"What?" Beth Ann puts a hand to her hip. "And miss our stellar display of manual dexterity?" She tries to get me to high-five again and we keep missing each other.

Then Marissa joins in and we're all laughing, slapping our hands together clumsily, purposely missing and stumbling around. I can hardly believe it, and I'm not delusional enough to expect it to last. But I'm here in the moment, I'm part of the action. It's real, not vicarious.

And I am breathing just fine.

Mom keeps my phone all weekend. And I don't really miss it, because the only person I ever called was Jenna. Lipton knows to email instead of text, and I can check Vicurious from my computer. But it still feels weird to be without it.

When I ask my mother if I can have the phone back on Monday morning, she just replies, "Password?" And I say, "Never mind."

Same conversation on Tuesday. I try with Dad on Wednesday morning but he just shakes his head.

By Thursday, I stop asking.

Instead, I live in the moment. I exchange notes and smiles and awkward attempts at conversation with Lipton. I slip into Mrs. Greene's office when I'm feeling overwhelmed, like when Beth Ann tries to high-five me in the hall and everyone sees me fumble it and starts laughing.

Marissa mopes around the yearbook office, and Adrian forms a lunch table with kids who usually sit by themselves. I want to make her feel better, but I don't want him to stop.

"I could walk through the cafeteria naked and he probably wouldn't notice," she says on Thursday. "I even messaged Vicurious to see if she'd post a photo of East 48 for their gig this weekend."

"If you can't beat 'em, join 'em?" says Beth Ann.

"Yeah." Marissa flops into her chair. "Something like that."

When I get home from school, I see that Marissa has put up some new photos on the East 48 website. She's dancing right out front in most of them, the center of attention. But there's one where she's in the background, by herself. Nobody's watching her. It's perfect.

If I do this, maybe Adrian will realize that she needs to be seen, too?

I can't check my direct messages to find hers, because the computer version of Instagram doesn't show them. But I can pretend I did. I can post a photo and thank Marissa for inviting me. Adrian would be psyched, Marissa would be happy, and Vicurious would be . . . a student at Richardson High School?

I brush off the risk of exposure. I Photoshopped myself into lots of random pictures from followers in my #Iseeyou series. Why not one more? I'll do some others in the next few days so it doesn't seem strange.

In a matter of minutes, Vicurious is dancing with Marissa DiMarco in the background of an East 48 concert. Now I just need to figure out how to post the photo from my computer, since Instagram only makes that possible from handheld devices. But there's an app for everything. I quickly find one that not only enables me to post from my desktop but also lets me schedule the image to appear at a specific time. I set it for 12:15 tomorrow. Lunch period. I'll be in the yearbook office working diligently. They'll never think it's me.

On Friday morning, Lipton is extra fidgety in class. He drops his pencil three times, then flings it halfway across the room trying to catch it before it falls a fourth time. He and Adam exchange a series of eye-bulging facial expressions, like they're trying to impersonate lizards.

I wait for him to pass me a note, but nothing comes.

After class, he follows so close behind me out the door that he gives me a flat.

"Sorry. Sorry," he says.

"It's okay." I stumble to pull my shoe back on.

Adam is standing nearby, rolling his eyes.

"I, um . . . was wondering," says Lipton, "if I could have a word with you." He sounds like the principal inviting me to his office for a detention slip.

"Okay." My heart rate ticks up a few notches.

Lipton cups his hand under my elbow and guides me to the same little alcove I crouched in that day I was pretending to tie my shoe. He releases my arm and sweeps a hand through his hair, which immediately falls back into his eyes.

"I wanted to ask you." He swallows. Sweeps his hair again. "I was wondering if you might like to go to a concert. East 48." He pulls a postcard promoting the gig from his pocket, probably the same one Adrian gave Raj, and shoves it into my hands. "There. That."

"Saturday?" I say.

"Yes, Saturday. Did I forget to say that? Saturday. Tomorrow."

I smile at Lipton. A weird thing is happening. His nerves seem to have a calming effect on me. The more awkward he gets, the less I am.

"Adrian Ahn invited me," he says. "It's his band. He's the drummer."

"Yes," I say, though I can't believe I'm saying yes to attending a concert. I may come to my senses later.

Lipton seems puzzled. "Yes, you know who Adrian is? Or yes..."

"I'll go to the concert with you."

"You will?" His whole face smiles.

I nod, pretty sure my whole face is smiling back at him.

"Um, okay. I'll pick you up," he says. "Well, my mom will pick you up. But I'll be in the car, of course. I mean, my mom will drive us. If that's okay. I don't have my license yet."

"Sounds good," I say, very cool and collected. "I'll see you then."

"Okay, great!" Lipton starts backing away from me, hands clenching his backpack straps near his shoulders, like a farmer tugging at his overalls. "See you then."

He turns around and walks straight into the side of the drinking fountain, which hits him square in the crotch. It buckles him over a bit, but he just shuffles sideways and around the fountain, and continues down the hall and into the boys' bathroom.

Adam comes up beside me. "Does he know where you live?"

"I don't think so," I say.

He laughs, and I'm hardly anxious at all. I write down my address and give it to him.

"I'll make sure he gets this. And you should know, he'll probably be ten minutes early to pick you up. He's always ten minutes early."

"Okay." I love that I'm having a conversation with Adam and barely sweating, but the hall is clearing and the bell is going to ring soon and I don't want to be late for class. "Thanks."

He sighs. "Just don't mess with him, okay? He really likes you."

I watch Adam turn and go, then hurry to my own class. The terror of going to a concert with Lipton doesn't hit me until halfway through my next period. I breathe in and out and try to focus on small details instead of the hugeness of it, like what am I going to wear? But that only makes me more anxious.

You can do this, I tell myself.

I run through all the things I've done in the past few weeks that seemed impossible a month ago. I've joined the yearbook staff. I've had several near-normal conversations. I have joked around with classmates. I have high-fived, albeit terribly. I've said hi to Hallie Bryce at least six times now. I have exchanged notes with a cute boy. I've had actual physical contact with that same boy on several occasions. I have spoken to him and even, dare I say it, flirted?

Most astonishing, I have walked into the school psychologist's office and sat in her chair and come very close to talking with her about all of it.

What scares me is something I can't help thinking: Would any of it have happened if Jenna was still here?

Am I better off without her?

"Help me find ones that don't suck," says Marvo, staring at photos of the random people we're considering for the special section. It was proving difficult to take photos of them all, until I mentioned their Instagrams and suggested we just ask them to submit their own.

So here we sit, in front of his computer in the yearbook office. We choose our favorite of the yarn bomber, then click over to Hallie Bryce's Instagram.

"None of these suck. They are the opposite of suck." He clicks through all of Hallie's pictures, and back again. "How are we going to pick just one?"

I point to my favorite. She's in a park, holding the back of a bench like it's a ballet bar. There's an old woman with a walker standing in the background. "Her turnout is perfect, and that lady behind her has her feet turned out, too. Like she's trying to do the pose."

Marvo laughs. "I didn't even see that."

I click to another favorite, where she's holding her leg up at an impossible angle, but also looking right into the camera. I used to think her expression was aloof, but now I see the sadness. "And this one," I say. "Her face."

"Oooh, yeah." He nods.

"No wonder Beth Ann didn't want to come today," says Marissa. "Listen to the two of you drool over Miss Perfect."

Marvo and I turn to stare at Marissa for a moment. Then

laugh. I know Marvo is probably thinking that Marissa is just as perfect as Hallie, while I'm thinking she's just as *not*.

Marissa isn't paying attention to us, though. She stands up suddenly, phone in her hand.

And screams.

Marvo leaps up. "What? What?"

I jump out of my chair, too, though I'm pretty sure I know what she's screaming about. "What's the matter?"

"Ohmygod, ohmygod. She did it. Ohmygod. Look." She shoves her phone in my face. It's the photo of Vicurious at the East 48 concert. "Look, look! She's dancing with me!" She points to the caption, which reads:

vicurious Thanks for the invite, **@marissadimarco**. #supportlocalmusic #East48

"She mentioned me! She answered me!" Marissa stops bouncing long enough to show Marvo. "Can you believe it? I have to tell Adrian! Oh my God."

She leaves her bag behind and runs out holding her phone up like it's the holy grail. Marvo and I look after her, then at each other.

"Okay, what just happened?" he says. "I couldn't even see what it was."

I scrunch my face up a bit to give the appearance that I'm not entirely sure, either. "I think that girl with purple-and-orange hair posted something about Adrian's concert on Instagram."

"Ah." Marvo nods. "Hmmm."

I return to the computer. "We should get back to work."

"Yeah, okay." He nods, a slow smile coming to his lips. "Will you be attending the concert?"

I swear he knows I'm Vicurious, the way he's looking at me right now. "Huh?"

"The East 48 concert. You going?"

"I, uh . . . yes. With Lipton. He asked me, so . . ."

"Oooh, big date." Marvo waggles his eyebrows.

I shove his chair so it rolls him away from the workstation, and turn my attention to the photos again. He scoots himself back, smiling, and points to the Hallie photo with the old lady.

"That's the one," he says. "It's the people in the background you really want to keep your eye on."

24

I SPEND FRIDAY EVENING TRYING on every item of clothing I own, and concluding that I have nothing to wear. It's a good thing my mother has confiscated my phone, or I would've texted Lipton to cancel. I could email him, and am thinking about it. But Adam's parting words linger. So I ask my mother if we can go shopping.

"I have a date," I mutter.

She almost explodes with joy.

We hit all the usual stores on Saturday morning; I hide from all the usual salespeople, and reject all the usual clothes. Finally, at a store that is blessedly understaffed and completely ignoring us, I choose a black turtleneck sweater that hugs my figure enough to satisfy my mother. She insists on a new pair of skinny jeans, too. And in a moment of weakness, I even let her maneuver me to the cosmetics island in Neiman Marcus, where a lady in a white coat applies some eyeliner and mascara. I try to concentrate on my breathing instead of the fact that a strange woman's face is inches from my own and everyone who walks past stares at what she's doing to me. When she's finished, I blink at my reflection in the mirror. My eyes look enormous. Mom buys the makeup.

I'm nervous in the car home, worried the sweater might be too snug to wear a T-shirt underneath, or the jeans fit weird, or the makeup makes me look like a clown. "I don't have shoes," I say. "What am I going to wear for shoes?"

"You can wear my black ankle boots," says Mom calmly.

I try to remember what her black ankle boots look like, if they're mom-ish. She hands them to me when we get home, and they're cute. I think. I really have no idea. I am trusting my mother for fashion advice and *oh, God, what have I done?*

I try everything on again and pull my hair into a ponytail. Mom takes one look at me and starts to cry. "You look beautiful," she says, fingers pressed to her lips. "I never thought—"

"You never thought I could look beautiful?"

"No, I *know* you're beautiful, with or without makeup. I just never thought you'd let anyone else see it. You're always trying to hide yourself."

I shoo her out of my room before I start crying, too. Because it's only three o'clock in the afternoon and I can't freak out yet. I take the new clothes off and put my usual ones back on. I sit at my computer to open my Instagram, so I don't have to think about the concert or my outfit or going on a date and what if Lipton tries to kiss me? I quickly click to my home page before that line of thinking goes any further.

Sometime in the middle of the night, Vicurious passed one million followers. I knew it might happen, and am surprisingly calm about this development. It's because of Ellen, I tell myself. Not me. She tells people to follow, and they follow. Rhyming Rhea started the ball rolling, and Ellen pushed it down a very steep hill.

Now at 1.2 million followers, my Instagram is nearly as big as the population of Dallas, Texas. Or the state of New Hampshire. But it's spread all over the country and the world. Some of the comments are in languages I don't even recognize.

I try not to think again about what all those people would look like gathered up together in one place. They come to me one at a time, I remind myself. I read their comments one at a time, respond to them one at a time.

One person isn't that scary.

I check the East 48 post. It has 98,300 likes and 2,400 comments. I spend the next hour scrolling through them. Marissa must've spent all night watching the feed, because about every twentieth comment is her announcing their concert Saturday. It's their biggest yet, at a venue that usually hosts national acts. If they pack the house, it'll be their big break.

I should've tagged the band. I edit my post to add it. A few minutes later, this happens:

east48rocks Thanks for the support, Vi! Wish you could be at our gig tonight.

vicurious Me too.

raychaelbee Me too!

anonymuskateer Me too.

hatemiselfee Me too!

marissadimarco Me too!!!!

And on and on. I log out, and wipe my browser history. I shouldn't have written "me too" this time. It takes away from the meaning of those two simple words that has developed among Vicurious followers. Sure, it started with the Foo Fighters post, people saying they were there, too. *Me too, me too.* But then it turned into something more. It meant "I'm scared, too" or "I'm alone, too" or, more important:

You are not alone.

And I'm not anymore. But it still feels that way, without Jenna. I keep thinking, maybe she didn't mean it, what she said about wasting all those years on me. Maybe it was all a huge misunderstanding. I could call her, or send her an email.

But that annoying little voice asks, *Why would you do that?* She's turned her back on me twice now.

Why would I set myself up for that kind of humiliation again? Especially now, when I think I'm making progress?

I wouldn't.

I won't.

I can't.

I . . .

Oh, God. I can't go on this date. What was I thinking, saying yes to a concert where I'll be surrounded? Crowds are the absolute worst. So many people, so many opportunities to humiliate myself.

I start sweating, the room spinning. I don't have a paper bag so I cup my hands and breathe into them, sitting at my desk chair to drop my head between my knees. From down here, where I can see the flaws of my room again, I hear the bleep of an email on my computer.

I sit up, too fast. The room's spinning again. When it stops, I reach for the mouse and click open my in-box. It's a note from Lipton:

> I can't wait to see you. I'm so nervous. I just put my
> shoes on the wrong feet. Please don't laugh if my
> clothes are on backward when I come to pick you up.
> It's like I no longer have opposable thumbs. Ouch. I
> just poked myself in the eye with my toothbrush.

I laugh out loud, and my nerves begin to slip away. Not completely, but enough. I write back:

> **Thanks, I needed that. See you tonight!**

I head to the bathroom, still shaky, and stare at myself in the mirror. The eye makeup that was so expertly applied is now all smudged. I wash it off and make three attempts at reapplying before it looks almost as good as it did when we left the store. Mom calls me for dinner and I try to eat, but my stomach is too knotted. For once, she doesn't give me a hard time. I excuse myself to get dressed. The new clothes go back on, and Mom's shoes. I even add a pair of earrings and one of Vicurious's bracelets, which I'm counting on not being recognizable by itself.

Then it's time, and my mother shouts, "They're here!"

I peek out the window and see a minivan in the driveway. I breathe. The doorbell rings. Mom is calling my name. She's answering the door.

I look at myself in the mirror one last time. Smooth my hair that doesn't need smoothing. Pull the ponytail tighter. Put my hand to the doorknob.

"Vicky!" Mom calls down the hall. "Gregory's here!"

Oh, God. Did she really just do that?

When I reach the living room, Lipton is saying, "It's Lipton, ma'am. Lipton Gregory."

"Oh, yes." Mom does an exaggerated head palm. "I knew that. I must be nervous for your date." She giggles.

I want to die, but I'm too busy looking at Lipton and trying to keep my jaw from scraping my knees.

He got his hair cut.

Gone is the bowl-shaped mom cut. In its place is the best

hair I have ever seen on a guy. It's cut super short around the sides and back, but the front is still longish. Kind of intentionally shaggy and . . .

"Your hair." I didn't mean to say that out loud. "It looks great."

"Yours too." He grins. Tooth gap, check. Dimple, check. "You look really nice."

My mother is teary-eyed smiling at us.

I grab my coat and the purse I spent an hour packing with a lifetime supply of mints, tissues, and an extra T-shirt rolled very small and squeezed into a Ziploc bag, just in case I sweat through the one I'm wearing. Which, at the rate things are going, might happen before we even get to the concert.

"Let's go," I say.

Lipton holds the door to my house for me, and even puts his hand gently on my lower back to lead me out.

"Would you like the front seat or back?" he asks.

I'm a little puzzled, because I figured we'd sit together. "The back is fine," I say.

He closes his eyes briefly before opening the car door. There's a girl sitting there, on the opposite side. She looks about eight. "That's my sister, Tammy," Lipton says. "Are you sure you don't want to sit up front? I can sit in the back."

I glance at Tammy. She smiles. "It's okay," I say.

We load ourselves in. Mrs. Gregory turns and introduces herself, reaching a hand out to shake, which I do. I hope she doesn't notice how clammy my palm is. Then his little sister reaches her hand out. "It's very nice to meet you," she says. "Lipton talks about you *all* the time. He said—"

"Tammy!" Lipton and his mother silence her in unison.

"Geez," she says. "I wasn't going to say anything *bad*."

"Don't say anything at all," he says, teeth clenched.

And thus commences the most awkward car ride ever. Lipton and I can't talk to each other, and his sister did the lip-zip-and-throw-away-the-key gesture. So, that leaves his mother to fill the silence with attempts at conversation.

"Have you heard this band before, Vicky?"

I swallow. Small talk with parents (or anyone, for that matter) is not my forte. "Yes," I manage quietly. "But never live. Only on YouTube."

More silence ensues. Lipton turns on the radio. It's Taylor Swift, and he immediately turns it back off.

"I like that song!" Tammy whines.

"We are all painfully aware of your fascination with Taylor Swift," he says.

Tammy turns to me. "Do you like her? If you like her, Lipton will turn it back on."

I pause to consider my options. Taylor Swift is not my favorite, but turning Lipton's sister against me right off the bat doesn't seem like a wise choice. "I like some of her stuff," I say.

"She likes her!" Tammy reaches forward to pound on the side of Lipton's seat. "Turn it back on."

Lipton twists around to raise an eyebrow at me. I can only

shrug. So he turns it on, and his sister bounces around to the tune. The moment it ends, she puts her eager face in front of mine and says, "Are you going to be my brother's girlfriend?"

My mouth pops open in surprise. "I, uh . . ."

"Tammy," Lipton's mother scolds. "Enough."

"Well, excuse me for living," she huffs.

I know Lipton is mortified, and I feel bad benefitting from his embarrassment, but it's the only thing keeping my own anxiety in check. If he was as smooth and cool as he looks right now, I'd have passed out. And here I am, still upright.

We arrive at the concert venue a few minutes later, and Lipton barely waits for the car to stop before he leaps out and opens my door. I manage to exit the car without any further embarrassment, except for the kissy faces I'm fairly sure his sister is making behind my back.

Lipton glares at her as he shuts the door.

"I'm so sorry," he says. "I had no idea my sister was going to have to come along. My dad had to work, and—"

"It's okay," I assure him.

We both turn to face the Clubhouse, and that's when we realize there's a line wrapping around the building and down the street.

"Did you get tickets?" I ask.

He shakes his head. "I don't think they even sold tickets in advance. I just have this." He holds up the little postcard Adrian gave him.

We get in line and shuffle slowly forward with everyone else.

"I didn't realize they were so popular," says Lipton.

"Me either."

The girl standing in front of us looks me up and down, then Lipton, sort of rolls her eyes, and turns back to her friends.

Lipton leans toward my ear. "Am I not dressed right or something?"

"You're fine." *Very fine*, I might add. He's got new, slim jeans on that fit perfectly, and a charcoal-gray shirt and black pea-coat.

It's late November and pretty cold. I shove my hands in my coat pockets and shiver. Lipton inches closer and puts his arm around my shoulder, slowly tucking me against him. A smile slides easily to my lips. Lipton notices and bestows one of his widest grins upon me. I feel a flush rising to my cheeks.

At least the cold isn't a problem anymore.

The line, which has completely stopped moving now, doesn't bother me, either. It's just me and Lipton, the warmth of his arm through my coat, the feel of his chest against my shoulder. His breath in my hair.

I know Lipton can't make me a different person. He can't magically vanquish all my fears or stop my irrational freak-outs. But right now, in this moment, in the space of his arms, I almost feel normal—at least, what I *imagine* normal to be.

Then someone comes out of the Clubhouse entrance and announces that the building is full to capacity and the fire marshal will not allow anyone else to enter. "I'm very sorry," the man says. "The band will be returning for three additional concerts, which will be announced on their website in the next few days."

There are cries of disappointment all around us.

A couple of girls actually start weeping. Some of them mob the guy at the entrance, begging to be let in.

The guy just shakes his head and keeps saying "I'm sorry" and telling them to check the band's website for information on future concerts. People start to disperse, noisily and unhappily. The girl standing in front of us gives Lipton and me another dirty look, as if we're to blame, and says, "Stupid Vicurious."

I startle backward. "I'm not Vicurious!"

"Yeah, no kidding. But it's all her followers that jammed the place."

Lipton takes a step toward her. "We're not followers of anybody. Adrian Ahn invited us personally." He glances at me. "Who is she talking about?"

I shrug.

Immediately, I feel bad. That shrug was a lie, which means I just lied to Lipton's face.

She snarls at us and stomps off.

"I guess we should've gotten here earlier," says Lipton. "I didn't realize."

"It's okay. Concerts scare me, anyway."

"You don't mind missing it?"

"I kind of have this fear of people," I say. "You may have noticed."

"Then it's not just me?"

"It's not you at all. Not anymore."

We stand there smiling at each other until the sidewalk is empty and the flush on our cheeks is no longer enough to keep us warm.

"What do you want to do?" he says. "My mom isn't picking us up until ten thirty."

We look around. There's not much to choose from within walking distance. An orthodontist's office, a bank, a 7-Eleven, and a bowling alley. I've never bowled in my life. It's probably not a good idea to start now.

But Lipton's eyes light up when he sees the bowling alley. "Do you bowl?"

I shake my head.

"You want to try?" He's bouncing on his toes a little bit. Grinning.

I blink up at the Bowl-a-Rama sign, then back to Lipton's hopeful face. He looks so relieved to have found something to salvage our date. I glance at the 7-Eleven, which is our only alternative aside from walking around freezing our butts off.

"I can teach you," says Lipton. "It'll be fun."

My head starts nodding before my brain has given it permission, and I hear myself say, "Okay."

"You sure?" Lipton takes my hand and squeezes it.

I am not the least bit sure about trying something new—a sport no less—in a very public place, but I squeeze his hand back and nod anyway. I can't live vicariously forever. "Just please don't let me make a complete fool of myself."

He laughs. "Don't worry. That's my job."

25

INSIDE THE BOWL-A-RAMA, THE NOISE is at first jarring. They're blasting the kind of pop music that makes your teeth ache, punctuated by the electronic beeps and buzzes of a dozen arcade games. Add the hum of people trying to talk over it all and you can barely hear the clatter of bowling pins in the background.

It's the kind of noise you can get lost in, though. And once I adjust to the volume of it, I like that nobody will hear me if I say something stupid.

"I still can't believe the concert sold out," Lipton says as we head over to the check-in counter. "Adrian must be out of his mind."

"Marissa, too."

"That girl in front of us, though. What was she talking about?"

"Something on Instagram, I think." It's a lie of omission, and I feel bad about that, too. But I'm not ready to tell him about Vicurious. I don't know if I ever will be. I rack my brain for another topic, anything to change the subject.

"Have you bowled here before?"

"A few times."

I glance at the nearest lane, where a guy wearing some kind of heavy-duty wrist supports knocks all the bowling pins down in one shot. He looks professional. If I have to bowl next to him, I'll pass out for sure.

Lipton leans down to talk low in my ear. "It'll be fun. Don't worry."

So of course I start worrying, because people never say "don't worry" if there is absolutely no cause for worry. They also don't say "be careful" if something is perfectly safe. Or "stay warm" if there isn't a distinct possibility of freezing to death.

Lipton smiles and swings my hand as we wait our turn in line. Our shoulders brush together and it is enough to pull me out of my head, away from all the stuff that is spiraling out of control. I lean into him, and he leans into me, and it's okay that we aren't very good at using our words.

I reach in my pocket for money when we get to the register, but Lipton insists on paying. Then we're directed to a different counter that is dwarfed by a towering wall of shoe cubbies, which are occupied by the ugliest examples of footwear I have ever seen. Flat-soled shoes with red on one side, blue on the other, white laces, and white heels.

Lipton notices the crinkle of my nose. "Sexy, huh?"

"People wear those?" I say.

He laughs and asks for a size ten. The guy at the counter looks down at us from his elevated perch, grabs a pair of shoes from one of the cubbies, and slams them on the counter in front of us without a word. "Uh, thanks," says Lipton.

He and Surly Shoe Guy both look to me then. The noise drowning everything else out falls away and I am suddenly on display. All my anxiety comes rushing back, and I'm convinced that I will say the wrong thing even if all they want from me is my shoe size. *It will be the wrong shoe size.* I'm sure of it.

I step backward and chirp, "No, thank you."

Surly Shoe Guy gives me a weird look, and Lipton leans to my ear. "You need shoes."

I drop my eyes to the ankle boots my mother loaned me. Not shoes, technically. But close enough. "I'm fine with these."

He smiles nervously, and immediately I know I'm doing something wrong. I can feel myself starting to sweat.

"They don't let you bowl in street shoes. You have to wear theirs, or bring your own." He turns over the pair in his hand to show me the smooth sole. "See, you have to be able to slide. Plus, it keeps the lanes clean."

"Oh. Okay." I glance up at the shoe guy, who is all head-shaking and eye-rolling.

"You, uh . . . want to go home?" says Lipton. "Do something else?"

"No. I'll wear the shoes." But I don't move, because I can't, because the shoe guy is judging me. I can only stand there hovering behind Lipton, avoiding eye contact with anyone who might look at me funny. Which is everyone.

Lipton touches my arm. "I'll get them for you. What size?"

"Eight," I whisper.

He returns to the counter and says, "Size eight, please."

Shoe Guy scans the size eight cubbies and grabs the most scuffed pair he can find. The laces are frayed and dirty, and the suede is completely worn off in places. Someone has taken a red Sharpie to the bare spots, even the ones on the blue side. They're hideous.

Lipton stares at the shoes. He lays his hands on the counter. I tug gently on the back of his shirt because a line has formed and everyone is looking at us and I just want to take the shoes and go.

But he doesn't pick them up. He says, "Do you have a nicer pair?"

"No. Sorry." Shoe Guy motions to the next person. "Size?"

The girl behind us glances nervously at Lipton before answering. "Um, eight?"

Lipton slides the grubby pair over to her. "This is all they have in size eight, apparently. You want them?"

She grimaces. "No, thanks. They're nasty."

Shoe Guy takes a much nicer pair of size eights from the cubbies and hands them to the girl. She receives them guiltily and hurries away. Which is exactly what I want to do.

I probably deserve the scuffed shoes. I don't even know how to bowl.

But Lipton is pissed. Off.

He lifts himself taller and gets right in Shoe Guy's face and says, "We'd like to trade these for a different pair, please."

"You'll have to go to the back of the line," the guy says.

Lipton's jaw gets very tight. I have never seen him like this, even when Jeremy was laughing at his *Minecraft* presentation. Instead of blushing and laughing it off like he usually does, he slides his arms wide so they block the width of the counter.

"No, actually, we'll wait right here while you reach *two feet* behind you, grab that pair of size eights . . . right there." He motions to the cubby directly behind the guy. "And pass them over here to me. Then we'll give you back this crummy pair that shouldn't even be in circulation anymore. Okay?"

Shoe Guy stares Lipton down for a minute, and I just want to disappear before this whole ridiculous situation draws any more attention. The guy finally takes the worn shoes away, and replaces them with the new pair.

"Thank you." Lipton smiles pleasantly, leaning across the counter so he can get even closer to the guy. "I'll be sure to mention the excellent service we received next time I see Mr. Pasternak."

The oh-crap expression on the guy's face is priceless. Lipton gives him an exaggerated thumbs-up and we turn toward the lane we've been assigned.

Everyone. Is. Staring.

But these are not the what's-wrong-with-her? sort of stares I've grown accustomed to. They are more of the whoa-did-you-see-that? variety. Still unnerving, but not as bad. When we reach our lane, Lipton sinks into a chair and lets out a slow, whistly breath.

I drop to the seat next to him. "You okay?"

He nods, but his hands are shaking. "My therapist says I need to stand up for myself. It scares the crap out of me, though. I'm not naturally assertive. You may have noticed."

Lipton has a therapist? This fact stops me, because of the way he mentioned it so casually. Like it's no big deal, when for me even walking into Mrs. Greene's office feels like a humongous deal. I desperately want to ask him about this, but instead I just say, "Well, you can tell your therapist you were great. I could never do that."

"Yes, you could. If you had to."

"But you didn't have to."

He smiles on one side, dimple tweaked. "And let you wear those awful shoes on our first date?"

I lower my gaze. "I wouldn't have minded."

"Well, I would've."

"So, you stood up for *me*, not yourself."

Lipton pinches his lower lip between his fingers for a minute, then sits up taller. "Still counts," he says. "I'm counting it."

"Okay." I smile. "Lipton, one. Judgey Shoe Guy, zero."

Lipton raises a fist in victory. "Yes!"

"Who's Mr. Pasternak, anyway?"

"The owner," he says. "He owns all the bowling alleys around here."

"You know him?"

Lipton grins sheepishly. "Never met the guy."

I laugh. Too loud. It's a guffaw, really. I slap my hand to my mouth. Lipton laughs, too, but at a normal volume.

He bends down to unlace his street shoes and I realize I'm going to have to take mine off, too, which is one of those weird things that goes on my list. I'm afraid to remove my shoes in public.

What if my feet are smelly?

What if there's a hole in my sock?

What if I misplace one of my shoes and then have to walk around with only one shoe?

Lipton is already lacing up the red-white-and-blue ones. He glances over, sees that I'm not doing the same. Sticks out his patriotic feet.

"Come on, they're not *that* bad," he says.

I laugh nervously. Still can't take my shoes off. "Is there a ladies' room?"

He points to where it is, next to the arcade.

"I'll be right back." I hurry away with bowling shoes in hand before I have to explain my shoe problem.

The bathroom is gross. I balance on one foot while changing the shoe on my other, so I don't have to touch my socks to the floor. I should change into a fresh T-shirt, too, except I'm afraid I might drop my sweater on the floor or into the toilet. Also, Lipton is waiting and if I don't get out there soon, the awkwardness of having spent too long in the bathroom will ensue.

I quickly finish and wash my hands and now it's been almost ten minutes since I came in here and he's going to think something's wrong with me.

This is pretty much why I should never leave the house.

I waste another two minutes coming up with eight different excuses to explain my lengthy absence. When I return to our lane, I don't have to use any of them because Lipton is not there.

Add "Being abandoned in a bowling alley" to my list.

I sit and wait, walking myself through various scenarios of what I will do if he never returns. Most of them end with me never leaving my house again.

A minute later, Lipton comes out of the men's bathroom. He gestures to my feet and shouts, "WHAT ARE THOSE?"

I want to die.

I mean, I know the meme. I've seen the videos on YouTube and witnessed kids at school shouting it at each other a thousand times. There's a reason I don't wear interesting shoes.

"Sorry," he says quickly. "You actually look really good in those."

I'm pretty sure my face now matches the red in the shoes, and I can't think of anything funny or clever to say.

A waitress appears, carrying a full tray of drinks and food. She rests it on the table behind us. "I've got two milkshakes and a large order of fries for lane thirty-eight," she says.

"That's us." Lipton stands again. "But I didn't order—"

"On the house." She nods toward the shoe counter.

Shoe Guy waves. All friendly-like.

"You've got to be kidding me," says Lipton under his breath. He doesn't wave, though. Just stares at the guy for a second and then gives the slightest of nods.

"He must really need that job," I say.

Lipton pops a fry into his mouth. "You think?"

I sit across from him at the table and we take turns dipping fries into the little paper cup of ketchup. Our hands brush every now and then, and it is ridiculous how much of an effect it has on me. Like I've been existing in some kind of suspended animation, my nerve endings grown numb from lack of use. Lipton is jolting them all back to life.

A trio of girls walks by on their way to another lane. One of them wiggles her fingers at Lipton. His eyes widen and he looks over his shoulder to see who she's waving at. But the only thing behind him is the empty bowling lane.

He blushes, and they giggle.

"Do I have ketchup on my face?" He wipes the back of his hand across his mouth.

"No." I smile and shake my head.

"What?" He runs a hand through his hair—his super-thick, flopping-adorably-over-his-eyes hair—and brushes some non-existent dandruff from his shoulders. "What is it?"

"Nothing." I can't tell him they think he's cute because that would be almost the same as telling him *I* think he's cute, which I do, but I can't *say* that. "They're just being friendly?"

"Oh." He glances at them and checks his shoes once more, then straightens his shirt. "We should get some balls now," he says, then quickly adds, "bowling balls."

He takes me to the rack behind our lane, where an assortment of colorful balls is available, and helps me choose one. Eleven pounds. Bright pink. I have no idea how to hold it, and I put the wrong fingers into the holes.

"No. Like this." He shows me how to position my hand. For a minute, I forget how open the bowling alley is. How on-display we are. It's like a little cone of privacy has fallen around us, just Lipton and me and my bright pink bowling ball.

"Then you lift it like this," he says, twisting my wrist around so the ball rests in my palm. His face is very close to mine, his voice low. "And use your other hand to steady it until you're ready to swing it back. Got it?"

"I think so." But that doesn't mean I want him to step out of our protective cone.

He lets his hands linger on mine for a few seconds longer than necessary. "We really don't have to do this if you're not into it," he says. "We could play arcade games, or just sit here and talk and watch the other bowlers."

"No," I say. "Let's bowl. I want to bowl."

I mean, how hard can it be?

Lipton smiles. He wants to bowl, too. And from the way he expertly selects his own ball and carries it, I'm guessing he's pretty good.

"Just don't laugh," I say.

"I promise." He sits at the controls for our lane. "You want to be Vicky, or . . ."

My eyes widen.

". . . Do you want to use a different name?" He starts typing, and the name "Gregor" appears on the scoreboard above. I wait for him to add the "y" but he doesn't.

"Call me Vic, then," I say.

Lipton types it in. *Gregor and Vic.* And we bowl. Or, rather, Lipton bowls and I attempt to roll the ball in the general direction of the pins, though it invariably ends up in the gutter. Luckily nobody is playing in the two lanes on either side of us, so I can almost pretend nobody sees me. *Almost.*

After five turns, my score is a whopping thirteen. Lipton's is fifty-eight, and I'm pretty sure he's purposely trying to miss. He keeps giving me tips. "Follow through," he says, showing how my hand should end up pointing in the direction I'm aiming.

"Okay. I got this," I say, with a confidence I usually reserve for Vicurious.

I approach, lift the ball, swing my arm, slide . . . and forget to let go. The ball arcs high and comes down with a loud thunk. *In the next lane.* It doesn't roll all the way to the pins. It just . . . it stops.

Lipton buries his head behind the scoring console. He's trying not to laugh. Or maybe pretending he doesn't know me. His shoulders are shaking. And people in other lanes, all the way down the alley, are looking. And pointing.

I scurry to the seat behind him and hug my knees to my face. "You said you wouldn't laugh," I mumble.

He comes back to sit next to me. "I'm not laughing at you—"

I snap my head up. "Don't even say it."

"Just kidding. It's okay." He bites his lip. "People do that all the time."

"Seriously?"

"Uh-huh." He nods, then shakes his head. "Actually, no. I have never seen that in my life. Do you know how much oil they put on those lanes? They're super slippery. I didn't think you could stop a ball like that even if you tried."

I bury my face again. "Not helping, Lipton."

"Sorry." He lays his hand on my back, just below my neck, and rubs small circles. He has now touched me in four different places.

"You want me to get you a new ball?" he says.

"How about I just watch you?"

"That sounds like the worst date ever. I bowl, you watch? No."

I sit up straight. "I'm serious. I want to watch you bowl. I bet you're really good at this. Show me your best stuff."

He scrunches his face up. "Really?"

I nod. "Really."

He sighs. "This is weird."

"And when has that ever stopped you before?"

"Ouch."

I laugh. "I mean that in the best possible way."

"Okay, but you have to sit up here at the console and talk to me."

I move to the console and try to look official. Lipton picks up his ball and rolls a strike. Then another strike. Some spares and another three strikes. He's playing my turns, too, so my score is looking much better.

"Wow," I say. "I might catch up to you."

Then he purposely gutter balls on his own turns so that I do.

"Not fair," I say.

He beams at me. Only two more rows or frames or whatever they're called left to play. It's his turn again, or time to play his turn, not mine.

"You're not going to let me win, are you?" I tease.

Lipton narrows his eyes at me and stands there longer than usual, then slowly begins his approach and sends a curveball down the lane. I'm not really paying attention to the ball, though, or how many pins he knocks down, because those new jeans he's wearing are a little distracting.

"Steee-rike," he says, grinning. "Your turn."

I blink up at him. "You mean, *your* my turn?"

"No, *your* your turn."

I shake my head.

"Come on," he says. "I'll even put the bumpers up."

"Bumpers?"

He points to the lane where three girls are playing. I hadn't noticed before, but there's a padded rail on each side. One girl stands at the foul line, holds the ball in both hands, swings it low between her knees, and lets it roll. It ricochets off the bumpers all the way down and ultimately takes out two pins. She squeals.

"See?" he says.

I do. I see a girl who possesses the kind of joyful abandon I've been seeking, but am too scared to embrace—even attempt—in my own skin. I need a disguise and an alias to enjoy that kind of freedom. She goes again, this time standing backward. She bends over and pushes it through her legs, then watches it go like that with her butt sticking up in the air. She doesn't care how she looks or who may be watching her. The ball hits the bumper once and then slowly moves to the center, knocking down the remaining pins. Her friends hoot as she celebrates with a little touchdown dance.

When I turn back to Lipton, I realize I'm standing. My body is braver than my brain, apparently. He hands me a ball. Not *my* ball, which is still sitting in the middle of the empty lane next to us, but an identical pink ball. I didn't even see him get it.

He walks right up to the foul line and kicks a lever on each side of our lane, and the bumpers pop up.

I hold the ball in both arms and shuffle to where he stands.

"Just let 'er roll," he says. "Any way you can."

I swallow and nod. Glance around. Nobody is watching, but I still can't bring myself to stick my butt up in the air and roll it between my legs. I slip my two middle fingers into the holes and grip the ball the way Lipton taught me.

"You got it," he says, backing away. Which is probably a good idea, considering my last attempt.

I wait until he is well out of range, step my left foot forward, swing my ball arm, and release.

It rolls mostly straight. Grazes the left bumper. Veers back to the center and ohmygod . . .

I knock them all down.

Lipton hoots. I turn around, hands pressed to my mouth, which is opened wide in a silent shriek, my shoulders pulled up to my ears.

"You did it!" He rushes toward me, wraps his arms around my waist, and spins me around.

I cling to his neck until we come to a stop and I feel the floor beneath my feet again. But he doesn't let go. It's full-body contact, arms around each other, chests and hips and thighs pressed together. Too many points of contact to count.

I'm pretty sure Lipton is as surprised as I am to find himself holding me like this, our noses mere inches apart. His whole face is open—eyes and mouth wide and smiling. Still laughing.

"You did it," he says softly now.

I might keel over if he lets me go, but not from embarrassment or humiliation or fear. No, this is something else entirely.

"I did it," I whisper, all breathy.

And before I can even consider the possibility, Lipton kisses me. His warm lips are on mine at first with a loud smack. A celebratory kiss that stuns me, and him, too, I think. Like he didn't really plan to do that. But still he doesn't let go.

"That was . . . I . . . ." His gaze drifts down to my mouth, then back up to my eyes.

His grip around me softens, his hands sliding to my hips. I rest my fingers on his shoulders.

And we kiss.

In front of the whole bowling alley and I can't believe I'm doing this. I'm scared of everyone who could be watching, but I really don't want to stop.

I could've died happy with the hand-holding alone. But the kissing? This is something worth living for.

Lipton's lips release mine and break into a shy smile, which I return. Then he's grinning. His lips are truly exceptional. Kissing. Smiling. Grinning. Smirking. You name it. Lipton's lips excel at everything. They should have their own Instagram.

"Should we, uh"—he looks around us—"finish our game?"

I couldn't care less about finishing the game, but people are watching, and now that the kissing has stopped, I feel like I might start hyperventilating a little. We walk back to the console, and he points up to my score. "Look. You're winning."

I steady my eyes on the display, not really caring what it says but needing something other than Lipton's lips to focus on. I am breathless, and happy.

If I am winning, it is not against Lipton. Tonight, for the first time in my life, I am winning against the fear of *being*—of taking up space and getting in the way . . . of being wrong or stupid or pathetic or not good enough. Of being laughed at.

Finally, I am winning against myself.

26

WE DON'T FINISH THE GAME, because we realize the concert's supposed to be over in ten minutes and Lipton's mom will be picking us up in front of the Clubhouse. We return our rented footwear to Now-Humble Shoe Guy, and run into the cold. Compared with the din of the bowling alley, the night air is quiet and peaceful. We can hear and see our breath as we hurry down the hill toward the Clubhouse.

People are streaming out, still buzzing with manic energy from the concert. They are flushed and sweat-soaked and *alive*. One very tall head bops above the crowd. Raj weaves his way to the sidewalk where everyone who's waiting for a ride is gathering, and notices us.

He bounds over. "Wasn't that amazing?" His voice is louder than it needs to be. "I didn't even see you guys in there. It was crazy!"

"Yeah, we—" Lipton starts to explain that we didn't get in, but Raj is spinning. Literally. He turns to some girls standing near us.

"That was so amazing!"

They shout their amazement at an equal volume, and then they're taking photos together. Raj is in selfie heaven, maybe because he's not alone for once.

Lipton leans close. "You're not upset we missed it?"

I blink at him. "Missed what?"

He laughs.

If time could stand still, this would be a pretty good moment to press the pause button. I am in a crowd but not terrified of it, in the company of someone who knows I have issues but likes me anyway. My lips are still vibrating from our kiss in the bowling alley.

Then Raj is upon us again, his shoulder pressing against my ear, squishing me between him and Lipton, phone raised at the end of his long arm. I don't have time to slink away or be nervous before he snaps the photo. I'm still smiling.

"Hey, there's my ride." He moves toward the line of cars and waves. Several people—none from our high school—wave back and call out good-byes.

It appears Raj Radhakrishnan has found his people.

Lipton's mother is alone when she collects us in the minivan, so we sit in the back together and hold hands beneath our coats—not that she would care or say anything. All she asks is if we had a nice time and we say, "Yes." She doesn't grill us like my mom would.

When we get to my house, Lipton walks me to the door, and I

am 99 percent sure my mother is looking through the peephole, so I give him an awkward hug.

He says, "Thanks" and "See you Monday" and "I had a really good time" and I say, "Me too," and silently curse Vicurious for weaseling into my thoughts. I vow to henceforth say "likewise" or "so did I."

They don't drive away until I am safely in the house, though it felt safer outside with Lipton than it does in my own living room, where my mother is ready with her questions.

"Did you have a good time?"

"Yes."

"How was the concert?"

"Great." This is not a lie, because it was by all reports a great concert. I don't know why I'm keeping the bowling secret, except that it feels like a special thing between Lipton and me, and sharing it might ruin that.

"Did you see anyone else you know?"

"Raj Radhakrishnan," I say. If she goes searching for him, she'll likely find photographic evidence that I was there.

I manage to extricate myself after just three questions by claiming exhaustion, though I've never been more exhilarated in my life. Mom hugs me and Dad says, "Night, sweetie," and I can't wait to get to my room and lie on my bed. Not to rest, but to *feel*:

One hand warmer than the other.

Lips tingling.

Skin like memory foam, imprinted with his touch.

Heart buoyant, not thudding in my chest but bouncing there.

Breath light and fast in my throat until I slowly force it to go calm and deep.

The only thing missing is that I can't tell my best friend about my first date or my first kiss or even my first time bowling. It makes me wonder if Jenna is having firsts of her own without me, and if she has anyone to tell.

It's four o'clock in the morning when I wake up in my clothes. I change into pajamas and try to go back to sleep, but can't. I would lie in bed with my phone if it wasn't still hidden away in my mother's room, battery most certainly dead. I toss, try to recover the feeling I had when I got home from my date, but a stronger one is nudging me. Not curiosity, exactly. It's more a sensation of missing something. Or missing out. People are talking, things are happening, *without me*.

Vicurious is calling, and I can't resist.

I climb out of bed and sit at my desk, stare into the computer's dark screen before touching the keyboard to bring it to life. I wonder if they will someday discover that an addictive substance was somehow engineered into the internet, just like with cigarettes. How else does it keep drawing us in the way it does? It can't only be the worry of being left out. Can it?

Because the lure has become a physical one. A fidgety rest-lessness. I need to *know*.

I click open Instagram and type in my password. The post about Adrian's gig fills the screen. I scroll through hundreds of new comments, which fall into two categories: complaints from those who couldn't get in and celebration from those who did.

Some thank me for letting them know about the concert; others blame me for telling too many people about the concert. They clearly don't need me to continue their conversation. Their comments are still coming in, and have been for hours now without a word from Vicurious. They could just as easily gather on East 48's page, or the Foo Fighters', or Neil deGrasse Tyson's, or whoever else strikes their fandom.

Again, I am tempted to delete the whole account and commit to living my own, real life. Not a vicarious one. I may never surf a mosh pit, or walk the red carpet, or explore the cosmos again. But I will hold hands with Lipton Gregory. I will be kissed in bowling alleys. And I will feel alive.

I will *live*.

I slide the cursor to "edit profile" and click on the "temporarily disable" link. But Instagram does not want me to make any rash decisions. I may regret seizing this rare moment of bravery. Everything will be hidden, they tell me, but I can bring it all back to life simply by logging in. Better yet, I could set my posts to private, or block people.

Instagram does not understand that I am the one who needs blocking.

I click through the reasons I must choose from to explain why I wish to disable my account:

Just need a break
Trouble getting started
Created a second account
Privacy concerns
Want to remove something
Too busy/too distracting
Can't find people to follow
Too many ads

But my reasons aren't there. There's no "Need to get a real life" or "Can't hide here forever" or "An actual smile is way better than a picture of one" or even "I've been keeping this thing a secret for way too long and really need to get rid of it before anyone finds out."

There's that final, catch-all "Something else" choice so I click on that and I plug in my password. The arrow is hovering over the "submit" button when I think of why I started Vicurious in the first place. To be seen . . . by Jenna. What if she does see me? What if she tries to send me a message? What if I miss it? What if I already have?

I decide to look for her just one more time before I shut

Vicurious down, in the last place justjennafied made contact. It was the photo of Kat. I go there and scan the comments that followed, but don't find her. The only other place I think to check is the fuzzy sock cocoon, where justjennafied left a "me too." I click to the photo and start scrolling. Interspersed between oohs and ahhs of fuzzy-sock-loving fans are the tiny voices of those who kept me from deleting my account the last time. I didn't see them in the comments of the East 48 post, but they're still here, hurting and alone:

> **exitstagebeth** Nobody cares about me.
>
> **ihateme2ew** I don't know why I'm even here.
>
> **problxems** My teacher told me I'm a waste of space.
>
> **sadlyghostly** All I want to do is sleep.

There's more. One girl writes a long paragraph in the comments, about a group of boys at her school who rate girls on a hotness scale of one to ten. She doesn't care if they give her a ten or a two, either way it makes her feel worthless.

Another writes that she's been eating pears lately. That she can't stop. It seems a harmless addiction until she adds, "I'm allergic to pears." And a few more lines down she elaborates, "Like, rush-to-the-hospital, EpiPen allergic."

I sit back, staring at the screen. I was ready to let Vicurious go. Really, I was. But my followers are not. They need me. No, they need *her*. So I start replying. I offer the hand they are reaching out for, the shoulder they need to cry on.

I tell the girl who is being rated on her looks to ignore them. Her body is not for boys to judge and their ratings do not decide her worth. I make the pear-eating girl promise she'll never do that again. I try to respond to everyone who believes they are unloved or unwanted or uncared for.

I care, **@exitstagebeth**

@ihateme2ew You're here to find your people. We are your people! And we care.

Hey, **@problxems**—your teacher is a jerk. Don't listen!

@sadlyghostly I feel the same way sometimes.

I'm not sure what advice to give to someone who sounds depressed, like sadlyghostly. I don't want to say something totally useless like "cheer up!" because I know it's not that easy. I search online for a hotline or something, but there are so many, and I have no idea where she lives.

The one person I know who can relate to the experience of having depression is Rhyming Rhea, so I go to her YouTube. I find the video where she rhymes about some of the ways she deals with depression.

She walks her dog, dances, reads books that make her laugh, watches TV, even takes a long bath (lots of bubbles in that shot!). It's fun, but serious, too. She talks about therapy and medication. I copy the link and go to my profile, which has thus far been completely blank. I write:

I make myself feel better by living vicariously. When that's not enough, go here:

I post the link. I hope she won't mind. I don't think she will. And I go back to commenting. Whenever I think it might help someone, I write, "click the link in my profile." But mostly I write, "I care" and "you are not alone" and "I see you."

I do it until the sun has been up for hours and Mom is tapping on my door asking if I'm awake and do I want breakfast. I devour the eggs and toast she makes for me, and return to my computer to write some more. There are so many comments, and the more I write, the more pleas for help I get. Clearly, no one else is listening to these people, or answering them. When I do, they want more. They write back. They challenge and question and doubt.

exitstagebeth You're just saying that to be nice.

ihateme2ew You don't even know me.

problxems Thanks. But what do I do? Drop out?

sadlyghostly I feel this way ALL the time.

And so many more.

I check the number of new comments. They are double what I had when I started replying. All the tingly lightness I felt after my date with Lipton is gone. It is hard enough to carry my own sadness and loneliness. But shouldering everyone else's will bury me.

I take a break, pace my room as if I can walk it off. But each second I'm away from the computer is another dozen comments.

Not all my followers are troubled. Most are happy. But I have to dig through their bursts of "LOVE THIS!" and "OMG you are the best" to find those who need my help. If the two kinds of followers would just talk to each other . . .

I scan my comments again, start tallying them up. There are about six positive comments for every negative one. Six happy, funny, silly, joyful (or at least trying to appear so) people for every one who is hurting.

I go to my closet. Pull out the wig. Throw on a black T-shirt. I won't need the skirt today, because this is only going to be a head shot. I choose the white cat-eyed sunglasses. They are the most serious I have. I get dressed, sit in front of the computer again, and open the Photo Booth. This will be as close up as any image I have posted, so I make sure all my hair is completely tucked into the wig. I apply lipstick. Neatly at first, then smearing a little outside the lines.

I snap the photo. One frame is all I need. But instead of uploading the image straight to Instagram, I print it out on my color printer. I dig through my desk drawers for all the thick, colorful markers I can find. Then, all around the edges of the page, I write the sadness and pain of my followers:

#Hated #Broken #Ugly #Fat #Nobodycares
#Wasteofspace #Unwanted #Unloved #Scared
#Alone #Weak #Sad #Depressed #Angry
#Hopeless #Ignored #Notgoodenough
#Seeme #Talktome #Listen

I write it like a word cloud, some words big and some smaller, but I curve them around my head, my neck, my shoulders, along the jagged edges of my hair and into all four corners of the paper. I fill the emptiness with despair. My own bleeds onto the page, too.

#Mybestfrienddumpedme
#Pathetic #Getalife

I thought Lipton might be able to fill the hole Jenna left, but he is carving out his own space in my heart. The one Jenna occupied is still empty, and still aching. Even though I pushed it all down, the feelings are still there.

Capping the markers, I put the picture on the scanner and capture a new image. A picture of a picture.

When I posted the #seeme images before, the plea for help was subtle. It was a nudge. A tip of my chin toward those in need. *Hey, look there. Look around.* See that girl? The one nobody ever notices? Say hi. *Notice.*

And some did. Adrian Ahn did. Without any expectation of a reward in return, he reached out.

This time, I pull the image into the app that lets me post from my computer, and let my cursor hover for a minute while I think of the message that will go with it. And this is what I come up with:

If you follow me, please find someone in the comments NOW who needs a kind word, a listener, a friend. Reach out. Be there for one another. I cannot do it #alone.

I post the image and log out before the comments start appearing, because I'm exhausted. And I know they'll do it. They have to, for when I'm not here to do it for them, which might be tomorrow or next week or months from now. I dive into bed. *They'll be fine*, I tell myself.

Will I?

27

I'M NERVOUS TO SEE LIPTON on Monday. Afraid that he came to his senses over the weekend and has realized I am not *all that*.

But I can't not look at him. And when I do, he passes me a note.

I miss you.

I quickly scribble my response:

I'm sitting right next to you.

His reply:

Not close enough.

I smile and tuck the note into my pocket and spend the rest of the class fighting the urge to inch my desk closer to his. After history, he offers to walk me to my next class, even though he needs to head in the opposite direction.

"You'll be late," I say.

He shrugs. "So, I'll be late."

We walk, shoulders bumping more than necessary.

"How was the rest of your weekend?" he asks. We are back to awkward small talk.

"Fine," I say, because truthful answers like "anguished" or "sleepless" or "emotionally draining" would only lead to more questions.

"I found out what that girl was talking about at the concert," he says. "About Vicurious."

I nearly choke, but pretend to simply be clearing my throat. "Oh?"

"It's an Instagram account. She's got like a million follow-ers. She posted something about the concert. Have you seen her?"

"I'm not on Instagram," I say.

"Me neither. I mean, not really. I haven't posted anything. I just signed up so I could see what all the fuss was about." He shrugs. "I thought maybe you heard of her. Everyone's talking about it."

I shake my head, lips pursed in a tight smile.

Lipton touches a protective hand to my arm, guiding me sideways so I don't run into some kid who is barreling down the hallway toward us. "She actually reminds me of you."

"I'm not on Instagram," I say again. "I don't know anything about it."

He chuckles. "Don't worry. There's not going to be a test or anything. I just thought you might be curious."

"Right. Sure. I'll check it out." We arrive at the door to my biology class. "Here I am. You better hurry."

Lipton says a quick "Bye!" and disappears.

I'm about to take my seat behind Mallory-of-the-bathroom when someone jumps up from the back row and says, "Vicky! Hey!"

It's Raj. I feel bad I never noticed him there before, because of keeping my head down, but I can't miss him now. He bounds to my desk and shows me the photo he took at the concert. "I'll send you a copy. What's your email?"

I give it to him and he types it in. Mallory says, "*You* were there?"

Suddenly everyone is staring at me and I can't answer. I can only blink at her.

"We both were," says Raj, chest puffed out. He holds his phone so she can see the photo.

Her eyes light up. "With Tea Bag Gregory?" She snorts and turns away from us. "Sounds like a great time."

"Actually, it *was*," says Raj, sticking his tongue out at the back of her head before returning to his desk.

I want to do more than stick my tongue out. I want to shove

her. Or yank her hair. The urge builds all through class, held down (barely) by the ever-present fear of drawing attention to myself. I seethe so hard my jaw starts to ache from clenching my teeth.

I could ruin her. Well, Vicurious could. Expose her to a million people. Call her out as a bully, a snob, a . . .

Wait. No.

I take a deep breath. Vicurious is not about vengeance. Or shaming people. Mallory isn't the nicest girl I've ever met, but maybe there's a reason for that. Maybe her home life is horrible or the boy she likes doesn't like her back. Maybe if I just talk to her, give her a chance to apologize?

By the time the bell rings I am calm, but pretty terrified over what I'm about to do. I stand and tap Mallory on the shoulder.

She turns, one hip jutting out.

"His name is Lipton," I say, trembling under her glare. I can feel my sweat starting and my stomach twisting in knots, but I need to say this. Lipton would do it for me. "Lipton Gregory, not Tea Bag."

"What?" She glances at her friends, laughing nervously.

"In the photo. Lipton Gregory." My voice is shaking, but I keep going. "You called him 'Tea Bag.' That's not his name."

"Fine." She rolls her eyes. "It's his nickname, then. Everyone calls him that."

"Not everyone," I say. "Only people who think it's funny to

make jokes at someone else's expense. Because that is not his nickname. It's name-calling. There's a difference."

She is briefly stunned, but tosses her backpack over her shoulder and says, "Whatever."

Her friends follow hesitantly as she stalks out.

I can't believe I'm still standing. I put a hand to the desk to steady myself and take a deep breath. I'll just wait here until everyone leaves. But then someone slow claps from the back of the room. It's Raj, I'm sure. I turn, thinking, *No, Raj, don't make it worse.*

But it isn't Raj. It's Jeremy Everling. I drop into my chair like someone just yanked the floor out from under me. Jeremy has made more jokes at Lipton's expense than anyone. He's probably the reason Lipton's seeing a therapist to learn how to stand up for himself. He walks toward me, his slow clap getting faster. A few smatterings of applause join his, but mostly everyone's waiting to see what he does. I brace for the punch line.

Jeremy stops clapping when he reaches my desk. He drops his hand in front of me, palm up. I bring my eyes to his.

"Guilty as charged, Decker." He shakes his head. "Guilty as charged."

"Dude," one of his friends says.

Somebody laughs.

Somebody else says, "Oh my God."

I stare at Jeremy Everling's palm. He's waiting for me . . . to slap it? I tentatively lift my hand.

He says quietly, "Low five, Decker." So I do it. I slap his hand and then wince, because I'm sure this can't really be happening. I am probably hallucinating the whole thing.

But he shrugs, says, "Hope there's no hard feelings," and leaves.

I stare at my hand. My low-fiving Jeremy Everling hand. It stings a little.

I don't know how long I sit there contemplating my hand. But when I look up, the class is full of the next period's students, and the one whose seat I am occupying says, "You're in my seat."

"Oh, sorry." I hop up and hurry out.

My heart is racing, but for once it's not because of fear or dread or anxiety. It's because I overcame those things. It's what I imagine it feels like to pump my fist in the air and shout at the top of my lungs.

Lipton is not entirely thrilled that I defended his honor. Mallory and some of her friends keep exaggerating his name when they say hi to him in the hall.

Now it's, "Hi, LIP-TON."

But it's nothing compared with the gossip and speculation going around about Vicurious, which reaches out to me like grasping tentacles. In the hall. In the locker room before gym. In the bathroom. On the bus. It's everywhere.

"You think she goes to school here?"

"How else would she know East 48?"

"I can't believe she'd pick them out of the blue."

"She could've."

"I bet it's Marissa. Put a wig on her ..."

"Doesn't look like her at all. She looks like ..."

I kick myself for forgetting to post some background shots from other places this week, which may have thrown people off. I put my head down and let my hair fall around my face, remind myself that my own mother didn't recognize me in that wig and sunglasses and lipstick. Still, it's like they're shouting "Get her!" every time they say "Vicurious." I can't stop flinching.

"Are you okay?" Lipton meets me at my locker first thing Tuesday morning. "You seem nervous."

I force a smile. "I'm always nervous."

"More than usual."

"I'm fine," I chirp.

"I can't even see you." He bends down to peek around my hair curtain. "Why are you hiding?"

I jerk away from him. "Sorry, I'm just ... I have to go to the bathroom." I spin on my heel and weave away from him, hating myself.

I expected all the fuss to die down by now, but it's only getting worse. Or *better*, depending on how you look at it. My classmates are not only speculating about a connection between Vicurious and East 48, they're doing exactly what I asked them to: finding someone who needs a friend and reaching out. And they're talking about it:

"I wrote to this one girl who wanted to end it all."

"What did you say?"

"Just that I'm here if she needs me, but she should definitely tell someone."

"I was on there for, like, an hour yesterday."

"Me too."

Laughs. "Yeah, that's what I kept writing. 'Me too.'"

"This kid said I was the first person to talk to him in three days. That nobody had even said good morning to him, or hi, or anything. *For three days.*"

"That's crazy."

"So, I followed him. Told him to DM me anytime."

"Cool."

I imagined a quiet army of helpers, doing their good deeds amid the relative anonymity of Instagram where I could safely check on them from the privacy of my own home. They would swarm the internet with selfless kindness. Not blab about it all over school every day.

It's like they're peppering me with bullets of my own making. Bullets of kindness, but still. I can't seem to avoid mentions of Vicurious and each one makes me nervous that I've been recognized. I duck into the bathroom and retreat to my usual stall, squeezing my head between my hands.

Nobody knows it's me.

They'll never guess.

I am nobody.

They don't see me.

It's a strangely comforting mantra, the opposite of what I've been recommending to everyone else. But it's my comfort zone. Invisible. *Safe.*

I give myself an extra hard head-squeeze before dashing to class. Lipton doesn't look at me when I walk in, but as soon as I sit down, he hands me a note.

I'm afraid to read it.

I go through the process of pulling out my world history notes, and my book, and lining up my pencil. I even consider walking to the sharpener, and I hate walking to the sharpener. I have a half dozen newly sharpened pencils in my bag to avoid that.

Lipton clears his throat and tips his chin to the note in my hand. I can't avoid it any longer. I unfold the small square of paper on which he wrote:

Is it something I said?

I almost sink to the floor with relief, then am shamed with guilt for making him worry that he'd done something wrong. I shake my head and scrawl a reply:

Just my stupid brain, messing with me.

He smiles and pretends to wipe sweat from his brow, like *whew!* And quickly scribbles another note.

Not to say I am glad your brain is messing with you. I am not. Tell your brain to piss off.

I smile. Before I can reply, he's sliding another note onto my desk.

Don't tell your WHOLE brain to piss off.
Just the part that's behaving badly.
The rest is perfect and should remain in place as is.

I pat my head, a gesture I guess is supposed to indicate that my brain is intact. He smiles and dips his head down to write one more note.

Can we talk after class?

The question takes away all the good feelings from our note exchange, because of course we can talk after class. We've been talking after class all week. Why is he making a special point of asking?

I nod, and spend the rest of the period imagining various reasons he might want to speak with me so officially, including all the ways he could break up with me. My brain likes to torment me that way, contemplating a future where everyone I care about leaves me behind.

My brain is pretty much an asshole.

After class, Lipton pulls me into the alcove where he asked me out only last week.

"I'm going away," he says, and my stomach drops to my ankles. I didn't actually think my brain was going to be right.

"Forever?" I whisper.

"What? No." He laughs and pulls me into the circle of his arms. Right there in front of everyone. "Just for Thanksgiving. We're visiting my aunt in Pittsburgh. Which sucks. I mean, she's great, but I'd rather be here with you. I just wanted you to know why I wasn't asking you out this weekend."

I blink at him.

"We could go out next weekend, though, if you want. To a movie or something, or get pizza, or I don't know." He lets his forehead knock against mine. "I'm terrible at this."

"No, you're not."

"Yes, I am."

I lean into him, crazily unconcerned with the nearby presence of the entire student body. "I'm terribler."

He hugs me tighter, and I hug him back.

It makes me feel like a real person.

And I need that, amid all the talk of Vicurious. I need a reminder that I exist outside the internet and that someone in the real world wants me *here*, more than my followers want me *there*.

28

THE LINGERING EFFECT OF LIPTON'S hug is like armor, shielding me from all the Vicurious talk. I'm only a *little* nervous when Marissa mentions her again in the yearbook office over lunch period.

"Adrian and I spent two hours on her Instagram last night," she says. "Which was great and everything—I mean, at least we were together for a change." She pauses and sighs. Lays her forehead on her calculus notes. "I just don't think I can keep it up. And why wasn't there a yearbook photographer at the game last night?"

"What game?" Beth Ann peers around her computer.

"*My* game. The biggest one of the season. I told you to assign a photographer."

"You did?" She flashes a glance toward Marvo for some backup, but he just shrugs. "Sorry, I—"

"Sorry, sorry, sorry. Everybody's sorry, but nobody gets anything done," says Marissa. "I have to do it all myself."

"Okay, Miss Perfect." Beth Ann wheels away from her desk. "I'll try to do a better job of reading your mind the next time."

"Don't call me that," Marissa snaps. "I'm not perfect. I missed an easy goal last night, looking around for that stupid photographer, and lost us the game. I'm going to fail this calc test, and Adrian expects me to be a damn Mother Teresa. I can't take it."

"Whoa. Hey." Marvo approaches Marissa with calming hands.

She spins away from him. "I am *not* perfect," she says again, voice wobbly now. "I can't do everything. I can't be perfect at everything."

"Nobody said—" Marvo starts.

"Nobody says it, but everyone expects it. Marissa can do it! Marissa can do everything! Manage East 48, book all their gigs? Sure! Marissa can do that! Can't you, Marissa? And keep up those straight As while you're at it. We're counting on that academic scholarship. Run the yearbook. Win the field hockey games! Look pretty and wave at the homecoming parade. And be nice to all the sad people on the internet!"

She stops, finally. Marvo, Beth Ann, and I are silenced, pretty much holding our collective breath to see if she erupts again.

Beth Ann is the first to talk. "Tell us how you *really* feel, why don't you?"

Marissa gives a half laugh, half sob. "I've just been under a lot of pressure lately."

"You think?" Marvo hands her a box of tissues from the bookshelf.

She snatches one and dabs her eyes. I'm kind of impressed at how un-perfect she looks right now. She's much more likable this way.

"Sometimes I wish I could be somebody else that nobody knows or expects anything from. Someone like—" She glances up at me, and for one frantic second I think she's going to say Vicurious.

"Like Vicky," she says.

My eyes widen. "Me?"

"Don't take this the wrong way. But when you came here to work on yearbook, I thought, *Great. Mrs. Greene is pawning her off on us because she can't do anything else.* I had zero expectations of you. Zip."

Beth Ann opens her mouth to object, but Marissa holds her hand up and continues. "And then you turned out to be amazing and brilliant, and super nice. You had nowhere to go but up. And you did. But when you start up here"—she wiggles her fingers high above her head—"there's nowhere to go but down. And everyone is just waiting for you to fall so they can pounce."

I'm not sure how to feel about being the poster child for low expectations, but did she just call me "amazing" and "brilliant"?

"Nobody's waiting to pounce on you," says Beth Ann.

Marissa snorts. "Oh, yes, they are."

"Not everyone," says Marvo. "Some of us are here to catch you. And hold you up if you need us."

"Yeah." Beth Ann throws an arm around Marissa's neck.

"Don't be so hard on yourself."

Marvo wraps his arms around both of them. Marissa is still half crying. "I am so going to fail this test."

Beth Ann says, "Who cares."

It's really sweet. I start thinking about all the Vicurious followers who are so hard on themselves, like Marissa is. It's not always a matter of others being nice and caring, or saying, "You're special." It's about giving themselves a break, too. I'm so absorbed in the idea, thinking of what Vicurious could do about it, that I don't realize Marissa is talking to me.

Her head is poked out of their little huddle. "Get over here!"

"What?"

"Group hug." She waves me toward them. "Get your butt over here."

I rise tentatively and she sighs her impatience. So I hurry over and their arms reach out to pull me in. Then we are head to head to head to head, hugging and swaying and laughing.

Well, the three of them are laughing, at least. I'm just trying not to cry, because they aren't Jenna, and they'll never be Jenna, but they've given me a place to belong. And it's such a relief to no longer feel like I'm floating away.

I only wish Jenna was the one who caught me, that she hadn't cast me off in the first place.

That night, I prepare the image inspired by Marissa's meltdown. First step is taking a new selfie in front of my computer, this time wearing the swirly X-ray-vision sunglasses and hugging myself. I scribble words of self-love and empowerment and putting yourself first all over it. Because sometimes, you can't be everything to everybody. You need to be there for yourself.

#Holdon #Behappy #Youarebrave #Fabulous
#Worthy #Wanted #Loved #Bestrong #Staycalm
#Hope #Laugh #Smile #Relax #Beyourself
#Breathe #Findyourjoy #Listentoyourheart
#BethereforYOU

I put that last line, "Be there for YOU," in a little speech bubble coming out of my mouth. The finished product makes me smile. I hope it does the same for Marissa and Hallie and everyone else who might be crumbling under the weight of expectations. Especially their own. The image looks a lot like the previous one, only with a smile and neatly painted lips instead of the smeary, sad ones. Hope instead of despair. I scan it and get it ready to post. The message is an easy one to write:

It's good to be there for one another. But don't forget to be there for yourself!

Instead of posting the image right away, I schedule it for Thanksgiving, two days from now. That way, I won't have to deal with the reaction until it's had a few days to diffuse. Tomorrow will be bad enough anyway, with Lipton taking the day off school for the drive to his aunt's.

I open my Instagram, but not to check on Vicurious. (She was nearing two million followers last time I looked, which makes me anxious, so it's better if I don't look.) But I'm worried about Jenna. I want to see if she's posted anything. It's weird that she hasn't been on there at all. At first I thought she went dark just to drive me crazy, knowing I'd be checking. But now, I'm starting to wonder if it's something else.

Her followers are getting fewer and fewer, too. After she moved, they jumped from about 27 to more than 100. When she started hanging out with Tristan, they climbed even faster . . . 300, 400, 500.

Today, she's down to 243.

And I just can't figure out what would make 250 people ditch her that fast.

I could text her a quick "You okay?" if I had my phone, but Mom's still holding it hostage. So, I open my email.

I write a message and delete it, write and delete and repeat. The messages I come up with are either too long or too complicated or too apologetic or too accusing or too . . . something. Finally, I settle on this:

Worried about you. Even if you hate me, will you let

me know you're okay? —Vicky

I hit the send button before I can change my mind, then wait for a reply. If all she writes is "I'm okay," then I'll know we're really, truly, absolutely done. But maybe she'll say more. Maybe it'll be the start of finding our way back to each other.

When my email in-box bleeps a few seconds later, I'm afraid to look. But I'm more afraid not to. So I open it and there it is:

Delivery notification: Delivery has failed

I stare at those five words for a really long time, because Jenna has had the same email address her whole life, and the only reason I can think for her to change it would be to stop someone from finding her where they've always found her. Someone like me.

When I get up from the computer, I don't even log out of email or Instagram or shut it down properly. I just reach around and flip the main power switch off. I crawl into bed and let the words I wrote for my followers swim in my head, over and over again.

Hold on . . . be strong . . . stay calm . . . breathe.

And I wonder if they'll help anyone out there at all, because they're not doing that much for me.

29

LIPTON IS WAITING AT MY locker on Monday morning and doing a pretty good job making me believe that he really did miss me. "The weekend is too far away. Can we go out tonight? Please say yes."

He is wearing the shirt and the new jeans he wore on our date. And his hair looks even better than it did last week.

"I have to work on my history presentation. I wrote the report over break but I still have to figure out—".

"I'll help you."

"You can't."

"Why not?"

"Because." I blink at him. "Cheating? Remember, I am a group of one."

"It's not fair that you have to do it on your own when everyone else had a group," he says.

I shrug. "I kind of brought that on myself."

"Maybe Mr. Braxley will let me help you. I'll just say I want to work on a second project. He should be happy to find a student so motivated, right?" Lipton crinkles his nose at me uncertainly.

I crinkle back.

So Lipton asks at the end of class.

"You want to do what now?" Mr. Braxley is understandably confused by Lipton's desire to do a second presentation, after the way he got skewered on the first.

"I'd like to help Vicky with her project. Since she doesn't have anyone else on her team."

Mr. Braxley squints at me over the tops of his glasses. "You okay with that, Decker?"

I nod.

"Fine, then," says Braxley. "You only get credit for one of the presentations, though. I'll count whichever one scores highest."

Lipton slides back into his desk next to me. "We are going to ace this thing."

"Didn't you ace the Battle of Thermopylae already?"

"Ninety-eight percent. We can do better." He notices the flash of panic on my face and quickly adds, "Kidding. No pressure."

It takes a couple of days to figure out how and where to work. Everything I've done on the project so far is stored on my computer, which makes my house the logical place to go. But Vicurious is on that computer. And I don't want Lipton anywhere near her. Even if I scrub my browser history, all the files that created her are there. I'm afraid he'll stumble upon the evidence.

So I lie and tell him we can't work at my house, that my mom won't let me have a boy in my room.

He offers his house. "We have a game room. We can work on the computer in there."

My mother thinks I'm working with Hallie Bryce on this project, so I go with a general, "Is it okay if I do homework at Lipton's house tomorrow?" I'm still expecting to be grilled, but she must be distracted by the fact that I am willingly interacting with other humans.

"Sure, sweetie," she says. "What time?"

"Right after school."

We decide to forgo the whole process of getting approval for me to ride the bus to Lipton's, because it involves a ridiculous number of permission slips and signatures from practically every person I've ever met, in triplicate. The idea of getting on a different bus also isn't my favorite—all those kids staring and whispering and nudge-nudging and, yeah, not a good idea. My mother drives me instead, and makes a little "hmmm" sound when she sees how close his house is to where she dropped me off for Marissa's party.

She stops the car in his driveway and starts to unbuckle her seat belt.

"You're not coming in," I say. "I'm sixteen, Mom. Not six."

She purses her lips, pauses for dramatic effect, and refastens the seat belt. "Fine. What time should I pick you up?"

"I don't know. Five thirty?"

"If you had your phone," she says, all syrupy, "you could call me when you're ready."

"If you give it back to me . . ." I mimick her tone. "I would be happy to do that."

"Password?"

I climb out of the car and say, "Five thirty is good," before shutting the door.

I've resigned myself to never getting the phone back, and I don't really miss it that much. The reason I got it in the first place was to text with Jenna. And any hope I had of that ever happening again has been officially dashed.

The only one I would text or talk to now is Lipton, but there's something magical about not knowing, not seeing, not sharing *everything*. It gives my imagination a place to go. It heightens the anticipation of seeing him again.

I could almost burst with it when he opens the door, smiling tentatively. He tilts his head to the side, and I take a mental picture that will only ever be *mine*.

"Hi," he says. "Come on in."

I duck inside. He leans out to wave to my mother. She'll like that.

Lipton shows me around the main floor of his house, which is easy since it's basically one huge room. There are exposed beams on the ceiling and a massive stone fireplace. His cat, Kitty, formerly of the shrubbery, is curled atop a fleece blanket folded on the wide arm of the couch. The kitchen looks out on the dining and living areas, which have wall-to-wall windows as well as skylights. It's bright and open and I've never felt so exposed and cozy at the same time.

Mrs. Gregory calls hello from the kitchen, where she's chopping vegetables. Lipton's little sister is sitting at a nearby table doing homework. She waves energetically, but is clearly under strict orders not to speak to me. She bites her lips and wiggles like she's got to pee.

I wave back.

"In here," says Lipton, leading me to a smaller room off the living area, which has a big L-shaped counter that runs along two walls. One side has an enormous Apple computer monitor, and the other side has trays and bins filled with every kind of paper and craft supply imaginable. The room is covered in artwork and accolades—including a whole wall of honor roll and perfect attendance certificates. There's a trio of beanbag chairs in the center of the room, facing a big-screen TV in the other corner.

"Wow," I say. "This is . . . wow."

"Homework slash game room," he announces.

"Wow."

"You said that."

"I just need to say it one more time and I promise I'll be done. *Wow.*" Then I notice the class pictures. Lipton in kindergarten, first grade, second—all the way up to sophomore year. He's pretty much had the same haircut the whole time. Until last weekend, that is. I point to the one where he's missing both of his front teeth. "Look at you. You're adorable."

His eyes go wide like he's completely forgotten the photos were there, and he dives to conceal the worst of them—grades seven through nine—behind his hand and forearm. "Not adorable. Promise you won't ever look at these again."

"How am I going to resist? They're hanging on the wall."

"Avert your eyes," he says. "Seriously. There are some things so hideous you can't unsee them."

I smile and look toward the opposite corner. "Might make it difficult to get our work done like this."

"Hold on." He darts over to the art supplies and shuffles around there, then back to the school pictures.

When he finally lets me turn around, he's taped some blank pieces of paper over the pictures. He scratches the back of his head. "Sorry. Thanks. So embarrassing."

I don't argue or try to convince him it's not embarrassing, because I hate when people do that—tell you how you should or should not feel. My mother is constantly saying "There's nothing to be embarrassed about" and "You're being silly." Which may be true. But having the validity of the feeling itself dismissed only makes it worse.

Instead, I lay my stuff on the counter. "You want to get started?"

Lipton's face relaxes, and we pull chairs up to the computer. I tell him this idea I have to combine images of the siege from centuries ago with present-day photographs. Show modern-day relevance of the historical event.

"Brilliant," he says, grinning.

I dump everything I have onto his hard drive, and he pulls up what he's collected. We go back and forth. He suggests using music, something classical and dramatic. I want to put the entire story on the screen in short paragraphs, so I don't have to talk at all. He convinces me to narrate.

"We'll record it. It'll be fine. You won't have to be in front of the class. All you'll have to do is press play and take a seat."

I give him a look. That's what he did, and we all know how that turned out.

"You can use your regular voice," he says, reading my thoughts. "We'll put it on a USB drive. No screen savers."

My heart rate definitely jumps up a notch, and my stomach churns. But it's not as bad as it could be. I've been diligently repressing any thoughts of my class presentation, afraid of how my body might react to the fear of something so big. And maybe there's a delayed reaction at work. Maybe I haven't even begun to process what I'm about to do. But having Lipton to help me is making it all so much less terrifying. Speaking into a recording device versus standing in front of the class? That's like night and day. Like yin and . . .

I push the thought aside, the feeling that I may never regain my balance. Lipton actually reaches out to steady me then, physically. He presses his hands to the sides of my arms. "I'll be right here," he says.

I nod. "Okay."

Still, I set about writing the briefest script possible. Lipton pairs up images of past and present. We're so wrapped up in it, neither of us notices how long we've been working until I hear my mother's voice. In the living room. Crooning over the Gregorys' house.

"Oooh. What a beauuuuutiful fireplace! And those beams. I've always wanted a house with exposed beams," she says, which is news to me.

I gather my things.

"Same time tomorrow?" Lipton asks as we're joining our mothers by the door.

"Sure," I say.

"You're welcome to work at our house, too," my mother chimes in. "Any time. Vicky practically has an entire Apple store in her room."

Lipton darts a curious glance at me. I told him she wouldn't allow it.

"We're all set up on Lipton's computer now," I say quickly. "They have a special room for homework and stuff."

"Whatever works best," she says, her smile forced.

We say our thank-yous and good-byes and, as expected, she's all over me in the car.

"How much homework do you *have*, exactly, that you need to meet every night?"

"It's a project."

"Oh." She adjusts her rearview mirror. "What project?"

"World history." I don't even consider lying to cover my previous lie.

"Another world history project?"

"No, it's the same one I've been working on. Siege of Jerusalem."

"With Hallie Bryce?"

"No." I swallow. "She's not in my class."

"But I thought you said—"

"I made that up."

She sucks in a breath. "You . . . Why would you lie to me, Vicky?"

I shrug.

"What on *earth* would compel you to lie about something like that?" Her voice has moved into its higher octaves.

I could lie some more to cover the lie, but I'm tired. It's getting so hard to always put a false face forward to hide the real one. I feel like Marissa did the other day—I just can't sustain it. I'm holding as much as I can carry and it's all going to fall apart if I don't find a way to lighten my load.

So, I sigh, and I spill. "I lied because it made you happy to think I was working on a project with someone like Hallie Bryce, who is beautiful and talented, rather than working alone, which is what I was doing until Lipton offered to help me. I lied to give you a rare opportunity to not be disappointed in me."

"Vicky, how can you say that?"

"It's okay, Mom. I've been a disappointment. It's understandable that you would be disappointed."

She glances at me, eyes watery. "I don't think you're a disappointment, sweetheart. Is that how you feel?"

"It's not a matter of feeling. It's a point of fact," I say. "I haven't lived up to any expectation you've ever had of me. I don't dress the way you like, or wear my hair the way you like, or have friends or activities or achievements you can brag about. By definition, I'm pretty sure that makes me a disappointment."

We pull into our driveway, and my mother kills the engine. She doesn't move, though. She just sits there, hands on the steering wheel at ten and two.

It's making me nervous. "Look, never mind. I was thinking about Hallie Bryce that day and I don't know why I said we were working on the project together. Wishful thinking or something. And it made that look on your face go away."

I fiddle with my backpack so I don't have to meet her gaze.

"What look on my face?" she asks.

I didn't mean to get *this* honest, but now it won't stop coming out. "That look of disappointment." I lift my eyes and see that she's got the expression on her face *right now*. She's disappointed in me even now. I point to her face. "*That* look."

She flips the rearview mirror down to see her face, then turns to me.

"Vicky, this isn't disappointment. This is concern. This is love.

316

This is a mother wanting everything for her daughter, wanting her to be happy, and trying desperately to figure out what will make her so. If there is disappointment on my face, it is disappointment in myself, for not knowing how to fix . . ." Her voice catches. "I can't stand to see you unhappy, sweetie. And I know you have been. But I don't know how to fix it."

"I don't need to be fixed," I say. "I just need you to accept me the way I am. I need you to understand."

She nods, wrapping her arms around her middle. "I can do that," she whispers. "I can try."

We sit there quietly for a minute and she keeps inhaling like she's about to speak, then stopping herself. Finally, she says, "I didn't mean to suggest that you need to be fixed, that I don't love you just the way you are. Because I do. It's just, if something's wrong or making you feel bad and you need help, someone to talk to . . ."

I scuff my feet back and forth on the floor mat. "Then why are you always telling me it's just in my head? That all I need to do is face my fears, and everything will be fine?"

My mother's face screws up, and I realize she's starting to cry. "I'm sorry, sweetie. I thought—" She reaches a hand to my knee. "I messed up. I see that now."

I blink at her, at the tears coming down her cheeks. I nod, and she reaches for me, pulls me to her, hugs me. I can't remember the last time she held me like this, and it doesn't make everything better, but it helps.

"I've been thinking I might talk to the school psychologist," I say.

"Okay." Mom leans away from me and looks in my eyes. "Is that what you want? Or I could find someone—"

"I like her. I think maybe she can help."

"Okay." Mom wipes her own tears, then strokes my cheek. "You just let me know whatever you need. Anything."

She hugs me again as Dad is pulling into the driveway. He gets out of his car and starts walking toward ours, sees us embracing, and gets the most adorably confused look on his face.

Mom lowers the window.

"Everything okay?" he says.

My mother turns back to me and smooths her hand over my hair.

"Not exactly," she says. "But it will be."

After Dad leaves us to head into the house, Mom makes me promise I'll visit Mrs. Greene. I'm nervous to open up what I've been trying to keep sealed for so long, but I know I have to.

"After my history presentation. I promise." I don't think I can handle both in the same week, because talking to Mrs. Greene is going to mean unveiling Vicurious to her, and I'm not quite ready to expose myself like that.

30

MOM TAKES ME TO LIPTON'S house after school the next day and the next, and Mrs. Gregory invites her in and they chat over coffee while we're working on the presentation. And it's okay.

I'm not saying she's a completely different person or anything, but I can tell she's trying. And I am, too. I put on a little bit of the makeup from Neiman Marcus. I reconsider some of the clothes she bought me and find a couple of sweaters that aren't too terrible.

Lipton says I look nice.

He says it in front of my mom, and she almost breaks her face smiling.

She even gives me my phone back. We're eating dinner Friday evening and she slides it across the table. She doesn't ask for my password.

"What's this?" I hardly recognize it.

"You may have it back," she says. "Under one condition.

You talk to me. I don't expect you to tell me everything you're thinking or feeling, but let me know if something's wrong. If I can help. Even if you don't think I can. Don't shut me out. Okay?"

Dad stops eating to look at her, then at me, like he's suddenly noticed a pair of deer have walked into the room and are grazing at the table.

"Okay," I say.

Mom nods and smiles, and dabs her napkin to the corners of her eyes.

Dad says, "And they all lived happily ever after."

We laugh, and for a moment it feels like that might be true. But my story isn't over yet, and I'm not sure how it's going to end.

I pick up the phone, which is completely dead, and it feels like a thin, smooth brick of nothing. I'll plug it in later, maybe, if I feel like it. But for now I feel like watching a movie with my parents, which is what I do. We pick *Boyhood*, a movie filmed over a period of twelve years, the length of my friendship with Jenna. It is weird to watch someone grow up like that, and grow away. But maybe that's what happens. People just grow away. Mom cries at the end like Patricia Arquette. I hug her, and she cries harder. I'm nothing like the boy in the movie, so I'm not sure why she's crying, and she doesn't say.

Sometimes you just need to let stuff out.

I set my phone on my dresser that night when I go to bed. I don't plug it in. I've managed to stay away from Vicurious all week, aware of her activity only by what I hear around school. I haven't posted anything since the self-care image on Thanksgiving, but Ellen has apparently Photoshopped us skydiving together. I've reached two million followers, so I've heard, and I'm not sure how I feel about that. It is both empowering and terrifying. It seems almost everything is a balance of yin and yang.

I add the mixed feelings over my growing number of followers to a new mental list of things I'll talk to Mrs. Greene about, when I talk to her. Which I will. Soon.

Most of my weekend is spent with Lipton, finishing the Siege of Jerusalem project and fiddling around on *Minecraft*. He shows me how it works. "Adam would give himself a concussion if he knew about this," he says.

But I'm curious, and I like the fantastical worlds you can create on there. Lipton has a whole island, with castles and waterfalls and farmland and shops. Even a bowling alley. He switches over to a different server where there are other players, and monsters, and he's this sword-wielding, fire-throwing ninja. When he comes across little figures who are standing idle, their "masters" having stepped away, he picks them up and tosses them off a nearby cliff.

"Did you just kill him?"

He grins at me.

"You totally threw a completely innocent person to his death. Without even blinking."

"He'll regenerate." Lipton shrugs. "Serves him right, standing around like that in the middle of a battle."

"Remind me never to go to the Grand Canyon with you."

He laughs as I pantomime falling off a cliff. And we get back to work. Aside from a kiss on the cheek when I arrive both mornings, we've managed to keep our hands off each other. Mostly. It helps that his sister keeps flitting in and out of the game-slash-homework-slash-craft room, making puppets out of paper bags.

Lipton gets permission to banish her when it's time to record my voice-over, though. He also gets permission to close the door while we're recording.

Even in my state of relative calm, I can't do the whole script without messing up, so we record it in sections. Lipton keeps saying it's great, but when he plays it back to me I sound like I've swallowed sandpaper.

"Is that what I really sound like? It's awful."

"Everyone's voice sounds weird to them because you only hear it from inside your head," he says. "It sounds different out here."

"It sounds awful."

"It sounds amazing."

"If you like the sound of fingernails on a chalkboard."

"I do," he teases. "I love that sound."

"Oh, God. Do I really sound like that? I can't do this."

"You don't sound like that." He laughs. "And you did it. It's done."

We layer the sound over the visuals. Lipton lowers the lights in the room and we move our chairs back to watch it all the way through. He leans forward to push the play arrow and then settles in next to me and takes my hand in his.

I cringe when I hear my voice, but it plays smoothly. The script matches up with the images. The ending is my favorite part. We show the modern-day photos of people at Jerusalem's Western Wall, including close-ups of prayers crammed into all the tiny crevices. I found some blog posts and articles written by people from all over the world who visited the wall and had really touching experiences there. I pulled quotes of hope and love and understanding from their stories, but instead of reading their thoughts aloud, I typed them in so they scroll down the screen with the photos in the background. In silence.

When it finishes, I turn to Lipton. "Do you think it needs music or something at the end?"

He clears his throat. "No."

"You sure?"

"I'm sure."

He gets up and turns the lights back on, but doesn't look at me right away. He busies himself downloading the presentation on two USB drives, just in case one of them is lost or malfunctions or gets swallowed or accidentally-on-purpose thrown out a window in an attempt to avoid the whole thing. (Though he made me promise I wouldn't do that.)

The way he's not saying anything makes me worried he's disappointed, that it's not as good as his Battle of Thermopylae and he won't beat his other grade.

"Do you think they'll ask questions?" I'm terrified of this prospect. Obviously.

"They're more likely to be stunned into silence," he says.

"It's that bad?"

Lipton closes his eyes and sighs. "You really have no idea, do you? It's brilliant. You're brilliant!"

I laugh. "And you're delusional."

He steps closer and tips his forehead down to touch mine. "It's great. Trust me."

"Okay," I say, unconvinced.

He leans away then, an incredulous smile forming. "You don't trust me."

"It's not that."

"You totally don't trust me." He thinks it's funny. Sort of. But there's a hint of hurt behind his eye. I know what it looks like.

"I'm just nervous," I say, "about getting up there. If they . . . what if they laugh? If they point and stare and I mess it up and I can't, what if I can't get up there?" My breath starts to get choppy. "I think I . . ."

"Whoa. Here." He holds me up by the arms and guides me into a chair. "You okay?"

I drop my head between my knees. Take deep breaths. The room spins. I lower myself to the floor. I curl up.

"What's happening?" Lipton is on hands and knees next to me.

I close my eyes. Try to breathe, deep and slow.

"Paper bag." Lipton is talking to himself now. "Paper bag." He runs to the craft supplies and grabs something and is crinkling it and then he brings it to my face. "Breathe."

And I breathe. I breathe again. And again. Slower, until the room stops spinning. Lipton's eyes are wild as he leans over me, holding the bag to my mouth. It's one of his sister's puppets, with googly eyes and a pink pom-pom nose. I take a few more breaths, watch the pom-pom move up and down with each inhale and exhale until my breathing is back to normal.

"I'm okay now," I say into the bag.

He takes it away.

We stare at each other for a minute, me curled on my side and he kneeling over me. The door is still closed.

"I'm sorry I'm such a freak," I whisper.

"You're not—"

"It's okay." I push myself up. "I know I am."

He starts to object again, but I press my fingers to his lips. He closes his mouth.

I take my hand away. "Don't try to convince me I'm someone different or better or stronger than I am. Okay? I'm doing the best I can, but sometimes it's not very good. Sometimes I have to lie on the floor and breathe into a paper bag. That's who I am."

"I understand." The expression on his face is, in fact, very understanding.

"Sometimes I am so scared of people, of being around people, that I have to hide. In the bathroom or, or . . . behind shrubbery or something."

He nods. "I get it."

"I say really stupid things all the time. I'll probably pass out trying to give this presentation. Or vomit. That happens, too. I could vomit all over the place. I'll never be able to show my face again. We should probably say our good-byes now."

"Stop it."

"I'm serious."

He drops from his kneeling position to sit on the floor next to me. "I don't care about any of that."

"Just wait till I vomit on you," I say.

He laughs. "Stop trying to scare me away. "

"I'm not." I drop my gaze to my lap. Fiddle with the hem of my shirt. "It's just, I lost the one friend I could be myself with, and I'm afraid—"

Lipton scoots even closer. His face is inches away. His eyes steady. "You can be yourself with me. I don't want you to be any-one else. Okay?"

I return his gaze. I nod.

He leans in, and his lips are on mine, and I do not want to be anyone else. Not even a little bit.

31

WE MEET AT LIPTON'S LOCKER on Monday morning. He's trying to be calm so I don't freak out, but I can tell he's nervous. Which actually helps me feel less nervous.

"I have something for you." He digs around in his backpack, opening all the zippered compartments and becoming increasingly frazzled when he doesn't find what he's looking for. I'm thinking he's going to give me another bag of M&M's, and why is he doing that *now*? Then he pats his pocket. "Here it is."

He produces a small rectangular box. It's wrapped in glittery silver paper.

I take the box in his hand. "What's this?"

"A present."

"What for?"

"For you."

"Why?"

He sighs. "Will you just open it?"

I look around to make sure nobody is watching, because it appears to be a jewelry box of some kind, a ring box maybe, and the part of my brain that isn't thinking clearly is a little worried that Lipton did something completely insane like buy me a promise ring. Which I sincerely hope is not the case because promise rings are the stupidest thing I've ever heard of and now is not the time to . . .

Calm down.

I force myself to stop the internal brain vomit, and I tear open the wrapping paper. The box is not from a jeweler. It's from the store at the mall that sells spiked bracelets and skinny, acid-washed jeans.

My eyes blink nervously to Lipton's.

"Will you just open it, please?" He is starting to look like *he* might vomit.

I pull the lid off the box. There's a necklace inside, a silver chain with a silver sword hanging from it. Kind of like the tiny swords the *Minecraft* soldiers were clicking together in his Battle of Thermopylae video.

"It's . . . a sword?" I stroke my finger over its surface, but don't lift it from the cotton padding.

"A diamond sword," he says.

My eyes bulge as I take a closer look.

"Not real diamonds. That's just what it's called in *Minecraft*." He shifts his weight, hands shoved into his pockets. "The diamond sword can protect you from almost anything. It makes you stronger, especially if it has enchantments on it. And I put all the enchantments on this one."

I take the tiny sword in my fingers. "How did you do that?"

"Well, in the game, you can buy enchantments with points you accumulate in battle. But this one, I just . . ." He shrugs. "I just pretended. It's for luck. For the presentation. Ward off evil classmates and all that." He shrugs again.

It makes me want to happy cry. I blink rapidly to keep that from happening. "Can you help me put it on?"

He takes it from the box and secures it around my neck after getting it tangled in my hair and then untangled. The sword rests right below the little hollow where my collarbones meet. My sweater covers it, but I can feel it there.

It helps me get through the door and into the classroom, but then I remember what I'm about to do and time starts to move really slowly. The roar comes back to my ears and takes on a slow-mo sound, the vacuum cleaners dropping to a lower pitch. My footsteps reverberate through the room with a thud . . . thud . . . thud. I can see every face, every smirk, every snicker as if captured on video and played back with a heavy hand on the pause button.

I'm pretty sure I've stopped breathing entirely.

Lipton breaks the horrible spell I'm under by whispering my name. "Vicky . . . Vicky."

"Huh?"

"Mr. Braxley said we can start now."

I grip the edges of my desk. I nod, but don't move. I don't even remember sitting down.

Lipton holds up the USB thumb drive. "I'll just put this in and push play and off we go, okay?"

I look up at him as he stands, the roar in my ears a swarm of bees now.

He leans down to whisper through the buzzing. "Nobody's going to hurt you. You've got the diamond sword, remember?"

I put my hand to the necklace, pinch the tiny sword between my fingers. Pretend or not, the enchantments seem to work. My shoulders relax, the roar quiets to a low hum. I manage to return Lipton's smile. He walks to Mr. Braxley's desk and puts the thumb drive in the computer. He turns out the lights and presses play.

The video starts, and the room gets quiet. I watch as if I'm having an out-of-body experience, floating above and looking down on my classmates. I brace myself for their laughter. For nudges and stares. But the whole class is strangely still, eyes glued to the screen. By the end, after my narration is over and the quotes by visitors to the Western Wall are scrolling, they are silent. The presentation is over.

I wait nervously for the reaction. A polite smattering of applause, perhaps. A slow clap? I'd settle for a slow clap. What I get instead are sniffles. Several of the girls are reaching into their bags for tissues, and dabbing at their eyes. Adam is not head-desking or face-palming but dragging a sleeve across his nose. I chose the quotes at the end because they moved me, but I get choked up at sappy TV commercials and reruns of *Little House on the Prairie*. I didn't expect my classmates to get this emotional. Mr. Braxley starts clapping then, and everyone joins in. I wouldn't call it uproarious exactly, but definitely enthusiastic. Jeremy Everling even gives me a thumbs-up.

I stroke the diamond sword at my neck. I will never, ever, EVER take it off.

Everyone's coming up to me and saying "Great job" and it's nice and positive and everything, but I feel like one of those whirling teacups on the ride at a fair. I'm dizzy and jittery, and I need to get out of here.

The bell rings. Lipton calls for me to wait up but I can't. I shoot him a pleading glance as I dart into the hall, hoping he'll understand.

I maneuver through the crowded hallway and head for the bathroom. But then I think of Mrs. Greene. This is my opportunity to talk to her. When I reach her office, the door is open. I practically dive through it and land on the comfy chair. She puts out the "Do Not Disturb" sign, plugs in the twinkly lights, and turns off the overhead fluorescents.

She doesn't prod me to talk. But I feel like I might burst if I don't.

"I did it," I say.

She doesn't ask what, just listens.

"My presentation for world history," I continue. "I didn't think I could. But I did. It was okay."

She smiles. "That's great, Vicky. Excellent."

"I'm sorry to barge in." I'm still panting.

"It's okay," she says. "That's what I'm here for."

I nod. Breathe.

Mrs. Greene offers me a cup of water. She has one of those big blue water dispensers.

I take the cup and try not to spill. My hand is shaking. "I don't know why this happens to me."

She waits a beat. "We can talk about it when you're ready."

"I'm ready," I whisper, and we spend the next fifteen minutes talking. Well, I do. She nods mostly, like she understands completely and I am not weird or wrong for feeling the way I do. I tell her all about the presentation, the roaring and buzzing and slow motion . . . everything.

At the end, Mrs. Greene says, "We can set up an appointment to talk some more if you like; discuss why this happens and how you can deal with it."

And I want to, because a weight has been lifted and I can breathe again. But I also feel dangerously exposed. Like I've taken off a bulletproof vest in the middle of a battlefield. I want to pull it back on and hide behind the nearest rock.

She leans forward to rest a hand on my arm. "It will all be completely confidential. Nobody has to know what happens in this room. Just you and me."

"Okay." I nod. "I'll think about it."

She gives me a pamphlet on social anxiety. A quick flip through it is like reading my résumé. "You can share this with your parents," she says. "Or not. It might help them understand what you're going through."

I try to imagine handing the pamphlet to my mother, watching that awful look appear on her face—the one she swears is concern and not disappointment, but I'm still not sure. I'd much rather give her something that makes her proud and happy, like a photo of me surrounded by friends, or a party invitation.

And what about Vicurious? What happens to her when I start talking about everything and—does telling the truth mean I have to give her up?

I leave at the end of the period, a jumble of conflicting emotions. Hallie Bryce is waiting in the hall to see Mrs. Greene. I hold the door for her. She pauses and turns to me before entering. "What you're doing is really special, you know."

I blink at her, because while seeing Mrs. Greene is a huge step for me, I'd hardly call it special.

"On Instagram," she whispers. "It makes a difference."

I start to stammer, to deny.

She holds a finger to her lips to quiet me. "Don't worry. I won't tell."

32

SO, HALLIE KNOWS. *HOW DOES Hallie know?* It brings the roar to my ears, and I want to run right back to Mrs. Greene's comfy chair. But Hallie is sitting there now. She said she wouldn't tell, but if she figured it out, will everyone else?

I walk to precalc. I do my work. I hold it together. I help Marvo pick photos of the dog walker, the skateboarder, the car builder.

I see Hallie again at the end of the day, by our lockers.

She says, "Hi," and I say, "How . . ." Because I need to know.

"Your hands," she says. "I notice hands."

I look down at mine, the right one holding my backpack and the left one balled tight at my side, as opposed to Hallie's, which are positioned as gracefully as if she were dancing.

"You clench your left fist all the time," she says, then lowers her voice to a whisper. "So does Vicurious."

"Oh." I stretch out my fingers.

"I don't think anyone else will notice," she says. "I'm kind of a freak that way. Hands, feet. I can tell you who bites their nails and who's pigeon-toed and who pounds their heels when they walk. It's one of my many useless skills."

"You're the only one who knows," I say.

"Really?" She lifts her eyebrows.

I nod.

"Wow." She gets her books from her locker. "You haven't told Mrs. Greene?"

I shake my head. "Not yet."

"Well, your secret's safe with me." She smiles and says, "*See you.*"

I lift my unclenched hand to give a little wave. "See you."

I watch her glide down the hall. The girl I was once afraid to say hi to is now keeper of my biggest secret. I'm not sure why, but it feels good for someone to know.

Lipton catches up to me at the end of the day, worried something's wrong after the way I ran out of class. "Did someone upset you? Did I?"

"What? No." I squeeze his hand. "I just needed to find a quiet place to catch my breath."

"Okay." He smiles. "You know you don't have to wear the necklace if you don't like it. I won't be upset."

I clutch it to the base of my throat. "Are you kidding? I'm never taking it off."

He laughs. "You didn't need it, though. The presentation was so good. I think Braxley was crying."

"Think he'll give us a perfect score?"

"I will dance in front of the whole class if he does," Lipton says, then does jazz hands combined with something slightly resembling the moonwalk and a little hokey-pokey. I'm too busy laughing to be embarrassed, though I do hide my face behind my backpack.

He walks me to the bus line and says, mournfully, "Will you ever get your phone back?"

"Oh! I forgot to tell you, I did! Now I just have to find my charger."

"Finally!" He walks toward his bus, grinning like crazy. "I'll text you later."

After homework and dinner, I log in to Instagram on my computer. Vicurious is up to 2.4 million followers. I try not to think of them as numbers. They are not my first and eight hundredth and two millionth followers. They are lonelyyy-girlll and dumbledorefanatic and tanyazeebee and kookiest-kimberly and ambivalentlessly. They are radhakrishnanraj and halliebrycedances and justjennafied.

I open the last photo I posted and scroll through the comments. Half of them are still exchanges between the helpers and those in need of help. But the others are panicked expressions of worry . . . about *me*. My followers have noticed my absence and they aren't happy about it.

Where are you, **@vicurious**? We miss you.

Are you okay?

Please come back. I can't do this without you.

Oh, God, if something happened to her I don't think I can take it.

And on and on. Some of them make it sound like I've abandoned them personally, and now I'm the one causing them pain instead of healing it. I lock my door and put on my Vicurious costume. The neon skirt is wrinkled from being balled up in a bag for so long. I smooth it out and get dressed, choosing the white cat-eyed sunglasses from my very first post. I open the Photo Booth camera on my computer and hang the white sheet behind me. I smile and wave.

Instead of pasting myself into another scene, I simply make a cheerful yellow background using a water-paint filter. I write:

Took a few days off and missed you all so much! Thank you for always being there for me, and one another. Please know: If I'm hiding, it's not from you!

I allow myself one hour to reply to comments, zipping through as fast as I can to reach out to as many as I can. It's a high, I can't deny it. As soon as my followers see me on there, they go a little crazy for my attention. When my hour is up, I can't stop. "Just one more . . . ," I keep saying. Until another hour has passed, and another.

Finally my eyes are bleary. I can't see the screen anymore. I write my last message and fall into bed.

In the morning, I find my charger wedged behind my dresser and plug my phone in before leaving for school. I can't wait to tell Lipton that we'll be able to talk and text soon, but he's not waiting at my locker as usual. I walk to his locker, uncomfortable breaking my usual routine and venturing beyond my safe route to find him. He's not there, either. I worry I've now missed him at my locker, but it'll take too long to go back to see if he's there and still get to class on time, so I head for Mr. Braxley's room. He's not there, either.

I sit nervously at my desk, glancing at his empty one. The bell rings and two seconds later the door opens. Lipton walks in, glances at Mr. Braxley, and mumbles, "Sorry." He crosses the room with his head down and scoots into his seat.

I wait for his smile, a note . . . anything. He doesn't acknowledge me. My stomach falls and my heart pounds. Lipton always looks at me when he comes in. Why isn't he looking at me?

Mr. Braxley starts teaching and my ears start roaring.

Something's wrong. I try to think what could possibly have happened since I last saw him. We were getting on the bus, he said . . . oh, shoot. He said he'd text me. Maybe he tried and now he thinks I'm ignoring him because I didn't respond.

I tear off a piece of paper and scribble a note:

> I didn't find my phone charger until this morning, if you tried to text. Sorry! ☺

I toss the note to his desk when Mr. Braxley's back is turned, and Lipton covers it with his hand. But he doesn't read it! He slides it into his notebook.

I clear my throat.

He finally glances at me. I mouth, "Are you okay?"

He nods, curtly, but still doesn't read the note. He looks like he's going to be sick.

Mr. Braxley hands us the grade on our Siege of Jerusalem presentation—a perfect score. I had expected Lipton to break into the hokey-pokey, as promised, but all he manages is a feeble thumbs-up and half a smile. The way he's looking at me is really strange.

Adam notices, too. He punches Lipton in the arm. "What's wrong with you?"

Lipton mumbles, "Not feeling great."

I try to talk to him after class, but he leaves in a hurry. "I think I'll go to the nurse" is all he says.

Adam stands next to me and shrugs. "Guess he's sick or something."

I nod. It's the "or something" I'm worried about. I kick myself for spending so much time on Instagram last night instead of searching for my charger before bed. Then I'd have my phone and be able to text him right now, find out what's going on. Or I would've been texting him last night, instead, and he wouldn't be mad at me at all.

He doesn't turn up at my locker between classes, either, so I go to his. I see Adam in the hall and approach him, my stomach in knots. "I haven't seen him," he says, before I can even ask. "Maybe he went home?"

I head to the yearbook office at lunch. Marissa, Beth Ann, and Marvo are there, but they all have exams, so they're studying rather than doing any yearbook work. I try to retouch some photos but can't concentrate. Even if Lipton were sick, he wouldn't ignore me like that.

Something's definitely wrong.

There's a knock at the door then, which is unusual since people generally just barge in. Nobody moves to open it.

"Come in!" Marissa shouts.

There's another knock, a bit louder.

"Jesus." Marvo takes the four burdensome strides to the door and swings it open.

It's Lipton.

"What?" Marvo barks. He's teasing, but Lipton doesn't know that and flinches backward.

"I, uh, was looking for Vicky."

I peer around from my workstation.

"Can we talk privately?" His voice breaks as he says it.

Marvo and Beth Ann and Marissa exchange looks.

I reach for my backpack. "Sure, I—"

"We were just going," Marissa blurts. "Weren't we?" She nudges Marvo and Beth Ann. "You can talk here."

They grab their stuff and scurry past Lipton as he steps inside. Beth Ann says, "See ya, Vic!" and closes the door.

I wait for Lipton to say something, but he just stares at me. He's breathing really hard, shoulders heaving upward and falling back down. "You said you weren't her. You said you weren't on Instagram."

Oh.

I shake my head.

"I can't believe, all this time . . ." He rakes his fingers through his hair.

"It's not me," I say, knowing there's no use denying it but desperate for Lipton to stop looking at me the way he is right now.

He leans over Beth Ann's computer and quickly pulls up Instagram on the browser. He types out my account name on the keyboard with a single finger, and with another click, the image I posted last night fills the screen.

"Then tell me why she's wearing the necklace I gave you."

My hand goes to my throat. The tiny sword is hidden under my sweater, at the hollow of my neck. But in the photo, Vicurious wears a lower-cut top. It's right there for all the world to see.

"Lots of people have that necklace, I bet."

"Lots of people who look exactly like you?"

I gesture toward my limp hair and baggy clothes. "I don't look anything like her."

He leans to the computer again and zooms in on the image. To my mouth. "That freckle," he says, pointing to the freckle above my lip. "You don't think I know that freckle when I see it? I've kissed that freckle."

I touch my finger to the freckle.

"See? You know right where it is."

I quickly drop my hand and lower myself to the nearest chair.

"You're Vicurious," he says.

I nod.

"I don't understand. How did you . . . why are you . . ." He shakes his head. "I just don't get it."

"It's hard to explain."

"Try." He sits in Beth Ann's chair and leans toward me. Waiting.

I pull my knees to my chest. "Jenna was my best friend, and she moved. She found new friends to replace me. I heard her tell them I was pathetic. I was alone. I didn't have anybody. So I created someone who is everything I'm not, who does things I could never do," I say. "She's better."

"Says who?"

"Says two million, four hundred thousand followers." I glance up at him. "Give or take."

"So, she's popular. Famous, even. And that makes her better?"

I swallow. "She helps people. She's there for them. Her followers are there for each other, too. It's, I don't know. It's a community of misfits and people who feel alone, like me. They love her."

"They love *you*."

"No! That's just it. I'm nothing like her. If they found out it was me . . ." I close my eyes. "They love Vicurious, not me."

"So, there are two million people who know this whole other side of you."

"She's not—"

"Can you stop talking about her like she's a different person? She's you! You're her!"

I drop my gaze to the floor.

"You could've told me," he says.

"It would've ruined everything."

"How?"

"I wouldn't have been just Vicky to you anymore. And you were the only one who liked me." I drop my head to my knees. "For me."

"God, Vicky." He kneels in front of me, puts his head to mine. "That wouldn't have changed. It won't."

343

I bring my eyes to his. "How do you know? Just look at how you reacted when you found out. You got sick. You had to go to the nurse."

"That's not because you're *her*. It's because you lied to me."

I shake my head. "It wasn't just the lie. You were totally freaked out."

He rocks back on his heels. "Okay, maybe I was a little freaked out. I thought I knew who you were and suddenly you're someone else entirely."

"Exactly."

"Wait. Exactly what?"

"You think I'm someone else now. You'll never be able to look at me the same way, and you probably won't even like who you think I am now. Nobody will be left to like who I was. It's as if I've totally disappeared and you were the only one who saw me anyway and now I'm just . . . I'm gone. That's why I didn't tell you."

He stands up and presses his hands to the sides of his head. "Okay, now I'm really confused."

"I'm sorry. I should go." I can't look at him anymore, knowing he'll never see me the same way again. "I don't want to be late for class."

Lipton backs away from me as I gather my things. "So, that's it? You're someone else now and I don't even get a chance to figure out if I like you?"

"I don't know who *this* me is," I say. "I don't even know if I exist anymore."

"Vicky, come on. That doesn't make any sense."

He tries to block my way but I push past him and out the door. It feels like I've been split in two—Lipton's Vicky is left behind, and I have no idea who the new one is, or where she's going.

33

I END UP BACK IN my favorite bathroom stall, where old Vicky would've gone, and I hide out there for the rest of the day. I could go to Mrs. Greene, but she'd want to know what's wrong and I'd have to talk and I can't talk right now.

I can barely breathe.

So I balance my history book across the toilet seat and I sit and wait for the final bell so I can hurry to the bus. I don't even stop at my locker to get my coat. When I get home, I'm shivering, but not from the cold.

Mom asks how my day was and I start crying.

She immediately wraps me in a hug. "What's the matter?"

"I miss Jenna," I blurt out. It doesn't explain what's happened at all, or maybe it does. Maybe it all comes back to this.

My mother fusses over me. She tucks me in my bed with a cup of hot cocoa. She smooths her hand over my hair and asks if I want to talk about it.

"Maybe later."

"Why don't you call her?" She reaches for the phone on my desk and unplugs it from the charger. "You haven't spoken in a while."

"Maybe later," I say again.

She lays the phone on my nightstand and leaves, closing the door gently. Kat curls up next to me, her purring form vibrating against my leg. I let the mug of hot chocolate warm my hands, but I don't drink it. When it finally gets cold, I set it on my nightstand and pick up my phone.

It feels strange in my hands; it's been so long since I held it. I key in my password and the home screen lights up and the little green texting icon shows a red circle with the number 37 in it.

I'm afraid to look, because they're probably from Lipton. He was the last person I texted before Mom took my phone that day. He was mortified that she might've read what he wrote.

Now I know why.

Adam told me what Braxley said. Crazy.

You there? Helloooo . . .

Okay, I'm just talking to myself here. *Dancing with my sel-elf, ooh ooh ooh*

Awkward.

Must. Stop. Texting.

Vicky?

Do you like me? Circle one: yes no

. . .

That was a joke, btw.

So, obviously, you are not there, and I am making a complete fool of myself. Feel free to interrupt at any time. "You are not a fool, Lipton!"

Vicky?

Yep, I am totally a fool.

Hey, remember my cat? She misses you. She really likes you.

Seriously. So do I.

I'm going now.

See you at school tomorrow.

I will be the one with a bag over my head.

I read it over and over. He's so sweet and funny and I HAVE RUINED EVERYTHING. I press my finger to the little text window, and hover there for what seems like forever. But there's nothing more to say. The girl he liked is gone.

I close the text thread with Lipton, and right below it is Jenna's name. It says there are 21 new texts. I stare at the little red number.

Jenna texted me?

I click on the window and try to find the beginning, where the new ones started. I scroll back to the last one she sent that horrible day. "Have a nice life." It was back in October.

The new ones started before Thanksgiving, two weeks ago.

Vicky, I'm sorry. I was angry and upset and I wrote stuff I didn't mean. I never wanted to be friends with those girls. You are the best friend I ever had, and could ever want. Forgive me?

Please. I take it all back.

I need you.

Vicky?

A few days later she writes one long message.

I really need to talk to you. It's Tristan. He wants to . . . He says he loves me. I like him a lot. But I don't know. I need to talk to you! Please, you have to forgive me. I don't have anybody else.

I scroll quickly to the next message. Three days later:

Never mind. It's too late.

"Nooo!" I call out, startling Kat. She jumps from the bed. "No no no no no no." Tears well up in my eyes. I wasn't there for her. I was helping people on Instagram, but I wasn't there for my best friend when she needed me. Yet she kept texting me. Almost every day.

She had nowhere else to go. She kept coming back to me, and I wasn't there.

He told all his friends I'm a slut.

Nice, huh?

Always wanted a nickname. Yay.

Got my driver's license. Drove Mom's car to school today. Some guy asked me if I'd show him the back seat. Asshole.

I know you're Vicurious, by the way. Nice cat.

I guess you don't need me anymore. You have a million friends. Must be awesome.

I have nobody.

You're my best friend.

You are, or you were.

You always were.

Vicky?

I can't handle this without you.

The next date stamp catches my attention. It's today. Less than an hour ago. I was in the kitchen with Mom, crying, and Jenna was texting me.

I don't want to be here anymore.

I don't want to be anywhere.

There's a picture, too. A photograph of a cliff overlooking a lake. What does *that* mean?

I sit up, thumbs speeding over the keypad of my phone, and text a reply.

Jenna. I'm here.

My mom took away my phone weeks ago.

I am just seeing your messages.

I'M HERE JENNA. I love you. I'm here.

I press send after each line, but the little "delivered" notification doesn't pop up. I switch from text to phone and find her number in my favorites. I press on her name and it's ringing forever and a thousand years. Then it stops, and it's not Jenna's normal voice mail. It's an automated voice that says, "The person you are calling is not available."

I wait for the beep. "Jenna? It's Vicky. Are you there? Call me, okay?" My voice breaks and I can't talk anymore, not without crying. But *not talking* to Jenna is what started all this in the first place, so I blurt the rest out through my tears. "I'm sorry, Jenna. I'm so sorry. Please. I'm here. I'm . . . I hope this is your number. I'm here for you. I'm here . . ."

The call cuts off when my voice gets too soft to be heard, and I'm listening to a dial tone over my own shuddery breath. I sit on the edge of my bed, trying to figure out what to do next. There's no time to hyperventilate or curl into a ball feeling sorry for myself. But my brain feels slow and dull. I don't know what to do.

Then I remember how Jenna called me on our home line, that she probably has one, too. I text my mother:

Do you have Jenna's home phone number?

She sends me a link to Jenna's mom's contact info without even giving me grief about texting her in the kitchen from my bedroom. I click on the home number and it rings four times and then goes to voice mail. I try to sound calm and normal but it's not working.

"Jenna, it's Vicky. Are you there? Please pick up. Jenna?" I start full-on crying and hold the phone away from my mouth until I can catch a breath. Then I quickly say, "Call me as soon as you get this," and hang up.

It feels like I'm leaving messages on dandelion seeds and blowing them into the wind. They'll never reach her. I open Instagram on my phone even though she hasn't posted anything in weeks, but it's the only other way I can think to find her. I pull up her jennaelizabethtanner page and leave a comment on the last photo she posted—the concert image that inspired my Foo Fighters posts.

vicurious Jenna, it's me, V. I'm here. Please let me know you're okay. I'm here.

I don't spell out my name, but she knows who "V" is. And I could swear she's justjennafied, too, so I click over to that page and leave another comment.

vicurious Is this Jenna of Wisconsin? I'm here, Jenna. It's me, V. I just got your texts. Please call me.

It's as close as I've come to identifying myself as Vicurious. Anyone who follows Jenna will know she had a friend named Vicky. But I'm counting on the fact that it's such an old picture, it won't pop up on anyone's feed.

I toggle between the two posts for a while to see if she responds, but there's nothing. It's been over an hour now since I saw her text and I'm wasting valuable time, not finding her, not stopping her. I pace my room feeling closed-in and helpless, until I realize there's only one thing to do. And it's what I should've done first, and all along, with everything.

I walk to the kitchen. "Mom?"

My mother turns away from the computer to look at me. Her face twists into a knot. "Sweetie, what's wrong?"

"I need your help," I say, the tears coming back. "You have to help me."

Mom stands. "Of course. What is it?"

"It's Jenna." I explain what's happened and show her the texts. "We haven't spoken in weeks. I thought she dumped me for her new friends. She said I was pathetic, that she'd wasted all the years we've been friends. But she didn't mean it, look. She's been texting me all this time and I didn't know it. You had my phone."

My mother scrolls through the texts, her eyes wide. "Did you call her? Did you try calling?"

"I did, but she didn't answer. What do I do?"

"Let's try her parents."

"I called their home number. There was no answer."

"I've got their work numbers, and cell. Let me find them." I pace the kitchen while Mom scurries around looking for numbers written in an address book, then gets her phone and dials. "It's ringing," she says. "Voice mail."

She leaves a message on Mrs. Tanner's line. All the time I'm reading and rereading Jenna's texts. *I don't want to be here anymore. I don't want to be anywhere.*

"We need to call 911," I say when she hangs up.

"Let's try her father first."

She dials Jenna's dad's number but he doesn't answer, either, and she leaves a slightly more frantic message.

She hangs up and we stare at each other for a moment, breathless.

"Call 911," I say.

Mom blows out a sharp breath. "Okay. We'll call 911." Her

hand is shaking as she dials and brings the phone to her ear.

The 911 operator answers, and Mom says, "I want to report a possible suicide in progress."

Hearing her say that about Jenna makes all the air go out of my lungs. I press my fist to my mouth as tears roll down my cheeks. I'll never forgive myself if something happens to her. Mom holds the receiver so I can hear what the operator is saying. "Do you have a location?"

"It's in Wisconsin," Mom says.

"She's on a cliff," I call out. "There's a lake."

The operator says she'll connect us to the 911 service there. Mom smooths her hand down my hair and back, petting me, saying, "It's okay. It'll be okay."

"What if it's not? What if it's too late?" How could I have been there for everyone else, millions of total strangers, and not my best friend?

The wait is excruciating. Finally, a Wisconsin 911 operator comes on the line, and my mom explains the situation. But I can't sit idly by.

I take the phone. I am not calm. "Her name is Jenna Tanner. I think she might try to kill herself. She's on a cliff. It's somewhere in Wisconsin. I think she's going to jump."

"Do you have an address? I'll need a location to send an officer out."

"There's a lake," I say. "It's a cliff by a lake."

"I'm sorry, miss. There are lots of lakes in Wisconsin. Without an address, without even a name of the lake . . ."

Mom takes the phone back. "She lives in Madison. It would probably be somewhere near Madison."

We give them Jenna's phone number, see if they can use GPS to locate her that way. The dispatcher says it would only work if the 911 call came in from her device. They can't help. They can't do anything. Mom is realizing it as I am. We lock eyes. "Try her parents again," I say. "I have an idea."

I leave my mom in the kitchen and race to my room with my phone. I sit down at my desk and open the cliff photo Jenna texted to me in Instagram. Vicurious will not be making an appearance in this scene, but it's the most important one I'll ever post. It may very likely be the last one I ever post, because if Jenna . . .

No. I can't think that. She wouldn't. She can't.

I quickly write a message to attach to the photo:

SOS. I need your help! My best friend is in trouble. Her name is Jenna. If you're in Wisconsin, please help me find her. Do you know this cliff? Please, go there. Tell her I love her. Tell her—

I stop typing. What I'm about to do will change everything. I'll lose Vicurious for good. I may lose myself. But I can't lose Jenna.

Tell her that VICKY DECKER LOVES HER.

I click send and watch and wait. The image fills my screen. The photo starts getting likes, and I shout at the screen, "I don't want your likes! I want your help!"

Mom hurries into my room. "I left messages again, and I called Jeanette's office. I told her secretary, but she's traveling. They're not answering. I'm trying to think if there's anyone else we can call."

"Tristan," I say.

"The boy who . . ." Mom grimaces.

"He might know where she is."

"Yes, yes." My mother nods. "It's worth a try. Do you know his number?"

"No, but I can try messaging him on Instagram." I pick up my phone and swipe and tap until I'm on Jenna's page, on the photo she posted weeks ago of her and Tristan. She tagged him. I click through to his page and start writing a comment on his last post.

I'm looking for Jenna. She's in trouble. Is there a cliff over a lake near you? She might be there. Can you—

"Vicky." My mom taps me on the shoulder. She's looking over my shoulder at the computer, at Vicurious—the little circular profile image of a girl with purple-and-orange hair. She points to the screen.

"I'll explain later," I say.

"No, look," she says. "They're answering."

I turn to the monitor. Vicurious fans from Wisconsin are chiming in.

sasharocksscotland I know that place. It's Devil's Rock.

jesseethehiker Devil's Lake State Park

badasschristinio Anyone at Devil's Rock today?

I turn to my mother, who is still staring slack-jawed at the screen. She's trying to puzzle out what I'm doing on Vicurious's Instagram.

"Mom," I say. "Can you call 911 back? Tell them it's Devil's Rock."

She nods and hurries back to the kitchen to get her phone. I can hear her making the call, repeating all the information. But now with a location. She's pacing the hall outside my room.

I watch my feed. More Wisconsin followers chime in. They recognize Devil's Rock. They've been there before, but nobody's there right now. Until:

staceyfromindiana My brother's at Devil's Rock today, I'll try to reach him.

I drill my eyes to the screen, willing it to give me the message I want to see, but it's taking forever and my feed is so cluttered with everyone else leaving comments, I'm afraid I'll miss it. So I comment to her directly:

vicurious Any news, **@staceyfromindiana**? Did you reach him?

staceyfromindiana I can't get through. I forgot there's no cell reception up there.

The sound that comes out of my throat then is half scream, half groan, and my mother comes running. "What happened?"

I can't speak now; I point to the screen and she reads. Her phone is still pressed to her ear. "They're sending emergency responders. They'll be there soon. I'm supposed to stay on the line until they find her."

We both stare at the computer for what feels like hours. Mom occasionally says into the phone, "Yes, I'm still here" or "No, we haven't heard anything more." She nods and says, "Okay, thank you" a couple of times.

"It'll take them a while to get up the trail," she says to me softly.

I want to curl up on my bed until Jenna is found, but I keep watching my Instagram feed. It's cluttered with people asking if we've found her, if she's okay, if my name is really Vicky Decker. Someone even writes, "Vicky Decker from Richardson HS?"

I knew this was coming, but I didn't think it would happen so fast. I want to disappear, but I can't look away until there's news of Jenna, or the emergency workers find her. I keep scrolling, reading, crying.

Finally, someone writes:

hikerdude22 My friend is up there today. He borrowed my satellite phone. I'll see if I can reach him.

"Yes. Yes. Please," I whisper. Mom rushes to my side to see what's going on. She talks into the phone. "Someone's trying to reach a hiker up there with a satellite phone . . . yes . . . I'll let you know . . ."

We both wait and watch. Then:

hikerdude22 He's on his way down. Just passed a girl going up there so he's turning around to see if it's your friend.

I start typing frantically.

vicurious Her name is Jenna. She has long brown hair.

I try to write something else to describe her, but my brain is frozen and all I can think of are things like "she can't tie her shoes." Every single other memory of Jenna and our friendship and how important she is to me is knotted up in my chest and I can't seem to let any of it out or I'll shatter into a million pieces. All I can manage to write is:

vicurious @hikerdude22 Ask him to tell her I'm sorry.

vicurious @hikerdude22 That she's my best friend forever.

The minutes tick by like hours. What if he's too late? What if she jumps? What if she's not even the girl he passed on the trail?

I start crying again, face in my hands, because I can't stop imagining the worst. Jenna, out there by herself, standing on the edge of a cliff. Thinking she's alone, that I don't care about her anymore, that taking one step toward the horizon—into nothingness—will make it all better.

It won't make it better, Jenna. It will only take away the chance to make it right. We'll never get to see each other again. I'll never have a chance to say I'm sorry.

"Don't take that away, Jenna, please," I mumble into my hands. "You're the only one who knows the real me. You're the only one."

Mom rubs my back. She keeps saying, "They'll find her. Everything will be okay." And then she's talking to the 911 operator again. "Yes, I'm still here . . . No, we haven't heard anything more . . . I'm not going anywhere."

Then this happens:

hikerdude22 He's got her. Showed her your message. She's crying, but she's safe.

My mother starts sobbing and smiling behind me. She says into the phone, "Someone's reached her. A hiker."

The 911 operator tells my mom to stay on the line. They've got responders heading up the trail.

I put my shaking hands to the keyboard and type:

vicurious Thank you, @hikerdude22. Please thank your friend, and tell Jenna I can't wait to talk to her, to call me as soon as she can.

hikerdude22 He's walking her down now.

I want to write more, but all I can do is stare at the screen. *She's safe.* But is she okay?

My mother is talking to the 911 operator again. "They've reached her? Okay. Yes . . . I appreciate it. Thank you. Yes . . . Thank you." She hangs up the phone and hugs me. "They said they'd take her to the hospital for evaluation and keep her until one of her parents shows up," she says. "I should call her parents back. They'll be in a panic when they get those messages."

She sits on the edge of my bed to make the calls, and I listen to her for a minute before turning back to my computer. I write down the names of all the followers who helped me find Jenna, so I can thank them, then I erase the Devil's Rock post. I only used her first name, but I don't want to draw any more unwanted attention. Part of me was hoping I could slip quietly back into anonymity. But it's too late.

In the hour or so that post was up, tens of thousands of people saw it. Some of them reposted it, maybe trying to help and maybe to be among the first to reveal my identity. It's probably on Facebook and Twitter and who knows where else.

Ready or not, I am out.

My mother finishes leaving a third set of messages for Jenna's parents, then comes to stand behind me, hands on my shoulders.

"You want to tell me about . . ." She gestures toward the screen.

"That's my Instagram. I'm Vicurious."

"Yes, I see that now. But when . . ."

I turn and start explaining it to her. How I took the pictures, Photoshopped the images. She nods. She looks from my face to Vicurious's and back again. "It's you," she says. "And that time—"

She's remembering when I answered my bedroom door wearing the outfit. "How did I not realize it was you?"

"Nobody knew it was me," I say.

"You have two million followers, Vicky. More than two million."

"That's not why I did it."

"I know." She nods, scrolling through the feed. "I can see that.

I'm sorry I didn't see it earlier."

"It's okay."

She walks to my door, stands there for a moment. "I'm proud of you, Vicky. What you're doing with Vicurious, what you did for Jenna. It's courageous."

I try to smile at her. "Then why am I so scared?"

She laughs. "Never confuse courage with fearlessness. When you face your fears to do what's right, that's courage."

"But I started Vicurious to hide from my fears. I made her do all the stuff I'm afraid to do. She's a total fiction. How is that courageous?"

"Don't fool yourself, sweetie. Maybe you didn't fly to outer space or ride a hippogriff, but the important stuff on there?" She points to my computer, to the Instagram image on the screen. "You did that. You should be proud of yourself."

I flop onto my bed. "I just want it to all go away."

"Do you really?"

I hug my pillow, thinking of the followers who are counting on me, the ones who went into a panic when I didn't post for a week. "I guess not," I say. "But everyone's going to know who I am now. They'll be pointing and staring and laughing. It's like my entire Terror List realized."

"Your what?"

"Nothing, just . . . everything I'm afraid of at once."

"We'll get you through it, your father and I, and Jenna.

Lipton, too," she says. "And we'll get you in to see that counselor. Okay?"

I squeeze my pillow tighter. "I kind of ruined things with Lipton today."

She smiles. "Can you un-ruin them?"

"Maybe," I say.

"Then what are you waiting for?"

She leaves, closing my door behind her. I grab my phone and pull up Lipton's texts. I try to put into words how sorry I am, but I keep writing and erasing. Then a "..." appears on his side of the screen. And it turns into:

Are you there?
Yes.
Can we talk?
. . .
Please.
Okay.

I stare at my phone, waiting for Lipton's call to come through. But the ring I hear a few seconds later is the doorbell. And then my mom's calling me from the living room. I open my door and look down the hall and there he is. Lipton. He's standing right there, in my house.

I don't walk to him. I *run*. I crash into his arms. And he holds me and I don't deserve him at all but I'm so glad he's here.

"I'm sorry," I mumble into his neck. "My brain is an asshole."

He laughs, and my mother makes a tutting sound. I glare at her over Lipton's shoulder.

"I'll just be in the other room," she says, walking backward toward the kitchen.

Lipton pulls away just far enough to see me. "So, it's okay if I like you? *This* you."

"I can't believe you like any version of me at all," I say. "But, yes. Please."

He laughs again and then holds me closer and kisses me like, wow. Really good. I'm a little dizzy when he pulls his lips from mine.

"I should warn you," I say, "that *this* me is kind of a mess right now."

"I saw what happened," he said. "Are you okay? Is Jenna?"

I nod. "They found her. She's supposed to call me when she gets home." I realize my phone is still in my hand, pressed to Lipton's back. I bring it around to make sure I didn't miss her call. "She doesn't hate me, though, so there's that."

"Nobody hates you. I don't know why you would think that."

I shrug. "My brain is—"

"*Not* an asshole," he says. "It's *your* brain, and I like it just the way it is."

I rest my head on his shoulder and we sit in the living room for a while, until Mom comes and asks if we want something to eat. We follow her into the kitchen.

"I called Mrs. Greene," she says. "I'll take you to school tomorrow and you'll go straight to her office. Lipton, would it be okay if I gave you a ride, too? Mrs. Greene thought it might help if Vicky has a friend with her tomorrow."

"I can do that." He smiles.

"Unless you want to stay home, Vicky. That's an option."

I honestly would like nothing better than to stay in my room and not come out for a very long time, but putting it off will only make the fear of it even worse.

"I'll go," I say.

Jenna calls around midnight, after Lipton's gone and I'm in my pajamas but unable to sleep until I hear from her. I crawl into bed with my phone.

"They took me to the hospital," she says. "I had to talk to this lady in the psych ward and I told her I was fine, but they wouldn't let me go until my mom got there. She was freaking out for a while or I would've called sooner."

Jenna starts telling me what happened, how Tristan was really nice at first but everything was going too fast. He kept pressuring her to do things she didn't want to do. Every time she resisted he'd say, "I thought you were cool" and "I didn't realize you were such a tease." She was afraid to break it off with him because her only friends were *his* friends, and then she'd be completely alone.

I keep murmuring "I'm sorry" as she tells the rest, how he got her alone at a party, and kept pressuring her.

"I told him I only wanted to be friends," she says. "That I wanted to go home. And he got mad."

"He didn't—"

"No. But he wouldn't let me leave the room so he could tell everyone we did. Then he made it sound like I was totally obsessed with, you know . . . And the rumor spread and everyone was saying stuff about me and I just got really depressed."

"I should've been there for you. I'm so sorry."

Neither one of us says anything for a while, but it's not awkward. I can hear her breath. I'm sure she can hear mine. We've sat in silent togetherness a thousand times, just being there for each other. It's normal. Comfortable.

"I can't believe you found me," she says quietly. "On a cliff in the middle of Wisconsin."

I swallow, wanting to ask but afraid to know the answer, of finding out how close I came to losing her. "Are you okay? I mean, you're not . . . you wouldn't . . ."

"I wasn't going to jump or anything. I mean, I thought about it. I didn't want to go back to school. I didn't want to do anything. I just wanted it all to stop. But then I hiked up there and looked out over the valley. It was clear and I could see really far, and I guess I realized there's so much more out there, so much ahead of me. I really want to know what happens next. With you, with me, with . . . I don't know, the world." She laughs. "It gets better, right? I mean, high school isn't forever."

"Thank God."

Jenna laughs again. "I knew you were Vicurious. And she wouldn't abandon me. You wouldn't."

"But I did. I thought you were better off without me. I abandoned you."

"I deserved it, the way I was acting."

"No, you didn't."

"I don't know who I was trying to be. Someone I don't even like. And then you wouldn't talk to me and I texted stuff I didn't mean. I don't know why I did it. I'm so stupid."

"And I imagined the worst, and then it really was the worst. I'm like a walking, talking, self-fulfilling prophecy."

"We both screwed up, big-time."

"And then I made Vicurious."

"Which, holy crap."

We laugh, and talk about all the crazy images I posted, and the yin-yang, and even the name Vicurious, how it all started with our friendship. We make plans to see each other over Christmas. We're not sure where, but one of us will fly to the other. Even if my fear of the airport, and walking through security, and taking my shoes off in front of people, and sitting next to a complete stranger kills me . . . I *will* see Jenna in December.

"What about Vicurious?" she asks. "You going to keep doing it?"

I sigh. "I don't know. I guess I'll talk to Mrs. Greene about it. She's my, uh . . . therapist?" I say it like a question, because I've never really spoken it aloud. *I have a therapist.*

"School counselor Mrs. Greene?" says Jenna.

"Yeah. She's going to help me figure some stuff out, I guess."

"Mom said she's getting me a therapist, too. And I'm changing schools. I'm really going to need you, Vicky. Promise you won't disappear again."

"I won't. I promise."

We talk until we're both too tired to stay awake, but right before we hang up, Jenna says, "I hope you keep Vicurious."

And I feel a twinge, a jealousy of my own creation. "You like her better than me, don't you."

"No, dummy," says Jenna. "It's just that she's the only thing that got me through some days."

34

"IMAGINE THERE'S A TIGER IN the room. Right there." Mrs. Greene points to the far corner. "What do you do?"

My eyes dart to where she pointed. There's no tiger, of course.

"Would you fight it? Run?"

I shake my head. "I'd sit very still. Hope it doesn't see me."

"It sees you. It's walking toward you now. Getting closer."

I make myself smaller.

"It's right in front of you. It looks hungry."

It's been a week now since my unmasking as Vicurious, and this is my third session with Mrs. Greene. She's trying to help me understand why I behave the way I do, why I panic over normal, everyday stuff. The suggestion that I'm about to be eaten by a tiger is triggering some of my usual reactions. Palms sweating, heart pounding.

"When your brain senses danger, there are three defaults," she says. "Fight, flight, or freeze. You can try and attack the tiger, you can bolt, or you can do what you did, which is to freeze."

"And get eaten?"

Mrs. Greene chuckles. "Luckily, we don't run into a lot of tigers around here."

She pulls out a diagram of the brain and points to this little almond-shaped blob on each side. It's called the amygdala, and it's the asshole that's been ruining my life, apparently. Whenever it senses danger, it pulls an alarm. And in the absence of a fire or hungry tigers, mine has decided to pull the alarm for *everything else*.

Which explains a lot.

Like, how sometimes I can't speak at all and other times I can't stop. Or the way the roaring in my ears drowns everything else out. "When there's a tiger in the room, it's kind of hard to think about anything else except how to not get eaten," she says.

I'm hyper-focused on the tiger, or whatever is *my* tiger. Things like walking into class late, conversations with strangers, getting called on by a teacher . . . all the things on my Terror List.

I'm supposed to write them down now. My tigers. Then we'll figure out how to tame them. (Or keep them in their cages at least, and learn to trust that they won't get me.)

For now, it helps to have someone who sees my tigers for what they are, and tells me, "It's safe, it's not going to hurt you, you'll be okay, you can do this."

That someone used to be Jenna. Now it's Lipton, and Mrs. Greene, and my mom. Someday, I hope I can be that person for myself.

35

THEY STARE. THEY POINT. THEY whisper. They've been doing it all week, but it's my first time in the cafeteria, so they're ogling en masse rather than one at a time as I pass in the hall. Mrs. Greene convinced me it was time to venture out of her office for lunch. I suggested the yearbook office, but she didn't think that was a very big step.

And we're taking actual steps. She gave me this worksheet to fill out, which was basically a picture of a ladder. On each rung, I had to write one of my "tigers," from least scary to most. I could've come up with at least a dozen less frightening fears for the lower rung, but I put "cafeteria" down, so here we are.

Lipton's been my human shield all week. He blocks for me on the way in, and Adam is there with a table. Still, I can hear people talking. Some don't believe I could possibly be Vicurious.

Others remember that I had a best friend named Jenna who moved to Wisconsin, so they believe, but just barely. I'm too much of a nobody to be that big of a somebody. And I don't blame them. I can't believe it, either.

Lipton prompts me to breathe, per Mrs. Greene's suggestion. I've brought him as part of my "crisis plan," which is basically any distraction I can focus on to deal with an uncomfortable situation. I touch my sword necklace, and I also have the picture of Jenna and me from my locker in my pocket.

We sit at the table with Adam, and Lipton pretends it's all perfectly normal, that every single person in the room isn't staring at us.

Four kids approach us and I'm about to hyperventilate until I realize it's Marvo, Beth Ann, Marissa, and Adrian. I might hyperventilate anyway because they're making me want to cry, and "crying in the cafeteria" is definitely on the list.

Lipton squeezes my hand and smiles his gap-toothed smile and it pulls me out of my crazy, roaring head. Just like Jenna used to do. I squeeze back.

There's one seat remaining at our table and Raj shows up and asks if he can join us. Then I notice Hallie gliding over just as he sits down. She blanches a bit when she realizes she's stranded and starts looking around for somewhere else.

I whisper in Lipton's ear and he says, "Make room." And we all squeeze together and Hallie sits down next to Raj.

"I'm Raj," he says to her.

"I know." She smiles and is even more beautiful than usual. "I love your Instagram."

Raj's head explodes.

People at the tables nearby keep daring their friends to come up to me and ask if I'm Vicurious.

My friends—*my friends!*—shoo them away.

Jeremy Everling gives me a thumbs-up from across the cafeteria, and it's not that I care what Jeremy Everling thinks, but somehow that is the signal that tells me it's going to be okay. It's okay to be me—as flawed as the dusty, imperfect floor of my bedroom. To be afraid and weird. To blurt out whatever pops into my head, or refuse to speak. If Vicurious has taught me anything, it's that there are more people out there like me than I ever could've imagined. I can be myself, whatever form that takes, and I'll never be alone.

I look around, and it's pretty obvious that everyone's waiting for something to happen. Maybe they just need me to say I'm okay, so they can be okay, too. Maybe if I show them I'm just a girl with problems, too, they can all go about their business.

My friends are doing the most amazing job of pretending it's a normal day in the neighborhood; they're joking and laughing. Adrian is twirling butter knives and Marissa is threatening to break up with him if he stabs her. Beth Ann and Marvo are trying to twirl spoons and they keep clattering to the table. Raj and Hallie are looking at each other's Instagrams, pointing out the ones they like best.

Lipton is watching them, or pretending to, but he keeps squeezing my hand under the table. He's the only one who notices when I lift my phone and snap a selfie from behind my lunch bag. I hate it, of course. I'm so dull and white without the wig, sunglasses, and bright red lips. I crop out most of my face, leaving barely enough to prove it's me—one eye, cheek, jaw, shoulder, lots of hair. It reminds me of invisiblemimi, one of the first who reached out on Vicurious to share her pain.

I risk a glance around the room. Eyes at nearby tables dart away, not wanting to be caught. I lower my phone to my lap, open Instagram, and click on "edit profile." I leave "vicurious" as my username but change my name to "Just Vicky." When I tap "done" a murmur goes around the cafeteria. They have their phones out. They're watching.

"Breathe," says Lipton.

I smile. I breathe.

Then I pull up the cropped photo I just took of myself. No filter. And I write:

Hi. It's me. Real me. #faceyourfears#onestepatatime

I turn off the phone. Completely. Slide to power down and slip it into my backpack. The buzz of the cafeteria rises to match the roar in my ears. I can't hear anything else. But I see them, as they #seeme. And I know I won't ever be #alone.

ACKNOWLEDGMENTS

My first and biggest thanks go to you, dear readers. It has been my privilege to write for you.

A big thank-you to my editor, Karen Chaplin, for always knowing how to bring out my best work; to editorial director Rosemary Brosnan; to Andrea Pappenheimer and the sales team; to Emily Rader in managing editorial; to Olivia Russo in publicity; to Bess Braswell and her marketing team; to cover designer Katie Fitch; and to everyone else at HarperTeen who makes the magic happen.

To my agent, Steven Chudney, thank you for championing my books and guiding me through the sometimes puzzling yet always fascinating world of publishing.

Thanks to all who played supporting roles in the making of this book or its welcome to the world: Rhe De Ville, for naming Vicurious long before I knew who she would become; to my son, for reading chapters as I wrote them, plus all the lessons in Minecraft; Julia Barta, who shared her expertise on social anxiety and the role of a school psychologist; Amanda Mattei, who offered additional insights on how social anxiety affects students in the classroom; Joy McCullough-Carranza, Paula Stokes, and Sona Charaipotra, for their valuable input on an early draft; the many librarians and booksellers who have welcomed me and my books, especially Rebecca Dowling at Hockessin Book Shelf;

the Fearless Fifteeners and many other author friends who have been a constant source of support and friendship; and to all the book bloggers, booktubers, and bookstagrammers who make the YA community such a wonderful place to be . . . THANK YOU!

Finally, to my beautiful family: Rich, Sebastian, and Anna— thanks for being my happy place.

Anxiety and Depression Association of America
www.adaa.org

Teen Mental Health
www.teenmentalhealth.org

National Suicide Prevention Lifeline
www.suicidepreventionlifeline.org
1-800-273-8255

HelpGuide
www.helpguide.org

National Institute of Mental Health (NIMH)
www.nimh.nih.gov

Find a Therapist—Psychology Today
www.therapists.psychologytoday.com

Teen Health & Wellness
www.teenhealthandwellness.com

MindShift App
www.anxietybc.com